THE PUSH

NATALIE EDWARDS

Copyright © 2020 by Natalie Edwards

All rights reserved.

No part of this book may be reproduced in any form or by any electronic or mechanical means, including information storage and retrieval systems, without written permission from the author, except for the use of brief quotations in a book review.

Cover art by Kealan Patrick Burke.

For my family: Siân, Alex & Zachary

CRICKLEWOOD, LONDON
MAY 1972

She picked the lock with a hair clip. It was a flimsy thing, shield brass looped through a hasp staple, and it came away in her hands in half a minute - the time it might have taken another woman to prise it open with a difficult key in the dark.

When the padlock was in her purse, she stood up on her tiptoes and shoved the door upwards until it disappeared into the ceiling. It was lighter than she'd expected, but neglected, the metal beginning to rust. Some of the paint peeled off in her hand as she pushed, flakes of it gathering in the soft leather palm of her driving glove.

The garage was empty, as she'd known it would be, nothing but a stack of dusty cardboard boxes catching in the beams as she swept left to right with her torch. She kicked the boxes into the corner with the tip of one boot - then, conscious of any footprints she might have made in the dust, wiped them clean with a handkerchief.

The ground cleared, she crept outside and back to the grey Morris van idling outside the lockup, its headlights off. She kept them off as she inched it forward, past the open door and into the space the boxes had left behind - trusting her night vision to steer her away from any obstacles she might have missed on first inspection. Then she turned off the engine.

In the dark, she stretched out a hand to the holdall on the passenger seat beside her; unzipped it and, with the torch, scanned the contents: three antique shotguns, the muzzle of one spattered with dried brown spots of what might have looked, in a better light, like blood.

She'd wiped them down already, more than once. But, reasoning that it wouldn't hurt to err on the side of over-caution, she took a chamois cloth from the pocket of her coat and wiped all three of them again, stock to barrel - making sure to leave the might-be-blood exactly where it was.

From the same pocket as the chamois she took a sheaf of bank notes, the tens and twenties thickly stacked and held together with a cashier's roll of paper ribbon, and let them drop to the floor of the van with a flutter.

Finally, from her other pocket, she withdrew something thin and circular and bound in clingfilm. She unwrapped it; turned it around in her gloved fingers, letting its edges catch the torchlight. It was a pendant - a cheap gold disc on a weak link-chain, a haloed St Nicholas carved into its face.

This too she let drop to the floor.

She slid from the driving seat and out of the van; shuffled backwards out of the lockup and, again on her tiptoes, grasped the garage door with both hands, pulling it closed behind her. Through the hasp staple she threaded a new magnetic padlock, more robust and more expensive than its predecessor, and secured it with a small silver key, which she slipped into her purse once its purpose was served.

Satisfied she'd done everything she needed to, she

buttoned up her coat and strode purposefully away from the lockup and down the brick-walled path that ran parallel to the unit of rentals, letting herself disappear into the warren of alleyways separating the narrow residential streets from the Cricklewood Broadway.

She reappeared not far from Willesden Green station, and made for the squat convertible car she'd left parked next to the bus depot. It was a Chevy Corvette, an original 1953 model: incongruous in the North London suburbs but perfectly preserved, only recently delivered to its owner from California.

She jumped into the driving seat without opening the door, a move that under normal circumstances would have brought her a shiver of pleasure, and sped off towards Hendon and the A5 back to Edgware - though not home, not straight away. There were things she had to do, still.

Plans to put in motion. Calls she had to make.

FROM THE DAILY REGISTER
11TH FEBRUARY 1955

Textile Heir's Baby Snatched From Crib

Mother and Father Taken To Hospital; No Ransom Yet, Say Police

The infant daughter of textile heir Edward Wainwright and wife Gillian has been kidnapped.

Little Ingrid Wainwright, aged just 18 months, was asleep in her nursery in her parents' house in Harrogate at 9 o'clock on Tuesday night when the masked kidnappers struck.

In a violent exchange, Mr and Mrs Wainwright were set upon with coshes and their wrists and ankles tied by two of the attackers, while a third man seized Ingrid from her cot and bundled her downstairs. All three kidnappers then fled the property, leaving Mr Wainwright unconscious and bleeding with what was later diagnosed as a broken nose and collarbone.

No ransom demands have yet been made, according to police, but this is assumed the most likely motive for the kidnapping.

Edward Wainwright is the son and sole heir of William Wainwright, founder of the million-pound Fine Cloth clothing company. A popular and flamboyant figure, the younger Mr Wainwright has served as his father's second-in-command since leaving school at age 15, taking Fine Cloth from a single stall in the Shambles area of York to a chain of 12 shops and half a dozen factories spread across the West and North Yorkshire regions.

Ingrid is his only child.

FROM THE CAPITAL INDEPENDENT
13TH APRIL 1972

One Killed, 2 Wounded In Woolwich Bank Shooting

An elderly man was killed and two others wounded today during an armed raid on a Woolwich building society.

Police said bank employees were handing over up to £20,000 at gunpoint when the robbers opened fire, shooting the customer point-blank in the chest and leaving two cashiers severely wounded.

The masked thieves burst into the Powis Street branch of the Blackheath Mutual at around 9.30am this morning and demanded that staff empty their cash registers, fleeing with the money when the shooting subsided.

Police have not yet named the dead man, but have identified him as a 79 year old resident of the Greenwich area.

FROM THE BRACKNELL STAR & ECHO
17TH APRIL 1997

James Marchant: A New Man?

Billionaire CEO James Marchant vanished last year amid a £20m embezzlement scandal and rumours of his involvement in at least one murder.

In the 9 months since his disappearance, numerous sightings of Marchant have been reported from eyewitnesses in New York, Mumbai and Buenos Aires, although none have been verified.

Others, including television psychic Trisha Langdon, have suggested that Marchant may be dead already.

Police state that there is "no proof whatsoever" of his death, and that investigations into his activities prior to his disappearance continue.

It's thought possible that Marchant used the money taken last year from his own Swiss bank accounts to buy a new identity, including a forged birth certificate and passport which would have allowed him to travel unnoticed to another countries.

And now, according to the woman who says she was his lover, he's working as a musician in a Sydney jazz bar.

Singer Nell Ryder, 41, claims to have enjoyed a passionate 3-month affair with Marchant in the Australian city, which ended only when she left for Melbourne to promote her latest album, Starwalker.

"It was lust at first sight, really," Ms. Ryder said. "I didn't know then who he was, but I knew from looking at him that he had to be *someone* important. He had that *look*, you know?"

Though she refused to disclose what Marchant was calling himself in the time she knew him, she indicated that it "wasn't a million miles away" from his real name.

"I used to call him Dizzy, after Dizzy Gillespie," she added. "You'd know why, if you ever heard him play."

Continued on page 3.

PART I
MAY/JUNE

CHAPTER 1
MAIDA VALE, LONDON
JUNE 1997

El didn't know what to eat.

It was an uncomplicated menu: Italian, nothing but pasta and pizza and, for the very ambitious, carpaccio and squid. Two wines, white and red; three desserts, two of which were gelato. The level of cognitive engagement it demanded of its diners was minimal, or should have been.

And still, she couldn't choose.

It had been plaguing her for a while, this decision paralysis - intermittently, then more constantly since she'd given up what she thought of as The Job, but what was, she was starting to suspect, less a Job than a Vocation. There was no small irony in this, she knew - a big decision effectively excising her ability to make even the most minor one, until she felt barely capable of picking tea over coffee (or Ovaltine, or hot chocolate) or matching a pair of socks to a sweater in the morning.

But *knowing* wasn't *helping*. And it brought her not a hair's breadth closer to alighting on a dinner order.

"Do you know what you want?" asked the woman on the other side of the table, looking down at her own menu.

El suppressed a laugh.

No, she thought. I can honestly say, I don't.

"What are you having?" she replied. "I'll have the same."

The woman, Rose - Lady Rose Winchester to the post office and Britain's more aristocratically-oriented celebrity gossip magazines - scrutinised El for a second, then nodded.

"Let's go with pizza, shall we?" she said.

She topped up her glass, then El's from the complimentary bottle of red they'd been given on arrival - Rose's name on the reservation, El presumed, carrying some clout with the maître'd' even in this particularly exclusive enclave of Little Venice - and took a long, deep draught that left the glass half-empty.

"Thirsty?" said El, smiling.

Rose glanced down at the glass and, apparently realising what she'd done, pressed a hand to her mouth in embarrassment.

"I'm so sorry," she said, not meeting El's eyes. "I think I may have forgotten how to conduct myself in the company of adults."

This dinner, El knew, was her first evening out in months - the first time she'd felt able to leave Sophie, her daughter, at a friend's overnight. Sophie was thirteen now, and prone to minor acts of rebellion - most recently dyeing the fringe of her red hair canary yellow and studding her navel with a barbell piercing that, El had heard, continued to horrify her mother. But Rose was protective; zealously so lately. And her caution had kept them both indoors more than Sophie would have liked, the windows locked and the front doors double-bolted behind them.

Rose's anxiety over Sophie's safety - entirely justified though it was, after the events that had engulfed them all the previous year - had also prompted a change of address over the Easter holidays: mother and daughter exchanging their Notting Hill terrace, albeit grudgingly in Sophie's case, for a three-bed penthouse flat in Lancaster Gate. The flat was famed for its view of Hyde Park, its Olympic-sized basement swimming pool - and, most importantly for Rose's purposes, its in-house security personnel, a 24-hour response team recruited exclusively from the British and Israeli armed forces.

"We can talk about the Spice Girls, if you like?" El offered. She took a sip from her own glass, privately thankful that the decision to fill it had been made for her.

"Oh, the Spice Girls are out," Rose said. "It's all Tori Amos and Fiona Apple now. I have to remind myself when I walk past her bedroom that it isn't *Sophie* who's screaming."

El flashed back to her own teen enthusiasm for Siouxsie and the Banshees, short-lived as it had been. Even as a kid, her interest in music - like her interest in fashion - was negligible; in adulthood it had vanished altogether. She couldn't remember when she'd last bought a tape or a CD for herself - or *as* herself, for that matter. The shelves of her study at home held as many albums as they did books, an illogically eclectic audio library of Kraftwerk and Mantovani, Northern Soul and Appalachian bluegrass. But none of them belonged to her, in the strictest sense. They were Jill Taylor's, Carla Finnegan's, Lydia Chopra's, Claire Brandon's - even Alison Miller's. And taken together, they were an archive: a room-sized testament to the tastes and curiosities of the women she'd been, the skins she'd worn and shed.

What they *weren't* were hers. You couldn't look at them - or at the books, or even at the artwork on the walls - and get any sense at all of who *El* was, what *she* liked.

Which was the crux of the problem, wasn't it? There was no record of the things she liked, because *she'd* never really liked much of anything, beyond The Job. She'd never stayed El Gardener long enough to cultivate passions or strange enthusiasms of her own.

And if she didn't know what she liked, how could she possibly be equipped to *choose* anything?

Across the table, Rose had stopped talking; was watching her, quizzically.

"Something wrong?" she asked.

El considered telling her, confiding a little of the new life-crisis that seemed to have overtaken her - perhaps even asking for advice.

In theory, Rose was the ideal listener, one of the very few people to have known El *as* El for longer than a couple of months - and not as Carla Finnegan, or Lydia Chopra, or one of the hundreds of other pseudonyms she'd accumulated on the job. And Rose knew first-hand what it meant to cast off a name and an identity for another, to reinvent yourself from scratch in the blink of an eye. In theory, she *got it*; she understood.

But telling her *what* would also mean acknowledging *why*. *Why* she'd stopped working; *why* she'd found herself saddled with the unenviable task of figuring out who she was and what she wanted - not at thirteen, like Sophie, but at thirty three. Which would mean, in turn, looking full in the face what she and Rose and the one-time colleagues they had in common had been dancing around since the previous year: the death - the *killing* - of Rose's father in her Notting Hill kitchen, and the fallout that had scattered all of them thereafter across the city, and beyond it.

Neither of them wanted that, surely?

"Tired," she said, washing the lie down with a second sip of wine. She doubted Rose believed her for a second - but was sure, equally, that she'd appreciate the effort to spare them both that particular conversational turn.

"Understandable," said Rose. "I haven't been sleeping well myself, though I can't imagine that's a revelation. I've seen how *these* look."

She gestured as evidence to the faint grey-green circles under her eyes; the touch of pallor on her already pale skin. Both were covered, proficiently, with what El recognised as very expensive, if not quite industrial-grade foundation.

"You look great," El said, and immediately wished she hadn't - aware of the weight of the words, the heft, however innocuous they'd seemed before she'd said them aloud.

This was the other problem with Rose - the reason she'd hesitated, momentarily, when Rose had invited her out for a catchup. There was a degree of awkwardness between them that hadn't been there when they'd worked together the previous year, one El attributed entirely to Ruby and Sita and their interference - to the persistent and poorly-concealed attempts they'd made over the last few months to bring Rose and El together, romantically.

Ruby and Sita were many things to El: friends, mentors, self-appointed fairy godmothers. They were family in all but blood, de facto aunts and co-conspirators de jure. They'd trained her; they'd *made* her. To Rose, they were more besides - in a very literal sense, she owed them her life.

And they were devious, wily - clever old birds, as Ruby herself so often put it. Any length of time in their company and you found yourself playing the mark in a particularly well-oiled game of Find The Lady, studying the rapid-fire movements of their hands for clues only to discover later that the card you'd been looking for wasn't up Ruby's sleeve or tucked away in Sita's handbag, the way you'd expected, but glued to the ceiling or clipped to the collar of a neighbourhood cat.

Sometimes there were benefits to this deviousness - as, for example, when they'd gifted El a substantial share of the £100m they'd acquired, surreptitiously, in the course of the last con they'd run together. But sometimes there were drawbacks. And the self-consciousness she now felt around Rose fell, she thought, very firmly into this latter category.

"Thank you," said Rose, with what seemed to El artificial lightness. "It's very kind of you to say so."

El considered her follow-up gambit - casting around for the question or statement that might guide them into safer waters and coming up empty. It came as a relief when the commotion reached their table, breaking the silence: male voices, low-pitched but resonant, speaking over one another in the kind of restrained disagreement that might rapidly abandon its restraint in a less public setting.

Rose cocked her head towards the sound.

"Is that who I think it is?" she asked after a moment, looking to El for confirmation.

El listened, picking up one word in three of what seemed to be an argument over access: one man demanding to be let into the restaurant, the second denying him entry in the absence of a valid booking.

The second man was the maître'd'; had to be.

The first was Dexter: Ruby's son and - along with Michael, his identical twin - the closest thing El had ever had to a brother.

"It's him," she told Rose, confused.

The voices came louder, closer to their table, and then Dexter was lurching towards them, the angry maître'd' at his shoulder. He was, El thought, markedly underdressed for someone so wedded to bespoke tailoring - the too-tight polo shirt, the denim cut-offs and the sheen of sweat on his forehead giving him the look, not of a moneyed professional on the hunt for high-end Mediterranean cuisine, but of a gym-goer who'd opted to forgo the shower after a tough workout.

Patches of dark maroon, only half-dried, stained the white ironed cotton of the polo shirt from neck to stomach. Worse still was his expression - a wide-eyed panic completely at odds with his usual insouciance.

"I tried to call," he said, the smooth posh-boy baritone he dialled up for clients and solicitors for the prosecution sounding scratched and raw. "Both of you, on your mobiles. But I couldn't get through, and Sita said I'd find you here..."

"I turned mine off," said El automatically.

They've got her, she thought. The police have got Ruby. I don't know what they've found on her, or what they've got her *for* - but they've got her.

Then: how did *Sita* know we'd be here?

"Is it Ruby?" Rose asked him, before El could speak, sounding every bit as panicked as he looked. "Dexter, is it Ruby? Has something happened to her?"

Dexter's brow creased in confusion, as if the possibility of something - anything - happening to his mother hadn't occurred to him.

"No," he said slowly, shaking his head. "No. Not Mum - Michael. Michael's been stabbed."

CHAPTER 2
WEST HAMPSTEAD, LONDON
JUNE 1997

It began with potatoes, of all things.

Michael, who'd offered that morning to make dinner, had wanted plain Maris Pipers, parboiled then roasted with sea salt and a sprig of rosemary; Dexter, who fancied himself the more creative and competent chef, had petitioned for the deep-fried dum aloo he'd been hoping to sample since seeing it brought to life on a cooking show the week before.

They'd squabbled in the kitchen while the oven heated, Michael refusing to put down the peeler and Dexter transferring oils and fenugreek seeds from the spice rack to the tabletop with passive-aggressive certitude. But the potatoes quickly gave way to other bubbling grievances - Dexter's over-use of the hot water, Michael's hoarding of the ironing board - which gave way in turn to the deeper ideological disagreement that had divided them since they were students: what Dexter saw as Michael's excessive caution and conservatism, and what Michael regarded as Dexter's dangerously freewheeling approach to being-in-the-world.

"I find it hard to believe," Michael had said, in reference

to the woman whom Dexter had brought back to the flat late one night the week before and tried, but failed, to smuggle out unseen the following morning, "that even *you* would be so irresponsible, when the whole purpose of this enterprise was to fly under the radar. Do you even *want* to keep Mum safe?"

It had seemed a good idea, when they'd signed the lease. Ruby, only just back from a cooling-off period up north after a job gone bad, would temporarily give up her flat in Edgware and move with the boys to a bigger, mansion house duplex in West Hampstead, one owned by a contact of Dexter's - a cannabis importer who'd elected, sensibly, to relocate to São Paulo before any arrest warrants could be issued. There, like Rose and Sophie in their penthouse, Ruby would be protected, not only by the presence of her sons but by the high electric gates and CCTV camera monitoring the building on all sides. Should anyone come looking for her, as both boys feared they might, she'd be far from the home she'd once vowed to leave only when she was carried out in a body bag - and neither alone nor vulnerable.

The plan's success, however, relied on two things. First, that all three of them were discreet, disclosing their new address only to their closest circles - a commitment with which Dexter particularly had struggled. And second, that neither brother killed the other before anyone else got the chance.

This too had proven a challenge.

It was a long-standing source of amusement for those who knew them, the differences in the twins' personalities - Michael's seriousness, professional good standing and reputation for incorruptibility the diametric opposite of Dexter's nonchalance, his moral flexibility. They'd qualified together, completing law degrees and training contracts in the same town at the same time - but from there their paths had diverged, Michael's leading him to commercial litigation and the City, and Dexter's to a discreet two-room practice on the Strand with a small, specialist client list to whom he offered a range of dedicated if somewhat unorthodox services.

("Straight as a die and bent as a nine-bob note," as their mother put it - in both cases, with a flush of pride).

But what had been entertaining for both men from the vantage point of separate apartments was less so at a distance of ten feet or less, and - much as they'd tried to hide it from their mother - the fraternal relationship was straining at the seams.

"I have to live," Dexter had said, banging a jar of asafoetida onto the counter with unnecessary force. "Bitch all you like, but I'm not prepared to retire to the monastery quite yet. Mum doesn't expect that, and neither should you."

"You can do all the *living* you want. Just don't do it here."

"So you don't have to think about what you're missing?"

This hit home, as Dexter had known it would. Michael's girlfriend, a Big Six accountant as strait-laced as Michael himself, had cut and run unexpectedly that Easter - packing up her things and transporting them from their house in Balham to a new one-bed in Limehouse while he was away on a late-season skiing trip with work, and leaving him to return from Chamonix to a home absent of furniture and a lone set of keys bunched forlornly by the answerphone.

("She didn't leave him *for* anyone," Dexter told El when it happened. "She just... left him. Absolutely tragic. So much worse for his self-esteem than if there'd been someone else").

Michael hadn't answered him directly, but had thrown

him a look of wounded anger before stalking out of the kitchen and then, or so the sound of the front door slamming suggested, out of the flat and into the communal hallway.

Dexter had been gleeful, revelling in his victory. Until he heard it: a ferocious, echoing bellow, so loud it was practically in the flat, followed almost immediately by a gasp, a sharp intake of breath and the sound of heavy footfall hitting the stairs, moving downwards.

He'd been on high alert all year, since the business with his mother and the dead man on Rose's kitchen floor, but the sound alarmed him regardless, and he ran for the door, yanking it open with such force that it slammed against the wall as it swung inwards.

And there was Michael, curled on the doorstep like an unwanted parcel - his eyes rolled back into his head with nothing but the sclera showing, blood staining the faded Cloud Cheetah apron Dexter had brought him for their thirtieth birthday and one crabbed hand clutching at the place on his ribs where he'd been stabbed.

"He'll be alright," Dexter told them, as they followed him from the restaurant to his car - a new one, El noticed, a black Range Rover rather than the Jaguar E-Type he'd been driving the last time she'd seen him. "He lost blood, quite a lot of it, but the cuts were shallow. It was a very amateur job, or so Barbara Potter says."

Barbara Potter, El knew, was a nurse: a former Ward Sister at the Royal Free Hospital, now retired, and another node in the wide-ranging obligation network of friends, associates and occasional enemies through which Ruby and

Sita got done the things they judged to need doing. Her husband, Terry, had been a respected antiques dealer, an authority on 19th century European glassware, and Ruby's go-to fence for much of the '80s; since his death, Barbara had brought in a little extra income patching up the minor workplace injuries of the friendlier end of the South East underworld, and of anyone else who'd rather not - for their own reasons, reasons she would never probe - take themselves to A&E for a couple of stitches and a tetanus shot.

Since Barbara refused unreservedly to minister to any patient she judged to require more intensive care than that she could provide in their living room, it was fair to assume, if Ruby had called her in, that Michael really *was* alright.

But still, Dexter looked as if he'd seen a ghost.

"You didn't want to get him checked out properly?" Rose asked, opening the door of the Range Rover and climbing up into the back seat.

"*He* didn't want to," said Dexter, slightly defensively, pulling himself up into the driving seat. "He thought admitting himself to hospital with a stab wound might draw attention - to Mum, not just to us. And he was perfectly lucid, so I wasn't about to argue."

Rose didn't reply.

It's guilt, El thought. A year later, and she still feels guilty for what happened - for what Ruby and the boys had to do.

Rationally, Rose had told her - late one Saturday night in January, when she'd called to notify El of Ruby's return from Rotherham and they'd spent two straight hours on the phone, a conversation that was neither therapy nor courtship but had a little of the flavour of both - she knew that she wasn't directly to blame for what Ruby had done, that day in the Notting Hill house. Or for what *Sita* had done, when she'd asked Michael and Dexter to dispose of the body Ruby had left behind when she'd stepped up to defend the rest of them.

But Rose had orchestrated the take-down of her father, had set in motion the events that brought about his death - and the involvement in the cover-up of Ruby and Michael and Dexter that its circumstances had demanded. And these events had led, ultimately, to the escape and disappearance of the probably vengeful and certainly volatile woman who now hovered on the peripheries of all of their lives like a coming storm - their Moriarty, unseen but no less unsettling for it. That made her, Rose reasoned, at least partly responsible for where many of them had ended up - for the fear that had driven them to change addresses, go underground, invest in ever more elaborate security measures.

El hoisted herself into the back seat beside her, considering the best way to phrase her next few sentences. She *knew* Dexter, the parts that worried her as well as the parts that made her smile and want to pull him into a hug - and the way he seemed now, his reaction to what had happened to Michael, was guiding her towards a question that was, and she was aware would seem to him, more rhetorical than it was enquiring.

"Dex," she began carefully, "do you know who it was, that stabbed him?"

He didn't answer immediately - took time, instead, to start the engine, angle the blunt nose of the Range Rover away from the pavement before accelerating forward into the oncoming traffic of Carlton Hill.

"Yes," he replied eventually.

"Was it someone you know?" she pushed, glad she couldn't see his face from where she was sitting. "A client, maybe?"

But he knew her as well as she knew him, knew she'd

never intentionally shame him or press him into a corner, and it wasn't anger or self-justification she heard in his voice when he answered - just the flat contrition of a man naming his sins in confession.

"It's worse than that, I'm afraid," he said. "It was someone who thought I was Michael. Or someone, rather, who thought Michael was me."

CHAPTER 3
SAFFRON WALDEN, ESSEX
MAY 1997

There had to be thirty machines in the hangar: saloons and 4x4s, box-fresh GTs and restored American muscle cars, single-seater racers shaped like bullets and armoured trucks so insectile Dexter couldn't fathom what purpose they might ever have served, on road or battlefield. And there were supercars, the kind that left his mouth watering and his fingers itching to grab for the steering wheel: a McLaren F1, orange as a Halloween pumpkin; a Porsche 911 Strassenversion, the chassis hanging dangerously close to the ground; a Dauer 962, high-winged and idiosyncratically yellow, that would on any other day have been the rarest model he'd ever laid eyes on.

They were arranged side-by-side in a vast, petal-like semi-circle, the grille of each one pointed towards the centrepiece of the collection: a long, lean Bugatti Royale, black and white, the bonnet more than twice the size of the cockpit. He couldn't pinpoint the year - somewhere between '28 and '32 was his best estimate - but was clearer on its price tag. Of the six Royales that Ettore Bugatti produced, he knew, only four had ever made it into circulation - and when one of those four went to auction in '87, it had sold for upwards of £5m.

He hadn't been there on the day, but his Mum had, and he vividly recalled her reaction to being outbid; the foul mood she'd been in when he'd called round for lunch that Sunday. He'd found out later that she'd been planning to buy it for his Dad, for his sixty-fifth birthday, and remembered wondering at the time whether or not she'd crack and look for a way to divert it to her own lockup before it was spirited away to Rome or Tokyo or Jeddah by its new owner. But then his Dad's first stroke had come along, taking his eyesight and with it his driving licence, and the Royale had been all but forgotten.

It was mounted on a raised platform built into the marble of the hangar's grey floor, a slowly rotating disc twenty five feet across that treated the observer to alternating views of its large spare tyre and the dancing elephant rearing up on its hind legs from the radiator cap. Its dark body gleamed in the overhead lights. Dexter was awestruck.

"Beautiful, innit?" said the man beside him, gesturing to the Royale with a moist pink hand loaded with sovereign rings.

"How much did you pay for it?" Dexter asked. Ordinarily he'd have shied away from a question that direct - one that Sita, if not his Mum, would have denounced as *vulgar*, as *beneath him*. But he had to know; needed confirmation that he really was seeing what he *thought* he was seeing, that the Royale - unique though it was - was an asset like any other, a commodity exchangeable for hard cash or harder credit, and not a mirage, an optical illusion.

Hartwood tapped his nose with one finger - a nose as pink and moist and unappetising as his hand.

"That's for me to know, mate," he said, grinning at

Dexter through capped, artificially white teeth. "For me to know and you to guess, 'cause I ain't telling."

Gary Hartwood had struck Dexter from the first as unusually unappealing in the flesh, more rat-faced than he'd seemed on the covers of the teen magazines he'd graced at the peak of his powers and far less charismatic than Dexter would have expected of a man who'd made his money, at least in the first instance, as the lead singer of a pop band. The band, Glamshell, had racked up eight Top 10 singles in the UK and Europe between 1984 and 1986, most of them to Dexter's mind eminently forgettable - but had had the good sense to make one of them a Christmas song. Hartwood, Glamshell's primary songwriter and sole owner of the publishing rights to its back catalogue, had reaped the royalties every January since.

He'd kept his hair bleached blond and gelled into the same high spikes he'd worn on Top Of The Pops, and the crystal fishbone earring that was his trademark still dangled from his earlobe, but the Barbour boots, the shooting stick and the twenty five-acre Essex estate on which he'd built a working brewery and an orangery as well as the climate-controlled storage space that housed his vehicle collection told Dexter that he'd moved squarely into the Country Gentleman phase of his career.

And his once-notorious vanity was still intact too, if the delight he'd taken in showing off the land, the half-mile of miniature racetrack and now the cars themselves was any indication.

Although it was entirely possible, Dexter thought, that he might have succumbed to a touch of vanity himself, with a Royale in his garage. And he couldn't fault the description: it *was* beautiful; spectacular really, a perfect convergence of art and science, from the leaf-spring suspension to the whalebone controls. He'd have sold... well, perhaps not his own *mother* for a chance to drive away in it, but certainly a more distant relative, a great uncle or a second cousin once removed.

"Shall we get down to it, then?" asked Hartwood.

Dexter returned, with some reluctance, to their conversation.

"With pleasure," he lied.

"I'll give you thirty large for the Jag," Hartwood said.

"It's worth forty."

"Forty cash, is that? 'Cause I got a big stack of fifties lined up in the safe, all ready to go. Leave the Jag and you can walk off with 'em now, today. I'll even get Gerry to give you a lift to the station."

He threw a thumb back at the quiet man in the suit and tie standing a foot or so behind them, the one Hartwood had introduced as his business manager. He was older than Hartwood, white and bald and luxuriously bearded - the combination of domed scalp and beard suggesting an eagle's egg incubating in a particularly well-thatched nest.

Dexter considered the offer.

He could certainly believe that Hartwood was good for the money. Whatever investments he'd made since his Glamshell days seemed to have paid dividends, and it was hardly out of the ordinary for a serious petrolhead to pay cash upfront. And Dexter *did* want rid of the Jaguar.

But there was also the matter of Hartwood's rodent looks and abrasive personality, the wide boy rudeness that had grated on Dexter from the first, the air of entitlement with which he'd refused point-blank to come into town to look at the Jag - insisting instead that *it* be brought to *him*, so *he* could take it for a run around *his* estate before he made the decision to keep it or throw it back.

The prospect of riling him a little, of forcing him to negotiate on someone else's terms - that too, Dexter thought, had its appeal.

"No," he said. "No, I think not. Thirty five, cash, or I'll be driving myself back to London."

Hartwood pursed his lips, irritated.

"It's like that, is it?" he said. "Thirty two. Last offer."

"You're not the only buyer I've been speaking to," said Dexter. "And yours isn't the only offer I've had. Thirty five."

"And yours ain't the only E-Type I've been looking at. So you can fuck off with your haggling."

Gerry The Eagle leaned in towards Hartwood and whispered something in his ear. Hartwood pursed his lips again, this time in a way that suggested he'd just swallowed something disagreeable.

"Yeah, alright," he told Gerry. "Alright."

He turned back to Dexter.

"Thirty four," he said grudgingly. "That's as high as we go."

It was probably as good as he was going to get, Dexter thought.

"Perfect," he said, giving Hartwood the lazy, self-satisfied smile he reserved for police and other people's solicitors after winning a settlement. "We have a deal."

"You got the keys?" said Hartwood.

"In my pocket. And you can have them, just as soon as we've finalised payment."

Hartwood glared at him.

You want to take a swing at me, don't you? Dexter told him, silently. You haven't quite got the guts for it, but I bet you'd *say* something, wouldn't you? If I were shorter, and scrawnier, and had a bit less melanin.

"Something wrong?" asked Dexter sweetly.

Hartwood didn't answer.

"Gerry!" he barked instead, spinning around so that he was facing his business manager. "Bring him his money, would ya? And get the paperwork sorted while you're at it. He ain't leaving here until I've seen a logbook."

∼

"I'm thinking there's more to this story than you selling him a car," said El. "So what happened? Was he scamming you?"

The Range Rover, creeping at a snail's pace through the surprisingly dense evening traffic on the Abbey Road, braked to a stop at yet another traffic light.

"He was," Dexter admitted.

"And you fell for it?"

Dexter sighed again.

"I did," he said.

∼

A fortnight later, the phone calls started.

The first was benign, in comparison to the ones that followed: a low-key message from Gerry The Eagle on the answering machine at the Strand office one morning, requesting that Dexter ring him back at his earliest convenience to discuss the sale of the E-Type. Something had cropped up, Gerry said - a small problem, nothing serious, but it would be terribly helpful if they could have a quick chat, for clarity's sake.

Dexter had been confused - not least since, to the best of his knowledge, the Jag had been in perfect working order when he'd taken it out to Essex. But he'd made a note to return the call sometime that day.

Which apparently wasn't quickly enough.

The second message, left while he was on another call, came from Hartwood personally. Though it was delivered via Dexter's secretary, the matronly and entirely unflappable Mrs Day, and though it had undoubtedly lost some of its bite and bile in translation, the point was clear enough: Hartwood was dissatisfied with his purchase, *extremely* dissatisfied, and he wanted his money back.

∽

"He said the engine had conked out on him," Dexter said, turning into a quiet street off West End Lane. "And it was his belief that I'd clocked it, before I'd sold it to him. That I'd taken a lot of miles off the odometer to increase its value," he added, for Rose's benefit - apparently assuming that El's knowledge of both internal combustion and the car con as a genre was sufficiently advanced to require no elaboration. This was only partially true, but El had no intention of telling him so.

"Which you hadn't, of course," said Rose.

"Which I hadn't," Dexter agreed. "That's Mum's game, not mine."

"So, what?" asked El. "He was shaking you down?"

"Like a chestnut tree," said Dexter. "But I wasn't biting."

∽

He ignored the second message; went about the remainder of his day, reasoning that Hartwood, having failed to provoke the reaction he was looking for, would eventually give up and move on to a weaker target.

Though it certainly gave Dexter more insight into how a

washed-up pop star best known for telling the nation that it was Time To Pull The Cracker had amassed those cars and that absurd country pile. If Hartwood and his *business manager* had been trying their luck with a reverse-clocking scam on even half of the people who sold to them, and if even half of *those* played ball - paying back the money but leaving the car in Hartwood's possession, perhaps under the not-so-veiled threat of police involvement or private prosecution - then the pair of them would have been sitting on a mountain of undeclared, untraceable cash in virtually no time. And the cars would have paid for themselves.

The third call came at 7pm that evening, when he was at home and working his way through a Lincolnshire Poacher and chilli relish combination he'd recently received in a hamper from a particularly grateful import/export client. Michael was, thankfully, out at the supermarket, and his Mum busy doing something unspecified with Sita; he answered the phone himself, expecting to find nothing more malign on the other end of the receiver than a wrong number or a telesales operative mispronouncing the name of the flat's previous resident.

Instead, he found Hartwood.

"You been avoiding me," he said.

"I've done nothing of the sort," Dexter replied. "I was intending to call you back earlier, but the day got away from me. You know how it is sometimes."

"I don't care *how it is*," Hartwood growled, in a way that was obviously intended to intimidate. "You think you can just pull one over on me and then skip away into the sunset? It don't work like that, friend."

The *friend* was pure Hollywood, an Essex boy crack at Dirty Harry or one of the Corleones. Dexter almost laughed aloud.

"Look," he said, trying to keep his voice even, "can we cut to the chase? We both know I didn't touch the milometer on the Jag. I appreciate you've got a con to run, and I'm sure you've found it very effective in the past, but you must believe me when I tell you that I would be an absolutely terrible mark. More to the point, I have no intention whatsoever of returning your money, however many times you call."

There was silence at Hartwood's end, punctuated by what Dexter thought was probably heavy breathing.

"I ain't fucking around," he said, when he spoke again.

"I'm very glad to hear it. And neither am I. So shall we agree to go our separate ways, no hard feelings?"

The growl this time was practically a splutter - an angry, disbelieving choke that sounded to Dexter not unlike the firing of an antique engine.

"You're gonna regret this, Mr Redfearn," Hartwood said, still channelling his inner De Niro. "I don't know what you *think* you know about me, but I'm not someone you ought to be talking to like that. I'm *connected*, you know what I mean? I got mates. Mates you don't want to be meeting down a dark alley. And they listen when I talk. So I'd watch myself, if I were you."

Dexter considered, for perhaps half a second, whether he ought to take seriously whatever kind of threat Hartwood was making. Then, deciding against it, hung up the phone and went back to his cheese and chutney.

∼

"I didn't hear from him again," Dexter said. "But this was last week. And for Michael, who to the uninitiated eye looks *exactly* like me, to get himself stabbed on our doorstep almost immediately afterwards... It seems likely that these two events are connected, doesn't it?"

El was inclined to agree that it did.

"Hmm," said Rose, as if chewing on a meaty problem. "I'm not so sure I think so. Taking out of the equation the possibility of a random act, a botched mugging or some poor soul acting out their troubles, and I'm certainly not saying that we *ought* to... You mother has her enemies, too. And it isn't wholly unthinkable that one of them might see an attack on her son as the best way of getting to *her*."

That's true, El thought. Except...

"None of them know where she is," said Dexter, answering the unasked question for her. "Michael's been fanatical about secrecy - about not giving out the new flat number and keeping us ex-directory."

"But you think that *Hartwood* worked out where you live?" Rose asked.

"He didn't need to," Dexter replied. "I filled out the paperwork for the Jag - contact details, everything. I gave him the address myself."

CHAPTER 4
STROUD, GLOUCESTERSHIRE
JULY 1997

El looked out across the fields from the top of the hill, watching the grassland below slowly filling up with cars and people.

"That," said a voice from behind her, "is a *lot* of old men."

She spun around, her spiked heels carving divots out of the turf, and there was Karen Baxter, resting casually back against the hood of the vintage Rolls-Royce Phantom El had come in.

"How do you know they're men?" El asked. "They look like ants to me from up here."

"This your first time at one of these?" said Karen. "They're *always* men. And they're always old. Nobody but old men has got the time to do this sort of thing or the money to plough into it."

She looked the same as she had the year before, El thought: still compact and muscled, still younger looking than her age, still draped in the ironic bemusement that covered her like a force-field.

The clothes were different, though - her standard

leggings and vest top replaced by a very well-cut charcoal suit with more than a suggestion of a collapsible baton in the bulge at the inside pocket. Her curly black hair was cropped short at the sides, slicked and parted; she wore dark glasses high on her head and a very visible comms device in one eardrum, the cable looping from her mastoid bone to her neck and then disappearing into the collar of her starched white shirt.

"You scrub up well," El said.

"What do you expect? I've done this before."

She'd been playing the hired heavy the first time they'd met, El remembered. And playing it convincingly then, too.

"It's the biceps," she said. "And that scowl on your face doesn't hurt, either."

"It's bloody typecasting is what it is. I shouldn't have to keep being someone's henchman just 'cause none of you lazy fuckers ever drag yourselves to the weights room."

"What is it you want to be, then? Zookeeper? Diamond merchant? Another dominatrix? Say the word, we can make it happen next time."

"*Next time*? I thought you were retired."

She'd hoped they'd be able to avoid the topic of her sudden return to the job - her conscription, as she'd been calling it, to herself if no-one else.

"I am," she replied. "This isn't me back. It's... a favour. Just a favour."

Karen nodded.

"Yep," she said sagely. "That's what I've been telling myself, too."

∼

Michael had been laid out on a futon in the living room when they'd arrived at the West Hampstead flat, thick layers of gauze and bandage criss-crossing his chest like a poorly-fitted toga.

He'd sat up as they'd entered, using the back of his head on the pillows behind him as leverage, then winced at the obvious discomfort the manoeuvre caused him.

"You need to stay *still*, darling," said Sita from the cushion-stuffed armchair across the room. "Keep thrashing around like a conger eel and you'll do yourself another injury."

She was heavier and more furrowed than she'd been in her heyday - back when, or so Ruby insisted, the sway of her hips and the dark cascade of her hair could stop more traffic than a pelican crossing - but every bit as glamorous, from the jewelled heels of her Giuseppe Zanottis to the sweep and fall of the cashmere scarf around her neck. Even in her sixties - after two children, three husbands and innumerable lovers drawn from every block of the global population pyramid - she was striking, memorable, the sheer force of her personality plugging the aesthetic gaps her age had left behind. If she were ever inclined to seek him out, El thought, husband number four wouldn't stand a chance.

Michael had allowed himself to sink, apologetically, back down onto the pillows.

"Good boy," said Ruby, crouching down next to him and touching a hand to his sweating forehead. "You listen to your Auntie Sita."

She was paler than usual, El thought; her lined face grey and her eyes red-rimmed, as if she'd been crying. Her hair, newly dyed an unlikely chestnut brown for reasons El suspected had more to do with her hibernation in Rotherham than with any con she was running, was loose and unbrushed. Her top, like Dexter's, was painted with streaks of dried blood.

"Has Barbara gone?" Dexter asked - still sounding penitent.

"Only just," said Sita.

"She stayed for a cup of tea and a chat, after," Ruby added. "Gets a bit lonely without Terry. And a bit of company's the least we can give her, after what she done."

"I can't help but feel she quite enjoys a captive audience," said Michael.

Dexter grinned; Michael grinned back, and El found she was relieved to see no hard feelings lingering between them.

"You tell 'em about Hartwood?" Ruby asked Dexter.

"In the car," he answered.

She turned her attention to El and Rose.

"What do you two reckon, then?" she said. "You think it was him that done it?"

"I think it's possible," said El, hedging her bets.

"What do *you* think, Michael?" Rose asked. "I imagine you have a better sense than any of us."

Michael shook his head.

"Unfortunately not," he said. "I'm confident he was male, whoever he was - he was very broad in the shoulders and at least my height, perhaps even taller. Large feet, too - I had a front row view of his trainers, from the ground. But as to his face or any other kind of identifying feature... I really couldn't say. He was wearing a mask - one of those rubber ones you find in joke shops. Unless he really *was* Prince Charles. In which case I believe we'd have ourselves an entirely different set of problems."

This earned a chuckle from Dexter and a scowl from Ruby.

"You want to take this a bit more seriously," she said. "And that's both of you I'm talking to. It ain't a joke."

"Sorry, Mum," said Dexter, chastened.

"Sorry," Michael echoed, equally sheepish.

"Alright, then," said their mother, mollified. "So, let's say it *was* him, Hartwood - or someone working for him, more like, if he's as much of a little weasel as he sounds. What do you lot want to do about it?"

∽

"You've not done bad yourself on the costume front," Karen said, as she drove them down the hill to the cluster of marquees that doubled as a registration area. "You gonna make him an offer he can't refuse?"

It was the trench coat, El thought. Long and dark and tightly belted at the waist, it gave her an old world mafiosa appearance that was faintly anachronistic, though no less intimidating for it. The rest, she hoped, was equally threatening: the blood-red lipstick, the cheekbones powdered and contoured high and hollow as a Milanese pinup's, the stiletto points sharp enough to weaponise.

"Shouldn't need to," she said. "We play this right, and he's coming to us."

∽

Nobody had answered Ruby. They hadn't needed to; all of them could see her cogs were already turning, that she had a scheme of her own for Hartwood already half-formulated.

She wasn't after their input, their help to extract payback or broker a resolution. She was looking for permission.

And not just permission, El had told herself.

Participation. She doesn't just want us to agree to whatever she's thinking. She wants us to sign up.

"What do *you* want to do about it?" she'd asked her. "You've got some sort of plan in mind, you must have, so you may as well come out with it."

Ruby had looked to Sita, who had looked back at her quizzically.

"You remember Turin in '82?" she asked.

"Of course," said Sita, surprised. "Who could forget that castle? And wasn't that the year that...?"

She'd paused, realisation seeming to dawn.

"Ah," she'd added. "I see."

"Well?" said Ruby.

Sita considered the unspoken question.

"I suppose it *could* work," she said. "But I must warn you, I go down far better with the Italians than the British in those circles. Englishmen are so... *mechanical*, so technically minded. All they ever want to talk about are pistons and exhaust pipes."

"I ain't thinking of *you*," said Ruby. "I'm thinking of El here."

"Me?" El had said. "What *about* me?"

They'd ignored her, the way they always did during these exchanges.

"She'd need an outsideman, for the rope," Sita added.

"I got someone in mind."

"And a second insider. Not to say a third body for the extraction, a strong one. Unless you expect the girl to do it *all* herself?"

Do what? El had thought. What is it I'm meant to be doing, exactly?

She'd felt it, then: the inevitability, the absolute unshakeable certainty that - regardless of what she did or didn't want, how much she did or didn't protest - she was going to be *in* this, front and centre and up to her eyeballs.

They were like waves, the two old women and their plots: rogue waves, unpredictable and impossible to fight. You couldn't run; all you could do was ride them out, and hope you didn't get flattened.

"You're dead right," said Ruby, grinning. "And wouldn't you know it, I got a couple of ideas about that, too…"

∽

When Angela Di Salvo stepped out of her Rolls-Royce onto the grass, heads turned.

Not because she was a woman, in what was - the attendees would be the first to admit - a decidedly male arena. Not because of the entirely impractical way she was dressed, or the flicker of exoticism that spoke to them of Mediterranean climates more temperate than Gloucestershire's, even in midsummer. And not because of the bodyguard, the young girl in the suit and headset who stepped out in front of Di Salvo as if she were getting ready to take a bullet for her.

No; heads turned for the *car*.

It was a Phantom V, a 1964 James Young model, hot pink and immaculate - among the prized possessions, though the attendees couldn't have known it, of one careful lady owner.

There were a lot of classics out on the field that morning, American and European as well as domestic: a Karmann Ghia, a Triumph Roadster, two Sunbeam Tigers and half a dozen Morgans. But none quite so spectacular as the Phantom, nor so beautifully maintained.

"What did I tell you?" said Karen, under her breath. "Old men, as far as the eye can see."

El allowed Angela Di Salvo a faint, thin smile.

They were barely ten feet from the car when the vultures began to circle: cagouled spotters armed with sharpened pencils, jotting the Phantom's specs into their notepads with breathless fervour; hobbyist photographers with SLRs around their necks and handheld video cameras at their shoulders; retirees with lunchboxes and flasks of hot tea, scouting around for the perfect space to park their folding picnic chairs. A tall fair-haired boy, younger than the rest but no less intense, his eyes flickering wildly back and forth between her and Karen and the Phantom – wondering, if El had to take a guess, how two women like *them* could possibly have acquired a car like *that*.

And a final group, more polished-seeming than their brethren - their equipment more expensive, the gazes they let linger on the vehicles they passed more appraising.

Professionals, El thought.

∼

"They just stroll around the fields, looking?" El had asked Ruby, astonished, while she was prepping for the job.

"That's the regional shows for you," Ruby had told her. "You might get the odd burger stand or an RAC bloke looking to pick up custom, but it's all about the cars, whether you're a dealer or a Sunday driver in a little red convertible. Looking at 'em, showing 'em off, seeing 'em race round. It ain't for everyone, but if you like that sort of thing…"

"Wouldn't it be a bit amateur for a woman like Di Salvo, though? A bit low-rent?"

Ruby had taken a sip of her coffee and a bite of one of

the Viennese butter biscuits Dexter had been buying her in lieu of her beloved custard creams, and thought it over.

"You ever been to a car boot sale?" she'd asked.

"Sure," El had said. "Once or twice, on the job."

But never for myself, she'd added silently. Never *as* myself.

"And what did you think of it? Of the stuff on the tables?"

El had let her mind drift back to what she'd seen there: to the cheap plastic action figures and My Little Pony knock-offs, the Jackie DeShannon records and the Barbara Taylor Bradford paperbacks.

"Not much," she'd replied.

"The thing about car boot sales," Ruby said, letting another section of biscuit dissolve into the coffee until a sugary froth developed on its surface, "is that most of what you find there is crap. Other people's crap, and all - whatever *they* don't want no more. And nine times out of ten, you leave thinking, *what did I bother with that for, when I could have been at home with a sausage butty watching David Frost?*"

"But the tenth time, you find something valuable? Is that what you're saying?"

Ruby withdrew the disintegrating biscuit from the coffee, scrutinised it and then, satisfied, took another bite.

"Valuable?" she said, through a mouthful of watery crumbs. "What good would *that* do me? If I wanted valuable, I'd take myself to Bonhams and pick a fight with all the other rich bastards over a hundred grand necklace or a bit of Queen Anne furniture. No - what you want from a car boot is something no-one else'd look twice at. Something nobody wants, but you can put a bit of elbow grease into and then take to Bonhams yourself to sell on for a song."

"Something with potential. Got it. And it's the same with

auto shows - people go looking for hidden treasures so they can fix them up?"

"If they're clever about it," Ruby told her, swallowing the remainder of the biscuit. "Though of course, if they're *really* clever, they'll go one better than that. If they're *really* clever, they'll go looking for something they can *tell* you is valuable that you'll pay up for, even if it ain't worth anything at all. And I reckon that sort of thing might be right up your woman Di Salvo's street, don't you?"

∼

They walked the rows of cars, El occasionally stopping to examine one model or another more closely before moving on, Karen three paces ahead of her.

Hartwood wasn't difficult to find. In the sea of sensible brogues, flyaway combovers and lightweight V-neck sweaters, his bleached blond head and fishbone earring called out like a beacon, in spite of his tartan slacks and quilted gilet.

He was standing by a battered-looking powder blue Beetle, deep in conversation with an older man whose gently protruding stomach, thick white hair and twinkling blue eyes gave him a sweetly Santa Claus-ish look. Both men were staring at her; Hartwood, especially, was doing a poor job of concealing his curiosity.

"That him?" said Karen, under her breath.

"That's him," El confirmed, just as quietly.

She paused, ostensibly to study the paintwork of a silver Jensen Interceptor; let herself count to ten, then twenty.

"Is he still looking?" she asked Karen, when she thought she'd waited long enough.

"Better than that," Karen whispered. "He's coming over."

"Len Wolf," Ruby had said. "He's the roper I been thinking of."

"Len Wolf?" Sita had replied, wrinkling her nose. "That... *stick-up artist*?"

There was something unsavoury, to Sita's mind, about using weapons - *real* weapons, ones that shot or struck or perforated - in the course of a job. Counterfeits were fine, El knew; Sita had never shied away from a replica gun in the handbag or a bladed letter-opener in the stocking, if it helped to sell a character. But real weapons, real violence - they were a kind of cheating. If you couldn't persuade a mark to part willingly with their cash or their possessions, to hand over the briefcase of fifties or that Georgia O'Keeffe in the attic with a smile on their face and thanks on their lips, then you didn't deserve to call what you were doing *work*, let alone *skilled* work. Pointing a shotgun at some poor cashier was extortion, plain and simple; money taken with menaces. For a woman to whom the con was an art, an impeccably choreographed dance, and the grifter herself both performer and stage-manager, bank robbery was a kind of destructive finger-painting; a heckle and a wolf-whistle released from the stalls in the third act of Madama Butterfly.

"He gave all that up years ago," said Ruby. "Been out of commission since he banged up his leg doing over that armoured van in Woodside Park. December '89, that must have been."

"And you're quite sure he's up to the job?" Sita asked, dubious.

"Bloke knows his cars," Ruby told her. "Spends just about every weekend on the circuit, at one of them events or other. And I seen him talk his way out of enough tight spots to know he's got the gift of the gab, so he'll have the patter down well enough to play the outsideman. Plus..."

She'd hesitated; thrown a dark, admonishing glance Dexter's way.

"He owes me a favour," she'd added.

Dexter had let out another deep, remorseful sigh.

"He's the one who introduced me to Hartwood," he said, before anyone could appeal for further detail. "I happened to bump into him at a Masters race at Brands Hatch, and when I mentioned in passing that I was selling the Jag, he suggested he might be able to put me in touch with someone he knew from the Classics shows. A potential buyer."

"Should have known better, bleedin' idiot," said Ruby, shaking her head.

It hadn't been obvious to El which of them she'd considered the greater idiot - Len Wolf, or her uninjured, loose-lipped son.

∾

Hartwood sidled up to them like a used-car salesman, all white teeth and insincerity - coming in so close and so quickly El worried he was going to try to slide an arm around her waist or make a grab for her arse.

Karen thrust herself between them, blocking his way.

"You want to back off," she told him, angling her body side-on and her head upwards, so that her shoulder grazed his chest and the corded tendons in her neck were directly in his line of sight.

"'S'alright, Jax," El told her, gesturing for her to move aside. "Let the man talk. I'm sure he's got his reasons for coming over here to introduce himself. Isn't that right, Mr...?"

She'd pitched the voice somewhere between Ruby's Cockney and a more generic Estuary, with just a little of the slip and slide of Calabria in the final, rising syllable. Angela Di Salvo, she'd reasoned, would be second-generation acculturated: Italian at home, English at school and then at work, and London to her core.

"Hartwood," he said, his manner an unlikely combination of nervous and peeved. Perhaps, she thought, because she hadn't recognised him, or responded in the way he'd been conditioned to expect from the general public after his brief flirtation with the A-list. "My friends call me Gary."

"And what can I do for you, Mr Hartwood?" she asked - disinterest dripping from every word, every downward flicker of her eyes.

He ran the palm of one hand nervously over his elaborately peaked hair.

"It's more a question," he said, "of what I might be able to do for you, Miss Di Salvo. Or can I call you Angela?"

∼

By the time El met him, Ruby had assured her, Hartwood would be primed. Primed, and a little frightened.

Len Wolf would have seen to it.

He'd make a point of running into Hartwood early on, before El and Karen arrived at the show; would make small talk about the races he'd caught up at Silverstone and Aintree, the Hillclimb at Goodwood and the Sunday Scramble over in Bicester.

Then he'd ask what Hartwood was selling, these days.

Like a lot of the collectors Ruby had known, Hartwood was a neophile - a novelty seeker, easily bored by the models in his lot and perennially in search of the next acquisition, the one that would set his pulse racing anew. And because of this neophilia, he'd become in the course of his collecting as much a dealer as a buyer - selling and swapping and trading up and out, switching an Alvis for an Alta or a Ferrari 250 Europa for a T-Bird, and swelling his own coffers in the process. Even when he wasn't running his reverse-clocking scam on the greenhorn petrolheads who approached him in good faith with a Healey Westland or a Peerless GT.

He'd be on the lookout for his next fix, Ruby was sure of it; and very likely his next mark, while he was at it.

But he'd also have an eye out for a new customer - for someone who might scoop up the stock he wanted to offload. Someone, ideally, with deeper pockets than the average.

"Why?" he'd ask Len. "You in the market for something?"

Len would laugh - a rueful chuckle suggesting that he most definitely *would* be, under other circumstances.

"Not sure the wife'd let me," he'd say. "She had a fit when I came home with the Alfa Romeo."

There would follow some light-hearted back and forth about the inestimable Mrs Wolf, who - despite her innumerable virtues - had never quite understood the love a man could feel for his motor, much less the seductive pull a reconditioned gullwing coupé could exert on the dedicated Mercedes admirer.

Five minutes or so would pass, Len checking his watch surreptitiously to time the conversation just so. And El and Karen would make their entrance.

"Bloody hell," Len would gasp, his eyes on El as she walked slowly among the parked cars. "I don't believe it."

"What?" Hartwood would ask.

"It's her," Len would say - slowly, as if not quite believing what he was seeing. "It's Angela Di Salvo."

"*Who?*"

And Len would tell him.

Angela Di Salvo, he'd say, was a legend - a name spoken in hushed whispers across the more clued-up corners of the London underworld. Hartwood couldn't be expected to know that, of course - he didn't run in those circles. But for a bloke like Len, an antique face who kept his ear to the ground... she was practically royalty. Practically folklore.

There were three things, he'd say, that you needed to know about Angela Di Salvo.

The first was the lineage. For all she'd done in her own right - and Christ knew there was a lot of it - she was Niccolo' Di Salvo's little girl, first and foremost.

Nicky Di Salvo, he'd say - may he rest in peace - just about ran Hackney in the '70s. Had a hand in everything: gambling, robbery, protection, loan sharking... just about anything but the drugs and tarts his staunch Catholicism forbade, the profits he made filtered through a chain of garages spread out across the East End. He was hard, Nicky, but fair, a proper old-school gangster - you didn't mess with him, and he didn't mess with you. You did him a good turn, and he'd do you one down the line, no questions asked.

When he died, in '86, it was widely assumed that his son would take over the business. But Piero was soft, and not too bright - loved his dogs and his birds, the racing pigeons he kept up in his loft, and not a bad bone in his body, but barely two brain cells to bang together, and hardly the sort you wanted fronting your operation. So in stepped Angela, barely into her twenties then, but a mind like a steel trap and twice as tough as even her old man had been. And before you knew it, the Di Salvo kingdom was an empire, stretching south to Lambeth and north to Finsbury Park.

The second thing was: she'd been away, the last couple of years. Not *inside*, Len would stress - it'd be a cold day in hell before the filth got anything to stick on Angela Di Salvo. But out of the country, somewhere in Palermo; a strategic retreat beaten in the immediate aftermath of a job gone bad - a job she'd overseen - at a safety deposit place up in Birmingham. There'd been no arrests, and not a penny of the £90m taken had been found, but the heat had been on, and Angela had known better than to hang around London waiting for the knock.

But now she was back. Back, and apparently happy to be seen.

The third thing to know about Angela Di Salvo, he'd say, is the cars. Rumour had it she lived a pretty austere life, by her Dad's standards: no yachts, no glitzy nightclubs, no fancy meals out when she could cook at home. But she'd grown up in Nicky's garages, hanging about with mechanics and repairmen. And there were few things she liked better than a Maserati A6 or a finely preserved Stradale.

"I heard she shipped half of her collection out with her to Sicily," Len would say. "And had the other half sold off while she was gone. Sad, really. I expect she's here to see what's on the market, so's she can start to restock. I know *I'd* be looking, if I were her."

Hartwood's wet, pink nose would twitch at this last revelation; his cupidity, if Ruby was any sort of judge, well and truly piqued.

"Interesting," he'd say, taking in Di Salvo and the bodyguard - the *female* bodyguard, no less - who seemed to be glued to her side. "Very interesting."

~

"I'm not sure we know each other well enough for you to call me anything at all," El said, surveying Hartwood now not with disinterest but with the displeasure of a woman plagued by an unseen mosquito in a dark hotel room.

Hartwood pressed on, undeterred.

"I heard you might be looking for a new set of wheels," he said. "Something a bit... special."

CHAPTER 5

KINGSTON, LONDON
JULY 1997

If El had harboured any expectations about how or where a young, very rich and very technologically literate thief might live, Karen's home would have bulldozed right through them.

It was a bungalow, that would have been the first surprise: a '60s one-storey, neat and squat, the kind of brown brick L-shape El instinctively associated with elderly widows. The suburban street on which it sat was beige and sedate; its front garden was well tended, planted with roses and hydrangeas and soundtracked by susurrating honey-bees and the beat of butterfly wings.

Further down the driveway, she saw net curtains - the nicotine-ivory backdrop for a set of ornamental hedgehogs arranged in size order in the front window. Two further hedgehogs, one large and one small, sat on either side of the doorstep - the hog and its hoglet guarding the frosted glass door with identical ceramic smiles. Above them, mounted on the brickwork, a rustic sign invited visitors to Bless This House With Friendship & Laughter.

The only possible occupant, El thought, was a little old

lady - on a fixed income now, and not as mobile as she used to be, but still house-proud enough to prune the bushes once a week and run a Hoover round the carpet. If she concentrated, she could see the old dear's plastic rain scarf and pinafore; smell the carbolic soap and tuberose on her hands and neck.

It was a good trick; a hell of a good trick.

She approached the step with care, mindful of the hedgehogs, and rang the doorbell.

∽

Inside, the bungalow delivered everything its outside promised: floral patterns on the walls and furniture, lace doilies on the sideboard, tasselled lampshades and off-white stucco on the ceiling.

"You've definitely got a theme going," El remarked.

"More reliable than a burglar alarm, this is," Karen told her, waving a hand at the wallpaper, the worn shag carpet. "You can pick just about any lock, hack into just about any system, but there's no better security than looking like you've got nothing worth robbing to begin with. Trust me on this - I know whereof I speak."

She pushed through the beaded drapes separating the hallway from the kitchen and beckoned El through; El followed, the rustling beads slapping down on her head as she squeezed between them.

Inside was what would have been the second surprise: there was someone in the kitchen already, filling up a plastic kettle at the tiny sink. He was Karen's age or thereabouts, white and carroty and thin to the point of scrawny, the bones of his freckled arms and collarbone poking out from the sleeves and neck of his baggy t-shirt. A pair of wire-framed glasses covered most of the top half of his face; the top of his right hand was scarred and stitched, the veined skin stretched to accommodate a slim rectangular slab of... *something*, something green and glowing and embedded in the flesh below.

"It's an implant," Karen said, catching her staring. "Rare-earth magnet with a couple of LEDs strung 'round it. Fucking stupid idea, if you ask me, but he seems to like it."

The boy looked up from his task.

"No-one's asking you to get one," he said - his voice mild, softly Scottish.

"Wants to be an android when he grows up, don't you Fergus? A little cyborg Pinocchio."

Fergus raised one disapproving eyebrow at her, and returned to filling his kettle.

"I didn't realise you lived with someone," El said, saving her questions about the implant for another place, another time.

"You never asked," said Karen.

"She likes to keep me quiet," Fergus interjected, switching off the tap and flicking the kettle on to boil. "Can't think why. You're El, I'm guessing?"

El was caught off-guard; the idea of Karen having not just a live-in boyfriend but a live-in boyfriend who *knew who El was* somehow antithetical to the mental image of the lone, maverick tech wizard she'd inadvertently cultivated. And raised a follow-up concern, altogether more worrying: if the boyfriend knew who she was, did he also know what she *did*? What she was right now *doing*, with Karen?

"That's me," she said, warily.

"Don't worry about Fergus," Karen said, apparently picking up on her need for reassurance. "If there's one thing he does well, it's keep his mouth shut."

"It's my best feature," he agreed.

"And he's got his own secrets, haven't you?"

"They pale in comparison to yours," he said, setting two chipped cups of coffee down on the countertop. "I've put milk in both," he added to El. "Hope that's alright. There's sugar and sweetener in the cupboard if you need it. I'm off out, so you've got privacy for whatever dark deed it is you're plotting."

He kissed Karen lightly on the cheek, gave El a strange half-wave and disappeared through the drapes in a jangle of beads.

"And don't get arrested!" he shouted to Karen as he opened the front door and then closed it behind him, releasing the scent of foliage and the low hum of insects into the bungalow.

If Karen was embarrassed, she wasn't letting it show.

"Shall we take these downstairs?" she said, picking up the cups. "There's something I wanna show you before we get going."

∼

The first time they'd done a job together, El had pictured Karen's workshop as something like a Batcave: a shadowy, subterranean lair replete with computer monitors and futuristic hardware, complex tools laid out on titanium desktops and mechanical components of unknown origin suspended from its pitch-black walls.

The subterranean part, at least, had been accurate.

They'd accessed the basement level that housed the workshop via a hidden passageway - concealed, to El's amusement, in the pantry Karen, and presumably Fergus, used to stockpile dried pasta, tinned tomatoes and wilted back-issues of Kerrang! magazine. Karen had pressed a thumb against what had looked to El like a speck of dirt on one shelf, and the back wall had separated into two, splitting down the middle to reveal another room behind it, well lit but barely the size of a wardrobe - and in *that* room a flight of stairs, leading downwards.

The workshop itself was vast and suitably cavernous, bigger by far than the bungalow above - but artificially bright and air-conditioned and well-organised, the drills and soldering irons mounted on an oblong rack and a line of elaborate-looking locks and slim silver lock-picks laid out on a tool bench next to them. There were only two screens, twinned with a pair of boxy grey consoles and a set of matching keyboards. Each computer had its own desk and padded swivel chair, giving the workshop the overall appearance of an extravagantly large two-person office. The office, perhaps - if the tilt-top drafting board in the centre of the room was any indication - of a newly-qualified architect, or a particularly fastidious carpenter.

Spread across the drafting board was something that looked from a distance like a blueprint: straight edges and intricate, mathematical whorls inked in black on a sheet of white A1 paper.

Karen went straight to it, urging El to join her.

It wasn't a blueprint but a map, El saw as she moved closer: an aerial overview of a house and grounds, heavily annotated in navy biro.

"Have a look at this," Karen said, tapping the paper. "A *good* look. And tell me what you see."

An hour later, they were on the road to Essex - Karen, now appropriately suited and booted, piloting the Phantom down the motorway at a more cautious speed than El would have predicted, had she allowed herself to presuppose.

Twice they missed the turning into Lambswool Hall, creeping back and forth along endless identikit hedgerows and acres of unoccupied greenfield at five miles an hour in search of the right dirt road, the right point of entry. When the narrow, winding track they were looking for presented itself, they spun right, letting the Phantom's wheels carve a deeper groove in the tyre marks already scored into the sun-baked mud until they reached the entrance to the estate: a black filigreed gate, ten feet high and set into stone pillars that were half as high again, the cataracted eye of a security camera peering out at them from the stonework.

"See what I mean?" Karen said, as the gate opened automatically for them. "You buy a place like this, you're *asking* to get robbed."

The grounds inside were better tended, the grass mown to a uniform two inches. Buildings passed them on both sides as the Phantom crunched a path through the gravel trail that led to the main house: stables, a carriage house, a tall outhouse packed with casks and barrels and brewing kettles, and finally, abutted by a small asphalt racetrack that seemed to El more suitable for go-karts than sports cars, a vast barn-like structure that could have comfortably accommodated a passenger plane.

That'll be the hangar, she thought; the place he keeps his collection.

Hartwood, and only Hartwood, was waiting outside it.

"I thought Dexter said he'd have someone with him," said Karen quietly. "His business manager, or whatever."

"He did," El replied.

The Phantom drew to a halt perhaps six inches from Hartwood's feet. He leapt back in alarm, swiping at his shoes as if they were on fire.

Karen adjusted her earpiece, unfastened her seat belt and, with no regard whatsoever for Hartwood's moment of panic, unlocked the driver's side and padded around to the rear of the car.

The left suicide door in the back swung open.

And taking her cue, El stepped out onto the gravel.

∼

"Not bad," she said, surveying the contents of the hangar with a connoisseur's eye. "Not bad at all."

Hartwood tipped her an unctuous smile that she guessed was intended to be charming.

"Like what you see, do you?" he said.

He ran a caressing hand over the vehicle closest to him - a cream Lincoln Roadster with more than a whiff of '30s Hollywood about it.

Another one for Ruby, El thought. She and Sita'd have a field day in here.

Brushing past him with barely a downward glance at the Lincoln, she traced a slow circuit around the Porsches and Ferraris, Maybachs and Lamborghinis that formed a three-deep girdle around the hangar's centrepiece: the high, lean Bugatti Royale, still mounted on its raised podium.

Every now and then, to gauge his reaction, she passed her own hand over the roof of a GT or a millimetre above the passenger door of a convertible. Sure enough, though he tried to hide it, he winced at every touch; no doubt, she thought, visualising the grease stains she'd be leaving on the paintwork, the industrial polish he'd need to employ to remove them.

When she'd done a full lap, Karen treading silently but imposingly in her wake, she circled inwards, to the second ring of cars. Which was where she saw the Jaguar: Dexter's E-Type.

She gave it a cursory once-over, scarcely more than she'd given the others - enough to suggest interest, but nothing like enough to demonstrate intent. Then moved on, and further inwards, until she reached the Royale.

She paused beside it; laid one splayed, proprietorial palm on the bonnet.

He grimaced, she assumed involuntarily, at the violation.

"How much?" she asked.

"You winding me up?" he said, very nearly choking on the words. "If you know what that is, then you know I ain't selling."

She stared at him, long and cold - Angela Di Salvo's displeasure inscribed in her narrowed lips, her widened pupils, her corrugating forehead.

"My mistake," she said, with the same cool detachment El imagined she might use on anyone reckless enough to cross her, in the seconds before she ordered the men on her crew to deal with them. "I thought I was here to buy a car."

She raised one finger in the air.

"Jax," she added to Karen, her gaze still fixed on Hartwood, "get the Rolls running, would you? We're leaving."

Hartwood froze, and she saw on his face what Dexter must have seen, the day he sold the Jaguar: the instinctive urge to tell her to go fuck herself, wrestling with - and pinned swiftly down to the mat by - the terror of what she might do to him if he dared. There was something else there too, she thought, something more mercenary: the pre-emptive fear of a lucrative deal lost, of a cash cow driven out of the cattle pen before any milk could be extracted.

His voice, if not his body language, turned placatory.

"Hey, hey," he said. "No need to be like that. I ain't saying *no*, no, am I? It's only the Royale I'm talking about. All the rest," he gestured around to the other cars in the hangar, "all this lot - it's all on the table. Even the Buick over there."

He indicated a hulking but perfectly preserved '40s saloon in the outermost circle, its proportions suggesting a machine built to a fractionally larger scale than the sleeker and more streamlined numbers that surrounded it on either side.

Angela Di Salvo, El thought - Angela Di Salvo who kept her purchases strictly European, Angela Di Salvo who'd never *dream* of driving American - would find the offer nothing less than a slap in the face.

"*That*?" she said, with a contempt she almost felt herself on Di Salvo's behalf. "What would I want with *that*? The only other thing here I'd even *consider* is that E-Type."

She pointed to Dexter's Jaguar.

Hartwood brightened.

"Good choice, good choice," he said, glossing over her tone in favour of the one clause that might lead the exchange to something approaching a profitable end. "I'm a big fan of that one myself. Lovely bit of equipment, innit? Iconic. And it handles like a dream, I'll tell you that. Like a *dream*. Fifty grand and it's yours."

She took a moment to ponder Dexter's inevitable reaction to the E-Type's new price tag, as Angela Di Salvo reflected on its costs and benefits.

"No, I don't think so," she said. "It's a nice looking set of wheels, and I've always been partial to an XK6 engine. But they're ten a penny at the shows, E-Types. Especially the Series 1s. That one there - I'd give you twenty for it, max."

Hartwood sagged, his shoulders drooping as he saw the cash cow gallop away from him and into a neighbouring pasture.

"'Course," El added, "if the Royale *were* for sale... that'd be a different story. There's not much I wouldn't pay for a work of art like that."

"It went for five and a half mil at auction," said Hartwood quickly - seeing, she thought, one last chance to lure the cow back to the meadow. "And that was ten years back."

"At the Albert Hall," she replied. "I know. I was there."

"It'd be more than that now. Inflation and that. You'd get seven for it these days, easy."

"We'll have to agree to differ on that one. And I can't say exactly how you managed to get your hands on it, but I think we both know it weren't legit enough for you to take it back to auction. Not one of the big houses'd touch it, as is. Now, me - I'm less fussy. So what do you say we split the difference? I'll give you six for it. Cash."

The long, sharp intake of breath that followed made her worry for his blood oxygen supply.

"*Cash?*" he whispered, every ragged syllable sounding as if it had been wrenched from his lungs by a fist. "Six mil, *cash?*"

She smiled - a dark, predatory baring of the canines.

"You think I'm not good for it?" she asked.

His tiny cogs were turning; she could almost see them grinding, almost hear him replaying what Len Wolf had told him out in Stroud.

A safety deposit place.
£90m taken, and not a penny of it found.
And now she was back.

"When?" he asked.

"That a yes?" she said, still smiling. "Tomorrow. I'd say today, but I need to have a quick chat with my brief first. Get him to... free up a few of my assets."

"*Tomorrow?*"

"Early as you like. I've never been much for lie-ins. You get things ready for me this end, and me and Jax'll bring you your money. Easy as."

His pink face was purple now. Globules of sweat mingled with the gel at his hairline.

"Get things ready?" he repeated, his mouth hanging open.

"The service book," she said slowly, visibly amazed that something as precious as the Royale could have ever ended up in the possession of someone as dim witted at the man in front of her. "I assume you haven't got the right registration papers, and I won't be asking for them, but I'll need to see *some* sort of proof you've been looking after it properly, keeping it maintained. That I can take it on the road without the engine dropping out the bottom."

He nodded dumbly.

"And another thing," she added, as an afterthought. "Throw in delivery for the twenty grand, and I'll take that Jag of yours as well. The Phantom does the job, but it's not exactly agile. Call me greedy, but I quite fancy a new little runaround."

CHAPTER 6
SAFFRON WALDEN, ESSEX
JULY 1997

When Ruby and Sita mentioned climbing, El had baulked; had seen herself clinging to a plate-glass skyscraper by her fingertips, night-dew forming on her ski-mask as her toes sought purchase on the impossibly smooth surface of the wall beneath her.

She'd fought them on it; insisted that, like Sita, she didn't *do* physical, when it came to the job. That she was a talker, not a cat-burglar; a grifter, not a thief. And that this position on larceny, on straightforward theft with no element of the con involved - it wasn't one she'd reached of her own volition, through any soul-searching or ethical objection. She just didn't have the chops.

And yet, here she was.

In the dark, under cover of one of the many elaborate topiary flamingos that littered the grounds of Lambswool Hall, she watched Rose scramble - quickly, deftly, almost exactly like a cat-burglar - up the exterior side wall of the boxy Neo-Renaissance manor house that Gary Hartwood called home.

She was heading, El knew, for one of the property's three

guest bathrooms - the one furthest from the master bedroom in which, Karen's earlier surveillance had told them, Hartwood typically slept, often drunk and almost always alone.

It was skilfully executed, the scrambling; anyone would have conceded as much. El had known, long before agreeing to the job, that Rose was a competent free-climber: that she'd been raised by a steeplejack with a sideline in breaking and entering who'd taught her much of what he'd learned before he died; that when she took a holiday, she was more likely to be found on the Potrero Chico or the Niagara Escarpment than sunbathing in Rio or shopping in Manhattan. But *seeing* it, seeing her scale the wall with a fluidity and confidence borne of thirty years' experience and nothing keeping her there but the spikes in her shoes and the tensile strength of her hands on the bricks... that was a different story. And El was surprised, and immediately thereafter embarrassed, to find it not just objectively impressive - a virtuoso display, akin to hearing a jazz trumpeter improvise a solo - but profoundly attractive, too.

Fucking Ruby, she thought - the idea that she and Sita might have been right, might have finally made an accurate prediction about El's romantic destiny sticking in her throat like a hairball. Fucking, fucking Ruby.

"You say something?" Karen whispered from an adjoining section of avian shrubbery.

El shook her head.

Just below the bathroom window, Rose paused; reached for the outside ledge with one set of fingers, then the other, and hauled herself upwards, bringing one foot and then another to rest on the thin sliver of granite until she was balanced, with feline precision, on the balls of both, her palms pressed against the brickwork on either side of the window.

"Amazing," said Karen, under her breath. "She's like a fucking gecko."

There was an automatic centre punch in Rose's backpack, El knew; steel-tipped and no bigger than a pen. A centre punch and a towel, thick and soft enough to muffle the sound of breaking glass, should any glass need to be broken.

But neither tool was necessary. Hartwood, as Karen had hoped, had left the window open on the latch - no more than a few inches, to let the warm night air circulate around the house, but giving Rose enough room to fold herself inside, head and shoulders first.

"And there are definitely no alarms up there?" El asked, suddenly anxious as Rose's legs and ankles disappeared through the frosted glass.

"I'm not even going to dignify that with an answer," Karen said.

∽

"The most obvious point of ingress is here, by the front gate," Karen had told her in the basement, as they'd bent over the map of the Lambswool Hall grounds. "But the gate's electric, connected to the guard hut - we'd need somebody inside to physically push a button to let us in. I can disable it, but it'd take a bit of time, and I expect Hartwood's got a camera there too, which'd give us another set of problems."

"Where did you get this?" El had asked.

"A friend," Karen had replied vaguely, before pressing on. "Now, I happen to *know* - and don't ask me how, I ain't gonna tell you - that Hartwood's got two other static cameras on the go inside: one by the front door of his house, and the other mounted outside the warehouse where he keeps his cars. Just here, look."

She'd pointed at a large, square shape in the centre of the map, marked "garage" in bold, even capitals.

"Once we're in, I can cut the feed to the one by the warehouse, no trouble. We'll *have* to sort that one. And we shouldn't have to worry about the one by the house if we're going in 'round the side. But I don't see why we'd wanna give ourselves more headaches than we need to actually getting *in*, do you? So I suggest we go in *this* way instead."

This time she'd indicated a wide, empty space in the right hand corner of the paper.

"What am I seeing?" El said.

"It's a field. Well, more of a wood, really, but whoever planted it weren't that generous when they scattered the seeds, so it's mostly grass. Common land - nobody owns it. Or everyone does, depending on how you look at it. But wouldn't you know it? It backs right on to Hartwood's estate. And for reasons best known to him, but in my professional opinion because the bloke's a fucking muppet, the most hardcore security he's put up at that end is a big fuck-off fence. A *wooden* fence, if you can believe it. Sort that gets knocked down whenever there's a storm. Should take us all of about 30 seconds to dismantle, and we can just drive through."

"I assume the house is alarmed?"

"Yeah. And a little bird tells me there's motion sensors all over downstairs. Good news is, they're not *upstairs*. So as long as we keep up there, we're sorted."

The same little bird who got you those plans? El had wondered.

"You said there was a guard hut," she said.

"And two guards - one inside the hut watching the security feeds, another walking 'round the place with a torch. A night watchman, basically. The one in the hut never goes out of it, so he's not a factor. Probably half asleep most of the time anyway, I know I would be. But the watchman might be one to think about. If Hartwood's half as protective of his car collection as it sounds, then I'd put money on him making sure there's someone keeping an eye on it day and night. Not sure *how* we'll deal with that one."

She's her father's daughter, El had thought - remembering what she'd heard about Leon Baxter, the robber king of '70s London, who'd walk away from a job before he used a weapon or his fists.

"There'll be a way around it," she'd said, not sure herself what that way might be. "There always is."

∽

Rose was in the house perhaps two minutes before the bathroom window opened fully and a pair of nylon ropes fell from it, slapping lightly against the wall as they descended to the ground - the other ends of both, El assumed, anchored to one of the bathroom's sturdier fittings.

"You good?" Karen asked.

"Should be," El said. It was a lie, but she hoped it might prove prophetic.

Karen took to the rope like a pro, shimmying up the brickwork with the practised ease of a circus acrobat. El was slower and more lumbering, the knots biting into her palms through her gloves as she dragged her body towards the second floor. At the ledge, she stopped to control her breath before pulling herself through the window frame - not, she told herself, because it mattered whether or not Rose might judge her, might think her incapable or out of shape, but because keeping quiet was one of the non-negotiables of housebreaking, and if something was going to give them away, it wasn't going to be her wheezing.

It was only this focus on her breathing that stopped her laughing out loud when she saw the room they'd landed in.

To say it had a theme would be, she thought, to do it a grave disservice. It *was* a theme, from the floor to the ceiling, and that theme was: race-car.

Through the faint yellow light streaming in from the hallway, she saw chessboard wallpaper the black and white of a chequered flag; a high-backed, low-slung toilet designed to mimic the layout of a Formula 1 cockpit; a pull cord weighted down by a miniature tyre. Best of all was the bathtub: a four-castered, red and white striped, aerodynamically shaped oval with a set of pedals and a full-size steering wheel built around the taps.

"I imagine it's even better in daylight," Rose said with a smile, when she caught El staring.

Karen touched a finger to her lips, and they fell silent, falling in line behind her as she walked out of the bathroom and down the hallway to Hartwood's more conservatively decorated bedroom.

He was asleep - flat on his stomach on top of the covers of his enormous bed, bare chested in boxer shorts, his arms and legs spread wide in a starfish configuration. The smell of sour whiskey and cigars hung over him; from his position, El guessed that he'd passed out rather than dozed off.

Rose reached around, and into her backpack. After a second or two of fumbling, she drew out a gun - a short-barrelled semi-automatic, the kind El thought Hartwood might recognise from American cop shows.

She passed it to Karen, who took it and, grinning,

twirled it around her index finger like an Old West marksman.

"Here we go," she whispered.

She took three long steps forward and, when she was close enough, pressed the muzzle of the pistol against the base of Hartwood's skull.

"Up!" she roared into his ear, the ferocity in her voice taking even El aback. "Out of that fucking bed, now, before I blow your head off!"

CHAPTER 7
SAFFRON WALDEN, ESSEX
JULY 1997

Hartwood's whole body twitched - so quickly and so violently it might have seemed to the casual observer as if Karen had shot him already.

"You fucking deaf?" she shouted, bellowing the words into his ear canal and thrusting the pistol harder into the back of his head. "Get up! Now!"

He flopped around onto his back, exposing the paunch of his furry white belly and the half-open fly of his boxers. A small, circular pattern of urine was forming around the button.

The terror already taking hold of the nerves and muscles of his face intensified when he saw who was holding the gun that was now at his temple - and who was standing behind her, arms folded.

"Hello, Mr Hartwood," El said, slipping into Angela Di Salvo like a pair of comfortable shoes. "Bet you weren't expecting to see *me* so soon, were you?"

"What are you doing here?" he said, half-whispering. "What do you want?"

"I *want* to cut off your bollocks and feed them to you," she answered. "But I'm not sure Jax here'd go for it."

"I might," growled Karen, curling her finger more tightly around the trigger of the gun.

"Please don't hurt me," he said - whimpering now. "Please, I haven't done nothing."

"Up," Karen told him. "Out of that bed and on the floor, before I lose my patience."

She pulled the pistol back an inch and he struggled out of the bed, almost rolling off the mattress in his haste to comply. He hit the carpet and pulled himself to his knees, his hands clasped together in supplication.

"Don't hurt me," he said again - more quietly, choking back tears.

El stepped into his space, forcing him to crane his neck to look up at her as she spoke.

"I can do what I like, Mr Hartwood," she said softly. "Exactly what I like."

"And before you say anything stupid, like how you'll scream and someone'll come running," Karen said, moving behind him and returning the gun to the back of his head, "keep in mind: we know for a fact there's no-one else in the house here with you. You might have your cleaner and your housekeeper and whoever else knocking around in the day, but they go home at night, don't they? Go home, and don't come back 'til the morning. So scream, if you have to. But all the screaming in the world," she lowered her voice and bent her head closer to his, until he was shaking and the hairs on his neck prickled out at horizontal angles, "won't do nothing but *piss me off*."

She shook the gun, very lightly, for emphasis. He froze; clamped his lips together with the fervour of an amateur ventriloquist.

El walked across to the side of bed closest to where he was kneeling and lowered herself onto the edge, studiously avoiding the wet patch in the centre of the sheets.

"Turn around," she told him. "Turn around and look at me."

He twisted his head, very slowly, towards her until their eyes met - the gun keeping constant contact with his scalp.

"Let's talk about that Jag you just sold me," she said. "And about my brief - the one who looks after my money. I think you know him? Bloke named Redfearn. Dexter Redfearn."

∼

Outside, El knew, Ruby would be sizing up the hangar; thinking through the best way of forcing the locking mechanism on the roller shutters, when the time came.

"The lock'll be a piece of piss," Ruby had told them at the outset. "They always are. It's what comes before that's trickier."

What comes before, as El had understood it, looked something like this:

At 2.03am, exactly three minutes after El and Karen had followed Rose up the ropes and into Hartwood's bathroom, an old woman would clamber - very carefully, with the caution befitting her arthritic hips - over the apparently blown-down fence separating the grounds of Lambswool Hall from the adjacent field.

She'd be grey-haired, ruddy-cheeked; decked out top to toe in the Gore-Tex jacket, walking boots and waterproof trousers of the dedicated hiker. A sixty five litre rucksack, almost as large as her, would be slung over her stooped shoulders and secured across her chest and stomach; a

Nordic pole would dangle from one fist, a Maglite torch from the other.

Once on the property, she'd make her way past the manor house - checking her ordnance survey map with the torch as she passed, and temporarily blinding the house's security camera with its beam in the process - and onto the warehouse that, though she *of course* couldn't know it, contained tens of millions of pounds' worth of vintage vehicle.

Somewhere in the vicinity of this warehouse, the old woman would be stopped by a security guard - a man, El knew, only a few years younger than the woman, and close to retirement himself.

The man would ask her - in severe tones that would leave the woman in no doubt that he was prepared to escalate things to the police if he didn't like her answer - who *exactly* she was, and what the *hell* she thought she was doing trespassing on someone else's property.

"Night rambling, old chap," the woman would reply, with all the gin-soaked confidence of the rural rich. "Can't beat it. Gets the circulation going, you know. And so wonderfully *peaceful* - none of your oiks raring around the place on their motorbikes and what have you. 'Fraid I might have taken a wrong turning somewhere. Ended up in yonder paddock."

Here she'd cast a finger backwards, towards the field whence she came.

"How did you get in?" the guard would say, suspiciously. "There's gates all 'round that grass."

The old woman's brows would crease, confused.

"Gates?" she'd say, shaking her head. "No, don't think so. No gates there. There *was* a bit of fencing, blown down by the look of it. But certainly no *gate*."

The guard would mutter something under his breath; curse the boss too cheap to upgrade to even a bit of reinforced steel.

"You know," the old woman would add, as if imparting great wisdom, "you might want to consider having that seen to. Wouldn't want intruders getting in, what?"

"I'm going to have to ask you to leave," the guard would say, his irritation with the mad posh woman growing.

"And go *where*, old chap?" she'd ask. "Could scarcely tell you where I was *before* I got here. Shouldn't have plodded off the beaten track, really, but the mind wanders in the dark, does it not?"

"You can't stay here," he'd tell her, more firmly. "This is private land. There's no public right of way."

The old woman would scratch her cheek, pondering the quandary in which she found herself.

"I don't suppose you might see your way to giving me a lift?" she'd say. "Not *home*," she'd add before he could protest. "Heavens no, that would be *far* too far. But perhaps into the village? I can make my own way from there."

He'd be forced to refuse; to tell her he couldn't leave his post, not even to run up to the village and back.

The woman's face would fall; she'd look, suddenly, ten years older, and a little frightened.

"Please," she'd say, a small tremor entering her voice. "One doesn't like to *ask* for help - it's terribly embarrassing, even at this time of life. But the thing is, you see... I'm not certain I'm able to make it back without assistance. The memory, you know... it isn't what it was."

The guard, whose own faculties weren't as acute as they'd once been, would feel a pang of guilt, then a bolt of sympathy for the old bird.

It was only half a mile, he'd reason. He could be there

and back in half an hour, and no-one would be any the wiser.

"Alright," he'd concede. "I'll take you. But just to the village, mind. No further."

"Of course, of course," the old woman would agree, clutching at the handle of the walking pole that would very soon leave debilitating punctures in three out of four of the guard's tyres.

And the two of them would make their way to his car, and then on to the village, where the old woman's son would be waiting to collect her and take her back to Lambswool Hall in his brand new Range Rover.

∽

"Redfearn's your lawyer?" Hartwood said, disbelieving.

El smiled.

"You seem surprised, Mr Hartwood," she told him.

He swallowed, the action causing his Adam's Apple to throb in his throat like a pulse.

"I didn't know...," he began.

"Course you didn't. Why would you? But it's a funny thing, coincidence. Always coming 'round to bite *someone* on the arse."

Hartwood's eyes darted left, then right; the eyes of a cornered rat, preparing to lie its way out of the trap.

"Whatever he told you," he said. "Redfearn - whatever he said, it ain't true."

Angela Di Salvo seemed to consider this new information.

"Just to be clear," she said calmly. "You're saying he *didn't* sell you the Jag you tried to sell to me this morning? And that *wasn't* you on the answerphone message he played me at his office, telling him that that Jag - to repeat, *the same Jag you just tried to sell me* - had been clocked?"

He looked away; lowered his head.

"Now," she continued, "*he* told me he'd done no such thing, and it was just you trying your luck - trying to have your E-Type cake and eat it too. But he's a bent bastard, same as you. He wouldn't be my brief if he wasn't, would he? Be just like him to clock a car and sell it on if he thought he could get away with it."

"So on the one hand, if he's telling me the truth, then the bloke I was about to hand over six million of my hard-earned to - that's you - is a scam artist who might be setting *me* up to fleece me, after the fact."

"And on the other, if he's lying and he *did* sell you a dodgy motor... I've got you trying to pass it onto me, *knowing* it was clocked."

"Do you see how neither of these looks good for you, Mr Hartwood?"

Karen pressed the safety catch on the pistol, which released with an audible click.

Hartwood shuddered.

"Cat got your tongue?" El said.

He looked up at her imploringly.

"I'd never," he said through chattering teeth. He was shivering now, goose-bumps breaking out across his skin. Another trickle of urine ran down his bare leg; pooled under him on the carpet.

"You'd never *what*?"

"I'd never scam you. It weren't like that."

"But you didn't mind scamming my brief?"

"I didn't know who he was. I never woulda otherwise, I swear."

"So you *did* set him up?"

He didn't answer. Karen twisted the handle of the pistol, digging through the greasy, sweat-drenched roots of his hair with the end of the barrel.

El crouched down in front of him so that they were face to face, her nose wrinkling in distaste as the smell of the urine hit her.

"I don't appreciate someone thinking they can take me for a ride," she said softly. "So I'm thinking that *you owe me*, Mr Hartwood. Nod if you agree."

He nodded.

"Glad to hear it," she continued. "Now, the good news for you is: I know just how you can make it up to me. Me and Jax here, we'll be taking that Royale of yours with us when we go. No questions asked, no money changing hands. That alright with you? Nod again, if it is."

He nodded again, even more vigorously than before, his head pistoning back and forth on his shoulders.

By now, she thought, Ruby and Dexter would be inside the hangar - hot-wiring the rings of cars that stood between them and the Royale and rearranging them like Tetris blocks until they had room to drive the one they'd come for through the doors and out of Lambswool Hall, across the field.

"Alright, then," she said.

She got to her feet.

"Just one last thing," she added casually. "Before we leave you to... clean yourself up."

He tried to speak but failed, his shivers so intense they impeded his effort to form words.

"What was that?" she asked, cupping a hand to her ear.

"I said, anything," he replied eventually. "Anything you want, you can have it. Just please, please don't hurt me."

She let her nose wrinkle a second time, Angela Di

Salvo's revulsion at his weakness and his cowardice a tangible presence in the room.

"It seems to me, now we've had this conversation," she said, "that you might not need telling. But I'll say it anyway: you send anyone else after Redfearn, anyone at all, and we're going to have words. You and *Jax* are going to have words. You understand me? He may be a bent bastard, but he's *my* bent bastard. And he's useful to me, very useful. So I really don't appreciate you trying to gut him like a fish."

Hartwood's head jerked up from his chest, fast as a bullet. There was surprise on his face now, as well as fear; surprise, and confusion.

"What?" he said.

∼

"You don't want to *hurt* Hartwood," Ruby had told them, back in her new West Hampstead flat - Michael bandaged on the sofa and the others crowded around him in a Nativity tableau. "But you *do* want to give him a scare. A bad one."

"That's it?" El had said, taken aback at the mildness of Ruby's vengeance. "Just scare him?"

"You reckon we ought to leave a horse's head in his bed?" she'd answered scornfully. "*Think*, girl. Most important thing, the *only* important thing is getting *this* one," she'd gestured a thumb towards Dexter, "out of the grave he's dug himself. That's your priority. And you do *that* by working that weasel Hartwood over 'til he's shitting himself worried you'll come back and do him if he so much as *sneezes* near one of yours again."

El had believed her; had trusted that what she was saying was the truth. But she also knew her well enough to be reasonably sure that what she was hearing wasn't the *whole* of the truth - that there was more to it, a twist somewhere in the tale.

"And the rest?" she'd asked.

Ruby had played it deadpan for all of half a second before she'd folded, the papyrus creases of her face collapsing in on themselves in a broad, knowing smirk.

"You ever met a petrolhead?" she'd said. "A real one, not one of them weekend warriors? They bloody *love* their cars. Love 'em like a wife, like a daughter. And when they lose one... it's like a death. They *grieve*. So if this goes our way, and we manage to get that Bugatti out of his lockup... believe me, it'll hurt him more than if we stuck him in the ribs with his own bleedin' knife."

∽

Hartwood fixed her with what she thought he might describe, in more lucid moments, as an honest look: one that said that what he was about to tell her was the truth, the whole truth and nothing but the truth, so help him God.

"I never," he said, the quake in his voice gone. He sounded sure now; certain of the veracity of what he was saying. "Christ as my witness, I never laid a finger on him."

She studied him. He wasn't blinking; wasn't licking his lips or touching his face. Nothing about him suggested deception.

"Call me a cynic," she said, "but I'm really not sure I believe you."

His breathing quickened - not, she thought, because he was gearing himself up to lie, but because he so badly wanted her to believe him.

"What would I do it for?" he answered, sounding desperate. "Yeah, alright, I tried to squeeze a bit of money out of him. But what would I get out of hurting the geezer? Think about it - it don't make no sense. I wanted paying, and he couldn't very well pay me from his coffin, could he?"

She couldn't deny the logic of it.

But if it wasn't Hartwood, she thought, who *was* it? Who else would want to go after Dexter, specifically? Or Michael, for that matter?

"If you're lying to me," she said, the suggestion of threat now explicit, undeniable, "you'll regret it, Mr Hartwood."

"I ain't lying!" he shouted. "Whatever happened to Redfearn, it weren't me that done it!"

She found herself believing him; wondered if Rose and Karen thought the same.

Karen's face, directly behind Hartwood's, suggested she might - her wide-eyed expression the antithesis of the aggressive certainty her body language still communicated.

"You got the ropes?" El asked Rose, without turning around.

"Yeah," said Rose gruffly, in a Mockney accent El thought she might have picked up from Eastenders. "Got 'em in the bag."

El nodded at Karen.

"Tie him up and gag him," she told her. "We're done here."

~

There was silence in the car as they drove away from the estate. It didn't break until they hit the dual carriageway - heading south, back to London.

"What are we thinking?" Karen asked, her eyes on the road and hands gripping the wheel.

"It wasn't him," said Rose from the back seat. "He didn't do it."

No, El thought; no, he didn't.

"I agree," she said. "But where does that leave us?"

"We'll need to tell Ruby," said Rose.

"Yeah," said Karen. "But she's on the road still. Her and Dexter both. And I don't fancy ringing Michael to tell him, do you?"

"Sita," said Rose. "Call Sita. She won't have gone to bed yet – she's always been a night owl. And she'll want to know how things went."

"Knock yourself out," Karen told her.

Rose took her phone from her bag: a new handset, El noticed, smaller and less blocky than her last, the casing a darker grey and the aerial more discreet.

She pressed a button, then another, and the echo of a dialling tone filled the car's interior, leaving El unsure about whether or not she ought to be listening in.

The dialling stopped abruptly, and she heard a voice - tinny and distant, its features indecipherable.

"Sita?" Rose asked - a look of uncertainty, and then of concern passing over her. "What? *What* happened?"

"What?" Karen demanded. "What is it?"

The voice spoke, as indistinct as before.

"No," said Rose into the mouthpiece - sounding urgent, panicked. "No, absolutely not. Stay where you are. Lock the doors, phone Barbara Potter and *stay where you are*. We're on our way."

She pressed another button on the mobile, apparently ending the call, and the voice vanished into the ether.

"What's going on?" said Karen, fingers tightening further around the wheel. "Don't fuck about, just tell us."

Rose looked stricken, El thought; utterly horrified by whatever she'd just heard.

"That was Sita," she told them, shaking her head. "She's been… it's impossible, completely impossible."

"*What* is?" said El.

Rose stared at the phone in her hand as if willing it to elaborate, to reframe whatever Sita had told her into some form of narrative coherence.

"She's been attacked," she said. "Stabbed. On her doorstep, like Michael. *Exactly* like Michael."

CHAPTER 8
SOUTH KENSINGTON, LONDON
JULY 1997

Looking out of the window: that had been her first mistake. Not the only one she'd made that evening, in retrospect. But certainly her first.

Midnight had been and gone when she'd heard the screech of braking tyres on the street below; the familiar rattle of van doors opening, of something heavy (and already, in her mind's eye, valuable) lifted out and placed gingerly onto the pavement outside her building. It was unusual, but not unheard of for her neighbours to receive their more expensive deliveries in the early hours; the standard English conventions of not drawing attention to oneself, not disturbing the peace, not *causing a fuss* were, she'd found, less rigorously policed among the obscenely wealthy denizens of Knightsbridge and South Ken than elsewhere in the capital. And practiced, certainly, with less ardour.

She'd *tried* to resist the urge to look; to see for herself what treasures - what Georgian console tables, what Regency desk sets - might be making their way even at that moment into one of the grander apartments of the Chatham Court complex. She'd prepared herself a lemon tea; smoked one of the few cigarettes a day she allowed herself, in her dotage; begun to heat the water for a late-night bath. And still the van had rattled; still the engine of the van had thrummed, calling out to her like the thump of a heartbeat under the floorboards.

When she could take it no more, when the temptation to know became too great to bear, she slid her bare feet into a pair of sandals, fetched a lightweight bolero jacket - now dishearteningly tight around the upper back - from her dressing room, slipped out of her apartment and down the three flights of stairs to the foyer.

She'd hoped to catch a glimpse of whatever was being unloaded through the reinforced glass of the outer doors. But the angle of the van - a dirty white van, she'd seen then, dusted with a layer of grime so thick that the number plate was almost entirely obscured - was such, its bulky chassis so poorly parked that she could see almost nothing of its cargo without stepping beyond the immediate bounds of the apartment block. All that had been visible of the mysterious item was the furthest end of the opaque plastic sheet that covered it, its particular distentions suggestive of a square-bodied shape, or possibly a rectangle.

She unbolted the foyer doors - top, middle and bottom - and stepped tentatively out into the dark, her eyes on the van.

∼

"And that was when he came at me," Sita told them - her damaged arm resting flat on the waxed mahogany of her dining table as Barbara Potter sutured together the tears in her skin. "He'd pulled a balaclava over his face, but a knife that sharp, that ornate - you really couldn't miss it. Thankfully he didn't seem to have a clue how to use it. Just came *slashing* at me, like something out of a horror picture. Got me *here*, as you can see," she gestured to her static arm, "but I imagine - frankly, I rather hope - it will be quite some time before the feeling returns to his wrist."

"You're saying you fought him off?" asked Karen, incredulous.

"I may be richer in years than I used to be, darling," Sita replied matter-of-factly, her speech barely faltering as Barbara drove the needle in, "but I'm faster than I look. And so much of self-defence is in the leverage, in the manipulation. Applying the right pressure in the right spot at the right moment. A principle all of *us* can get behind, I daresay."

She smiled, and El saw the scene as it might have unfolded: the man, face covered, approaching Sita with his strange arced weapon held high over his head; Sita's arm rising to block the blade as it flew toward her, her body spinning not *away from* but *into* his as the flesh of her forearm absorbed the blow; both her hands reaching down to his, seeking purchase on the wrist that held the handle and then *twisting*, up and round and over until his palm opened and the knife fell to the ground, its danger spent.

Barbara Potter shook her head sadly, regretfully - no doubt lamenting the foolishness of an old woman with such cavalier disregard for her own safety.

"Where did he go?" Rose asked - looking more serious than Karen, more frightened. "Or she?"

She's thinking of *her*, El thought. Of Hannah.

Bloody Moriarty.

Hannah D'Amboise, or whatever she was currently calling herself, was Rose's half-sister - a fact that had come as a greater surprise to Rose than to anyone, when it was finally made known. Dexter's certainty that Hartwood, and only Hartwood, had been behind the attack on Michael meant that none of them had named her in relation to his stabbing - though this certainty, El suspected, was only part of the reason. Since her disappearance and the events that precipitated it, even Hannah's name had seemed to El to possess a kind of power, a talismanic potency that prevented them from invoking it unless absolutely necessary - as if saying it aloud would cause Hannah herself to appear before them like a Fury, ready to extract vengeance.

It's why she's Moriarty even in my head, El thought. It feels safer, somehow. Less like I'm tempting fate.

"*He*," Sita assured her. "Most certainly a *he*. I'd inferred as much from his height, but the toe I was able to connect to his more... delicate parts rather confirmed it."

"Nice one," said Karen, nodding approvingly. "Like it."

"You were going to tell us where he went?" El said.

"Towards the main road," said Sita. "In that dirty white van, no less. He didn't *run* away - he *drove*. And I'm afraid I couldn't muster the energy for a hot pursuit, after my initial burst of heroics."

"It was *his* van?"

This was from Rose.

"His van, and indeed *his* pile of empty cardboard boxes under the plastic sheeting he left behind him when he fled. I'm rather embarrassed to say that what I took to be a furniture delivery may in fact have been a ruse."

"A ruse?" El said. "You think he was trying to lure you outside?"

"Fucking hell," said Karen under her breath. "*Fuck*ing hell."

"It sounds so unlikely, doesn't it?" Sita answered. "There are more than a dozen private apartments in my building alone, over thirty permanent residents. But given how he reacted when I *did* go outside... I'd say there's every possibility that it was, as Auntie Ruby might put it, *one of them setups*. And then, of course..."

She stopped herself; shot a brief, reflexive glance at Barbara Potter. El didn't think the others caught it, but it was a look she'd seen before on Sita, many times - a look that said she had more to tell, maybe a *lot* more, but that now wasn't the time to tell it.

"So he knew you," said Karen, sprinting towards the conclusion El had reached herself. "He needed to get you out of the flat and on your own so he could come at you, and late at night so no-one'd be watching and try to stop him, but he knew you wouldn't just be wandering round without a reason. And he knew what you're like, *what* you like - what sort of shiny antique bollocks he'd have to dangle in front of you to get your attention. He *knew* you, Sita."

"Yes," said Sita. "Yes, I believe he did."

∽

Barbara Potter finished up the sutures just as Ruby and Dexter arrived, the two of them bursting through the front door like a small, localised hurricane.

El wondered who'd called them - Karen, or Rose, or Barbara herself. That Ruby would have a key to the apartment was a foregone conclusion.

"Christ almighty, woman!" Ruby said, rushing to Sita and taking stock of her arm, the narrow row of butterfly stitches now holding the bruising flesh together. "What the bleedin' hell have you done to yourself?"

"She's been bloody lucky," Barbara told Ruby - the stiff Ulster vowels and vestigial lilt of an accent, softened only a little by forty years in London, clearly underlining her disapproval. "Very bloody lucky. Her and your wee boy both."

She dropped the needle into the disposable sharps box she'd brought with her; pulled first her left hand, then her right free of their blue nitrile sheaths.

"I won't be asking what it is youse all have got yourselves mixed up in," she added. "But I hope you've got yourselves an exit strategy, is what I *will* say. I might not be around to sew youse up, the next time."

∽

"That ain't all of it, is it?" said Ruby, when Barbara Potter had gone and Sita had related to her and Dexter an abridged version of the story she'd told El and Rose and Karen. "There's more to it."

She looked long and hard at Sita, now reclining like Ariadne on a Rococo chaise lounge - her eyes closed and the back of one hand resting on her forehead.

"Not now," she replied. "Later. We'll talk later."

When they're gone, you mean, El thought, with the irritation that prickled her whenever she became aware of the two old women conspiring to withhold information - some clue or piece of a puzzle they'd decided it wasn't necessary for El, for example, to know.

But Ruby - the firmest advocate El had ever known for keeping things from others for what she decreed to be their own good - seemed to El's surprise to have no patience for it either, here and now.

"I ain't interested in secrets," she said softly. "Not from this lot - not no more. If there's something to say, you ought to say it to the rest of them an' all."

El flashed back, involuntarily, to a scene in the kitchen of Rose's Notting Hill house the previous year - to another knife, thickened with blood and tissue, its grip clenched tight in Ruby's hand and its blade buried deep in the neck of the man who'd probably have killed them all, given the chance. To the others who'd watched it happen: Karen, her ribs smashed and jaw broken; Rose, paralysed with shock and fear; Sita, the only one of them with a clear enough head to decide what needed to come next, what would have to be done.

To Dexter and Michael - honest, law-abiding Michael - carrying the body out of the house in a Matryoshka nest of cling film, duct tape, rubber sheets and carpet, because their Mum and Auntie Sita had asked them to.

Maybe, she thought, there *weren't* many secrets worth keeping, after that.

"You know, don't you?" said Karen. "The pair of you know it weren't Hartwood that did Michael."

Ruby seemed genuinely stunned.

"It weren't Hartwood?" she said. "How'd you know?"

Karen sized her up, sceptically - then, apparently convinced that her shock was real and not feigned, answered:

"He ain't got it in him. He was shitting it when El started throwing her weight around. And he pissed himself when I had that water pistol of yours pressed to his head - *literally* pissed himself. Like he'd never seen a gun before, let alone had one pointed right at him. Bloke like that... he wouldn't have the stomach for real violence. And I can't see him having the sort of connections that'd do it for him if he bunged some cash their way. A proper criminal would've laughed in his face if he tried."

"I have to say, I agree," Rose added. "I can well imagine him making threats from a distance, over the phone where there was no possibility of an immediate retaliation. But in person? No."

"Bleedin' hell," said Ruby, half to herself. "And you're sure about this, are you?"

"Never been surer," said Karen. "Man who leaves a puddle on the bedroom floor when you put a scare on him ain't a man who'd put himself on the hook for murder. Just wouldn't happen."

El turned to Sita - Sita, who'd stayed conspicuously silent through this last exchange.

"*You* knew, though," she said. "*You* knew it wasn't Hartwood."

Sita opened her eyes; removed her hand from her forehead and sat upright on the sofa, her expression grim.

"Not before," she replied gravely - all trace of irony and melodrama gone from her voice. "You must believe me, darling - I'd never have sent you off to chase your tails in the provinces if I'd so much as *suspected* that someone else was responsible for what was done to Michael. That boy is as good as my own child - I've wanted nothing more than to see the creature who hurt him brought low."

"Before when?" asked Ruby - more mildly than El might have expected.

"Before tonight. Before... *this*."

She gestured to her own, wounded arm.

"You think the person who attacked you was the same person that attacked Michael?" said Rose.

It was a logical conclusion to draw, El thought. But it was baffling, just the same - the idea that the same assailant would go after *both* a man as straight as Michael *and* a woman as inherently crooked as Sita. For all their closeness, the two of them ran - at least by day - in very different circles, the Venn diagram of their professional lives overlapping only on those few occasions when Sita happened to be running a job on a banker or a broker in the City.

Unless it wasn't the *job* that had marked them as targets, but a more personal grievance altogether.

Sita didn't reply.

Instead, she got up from the chaise lounge and walked slowly, tentatively, across the dining room to a black lacquered chest of drawers El recognised as one of several pieces the old women had liberated from a stately home in Surrey three summers earlier.

She opened the topmost drawer and, turning her back on them, retrieved something from inside.

When she turned around again, there was a knife in her hand: a pocket Toothpick that, with its unexpectedly curved blade extended, reminded El of nothing so much as a scimitar in miniature. It was whetstone-sharp and cruelly thin; flakes of drying, glue-like blood lingered on the metal. The handle was plain woodgrain, but decorated – inscribed with logograms, Japanese or Chinese, above a carving of what looked to El like an animal's head. A dragon, or an Oriental lion.

"Mother of God," whispered Ruby.

"This," said Sita, her eyes on the knife, "was the weapon used to stab me. I thought it prudent to retrieve it, afterwards - better that than leave it on the pavement and there be *questions* later. It wasn't until I brought it upstairs and really looked at it that I realised what it was. *Whose* it was."

"Soames," said Ruby distantly.

"Soames," Sita confirmed. "I may be wrong - I very much *hope* that I'm wrong. But given the events of this evening, and the misfortune that befell Michael last month... I'm afraid he may be back."

CHAPTER 9
EDGWARE, LONDON
APRIL 1972

Before there was Barbara Potter, there was Judit Neumann – a Hungarian-born midwife whose respect for the rule of law had eroded considerably when her son was given five years in Pentonville for resisting the enforcement efforts of the local National Front with a snooker cue. And before there was Judit Neumann, there was Winston.

Unlike the women who succeeded him, Winston Redfearn had received no formal clinical training beyond the combat medicine he'd picked up as a much younger man in the latter days of World War II, and informally practiced in fits and starts across the battle zones of the Italian peninsula. He was a typesetter by trade and a gardener by inclination, but the knack for healing in a pinch had never left him - a knack that Ruby Wood, the blue-eyed girl with the quick fingers who would eventually become his wife, had spotted the night they'd met in a run-down pub on the Kingsland Road in the spring of 1949.

She'd been seventeen, working the factory floor of a place that made ball-bearings and dreaming of better things. But still smart enough to put three tables between herself and the Twelvetrees brothers, Mark and Harold, when the heated words they'd been trading about their mother's ashes had become an exchange of fists and flying pint glasses - and practical enough to be impressed when the tall black man she'd been admiring earlier at the bar had stepped in to wrap up Harry Twelvetrees' lacerated arm with a strip of cotton torn from his own shirt sleeve.

Because she'd never had a problem getting what she wanted, and because he'd been noticing her just as she'd been noticing him, they began courting that very week - an arrangement that progressed to their mutual satisfaction until they married, with Sita and Winston's friend Hadley as their witnesses, in a Westminster registry office in the summer of 1955, the day troubled by the presence of neither Ruby's surviving relatives nor the extended family Winston had left behind in Trinidad before the war.

She and Sita were a double act by then, running pigeon drops and pigs-in-a-poke in the fiscally salubrious districts of Chelsea and West Brompton and making friends across the full spectrum of the London demimonde - and it wasn't so many years after, when word had spread of her new husband's facility with a needle and thread and a bottle of antiseptic, not to say his iron-clad discretion, that the first of Winston's patients turned up in the courtyard of their brand new flat in Barnet, stinking of faulty explosives and missing both a trouser leg and a chunk of the calf muscle it had previously concealed.

The patient, Keith Monroe, had been a particularly loquacious man, and had chattered non-stop as Winston, more taciturn by far, had washed, dressed, stitched and bandaged his wounds - primarily about the bungled robbery that had taken a bite out of his leg, singed off his eyebrows and led him, finally, to Winston's doorstep.

Winston had let him talk, tuning out the man's chittering until it was so much white noise - interrupting him at the last only to let him know when the reconstructive work was done, and to advise on the aftercare that might, with luck, prevent infection from taking root in the mangled limb.

"Appreciate it, doc," Monroe had told him - shaking Winston's hand, and tucking five warm pound notes into his saviour's top pocket on his way out.

Winston had been speechless.

"Where's the harm in it?" Ruby had said, when he'd related the incident to her later that night. "I know you, Winston Redfearn, and you'd have done it for nothing without a word of complaint. So if the man wants to pay you for your trouble, bleedin' well let 'im. Besides which - now might not be a bad moment to start thinking about putting the odd bit of money to one side for a rainy day. I didn't want to mention it before, 'cause I weren't sure myself, but I nipped in to see the nurse this morning, and it looks like we might be having a little visitor come May..."

And so had begun Winston's second career as an unofficial field medic, tending this time to the injuries suffered by the London criminal community across their myriad urban battlegrounds. He was quick, and efficient, and every bit as circumspect as they said, and as his reputation grew, so too did his case load - with two, sometimes three patients a month appearing at the flat with a fistful of cash and a burning desire to be healed of their cuts and bruises, burn marks and bullet holes. They were, for the most part, *good* patients: friendly, polite and grateful for the attention they received from him. Just as importantly, for the salving of Winston's ethical code and conscience, the crimes that sent them his way were almost always non-violent - typically involving larceny of one kind or another, or so his wife had assured him. On this, as on everything, he trusted her word: it had been a central tenet of their marriage from the beginning that, whatever the jobs she worked or the cons she pulled on other people, they would never lie to one another, by design or by omission.

Until Charlie Soames came knocking.

~

He wasn't the affable sort. But if Charlie Soames had *had* friends, and those friends had been asked to describe him, they might have used words like *meticulous. Single-minded. Obsessive*, even.

He was a neat, clean little man in his middle thirties, always well-scrubbed and smooth-shaven. His style of dress tended towards the idiosyncratic: the dandyish flourishes of his polished spats, frock coat and pinstripe trousers suggesting a minor character from a PG Wodehouse novel. His voice was soft, the trace of a lisp discernible in his sibilants - entirely at odds with the rudeness of his manner.

Like Ruby and Sita, he was a grifter, his preferred marks wealthy widows twenty or thirty years his senior - ones lonely or vulnerable enough to be impressed by a dapper, solicitous young suitor who said all the right things, up until the day he disappeared into the ether with a solitaire ring, or a treasured coin collection, or a set of Russian Imperial dinner plates, leaving the women too flustered or too ashamed to report the matter to the appropriate authorities.

Ruby despised him.

"Bleedin' parasite," she'd mutter with a shake of her head when his name was uttered in her presence. "Not right, is it, what he does? Not right at all."

Winston had been shocked to see Soames, when he'd appeared at 9 o'clock one weekday morning outside the front door of the flat - not only because his wife's contempt for the man was public knowledge, but also because the *kind* of con he was made him an unlikely candidate for physical peril. In spite of the ostentatious pocket knife he carried with him everywhere, playing it back and forth between his fingers like a pair of Chinese worry-balls (more for the look of it than anything else, in Ruby's opinion), Soames' primary weapon wasn't a crowbar or an old service pistol but his instinct - his unerring predator's sense of which dowager would be receptive to his advances, and which would invite him to take his flowers and his flattery elsewhere. The firing line, for him, was a purely metaphorical proposition.

He'd been more shocked by the skinny, frightened-looking white girl half-hidden behind Soames' body – a girl so thin she seemed to him nearly transparent, her peroxide hair scattered around her pinched face like day-old candy floss and the troubled, otherworldly look in her puffy, bloodshot eyes much older than the sixteen or seventeen he thought she probably was.

"Can I help you?" Winston had asked Soames warily, half-wondering if he was at the wrong address, had pressed the wrong doorbell.

"I'm certain you can," Soames had replied, the c of *certain* reaching Winston as an aspirated *th*.

Winston had shown them inside; invited them - still puzzled, but as polite as always - to take a seat at the kitchen table. Asked what he could do for them.

Soames had shot a look to the girl, who - head bowed, eyes fixed on the table - had slid her emaciated arms out of her brown polo-neck and pulled it over her head, exposing her braless chest, her ribs, her concave stomach and the three bloodstained cloth bandages taped inexpertly to her hip, her navel and her right breast.

"Go on," Soames told her. "Show the man why we're here."

She reached for the tape, wincing as its grip on her skin loosened and came free, and pulled down the bandage across her breast, exposing the wound underneath.

It was a bite mark: raw and deep and bloody, a torn red crescent going all the way down to the muscle. A bite mark, the size and shape of an adult human mouth.

∽

"Lois, her name was," Ruby said. "I never found out much about her, even when I went digging, but Win weren't wrong about her being young. Way I heard it, she'd been shacking up with Soames a while already by then, poor kid. Couldn't have had no family to speak of - no-one to nip in and see she was alright, no-one to ask questions. And I know I ain't telling none of you what you don't know already, but a girl like that - the wrong kind of bloke can get away with doing just about anything he wants with her."

∽

Winston stared at the bite; couldn't look away.

The teeth that had made it, as far as he could tell, were straight and evenly-spaced - an entirely unremarkable set of canines and incisors, molars and bicuspids. Only one of the gouges they'd made in the girl's flesh was unusual - a clotting groove in the upper left corner of the bite, sharply tapered at one edge in such a way as to suggest that the eye tooth that had left it was cracked, or otherwise damaged.

Seeing it, he turned, automatically, from the wound to Charlie Soames' mouth, its parted lips allowing him a flash of Soames' fang-like incisors.

The left one was chipped - the jagged edge a perfect match for the bite taken out of the girl's mauled breast.

∽

"There were two more bites just like it under the bandages, Win said," Ruby continued. "And that weren't the half of it, neither. It weren't obvious, if you weren't looking. But when she'd took her kit off, and he could see her, *really* see her... well, it were there. Right in front of him."

∽

The ribs had been fractured. Probably not recently, or there'd have been more swelling, more bruising, but fractured all the same, and healed wrong - at least two of them slipped out of place, not where they ought to be below the intercostals. She must have known, he told himself; must have *felt* the misalignment, the stabbing pain in her chest when she coughed or sneezed.

Her fingers had been broken - he noticed that, too. Broken, but not set, the middle and index digits of both hands more knotted than the others, more crooked. He thought, though he couldn't say exactly why, that they'd been bent rather than crushed, deliberately peeled up and back until they snapped. With no effort at all he could imagine it: the crunch of the bones as they gave way under the weight of Soames' clenched fist; the pleasure, the malicious satisfaction on his face as she begged him to stop.

And those bites... Puppa Jesus, those bites...

~

"He were a sensitive soul, your dad," Ruby told Dexter, squeezing his hand. "A thinker, like your brother. A peacemaker, an' all. But that don't mean he was soft. He'd stand up for anyone that needed it. Anyone he saw couldn't stand up for themselves."

~

Winston rose to his feet; took three steps across the kitchen towards Soames until he was looming over him, close enough to see the fine white hairs of his earlobes, to smell his lemongrass cologne.

"You did this?" Winston asked him, the anger bringing out the old patois in his voice, lowering his pitch to a baritone.

"Should it matter to you *who* did it?" Soames replied, unfazed. "I thought the *point* of you was that you didn't ask questions."

Winston stretched himself to his full height, tension pressing his tendons to the upper surface of his throat.

"Imma ask you again," he said. "Did you do this to this girl?"

Soames smiled lazily, untroubled by the unspoken threat.

"What do you say?" he asked the girl. "*Was* it me? *Did* I do it?"

She swallowed, but didn't answer immediately - only fixed the table with the same dead-eyed stare she'd worn since they arrived.

"No," she whispered eventually, as unconvincing as anything Winston had ever heard.

He'll kill her one day, he thought, with sudden but absolute certainty. If she leaves here with him, if she *stays* with him... he'll kill her, as surely as I stand here now. And she'll suffer more and worse than this, before he does.

He clamped a hand to Soames' narrow shoulder, ready to pluck him from his chair and remove him, bodily, from the flat.

Soames barely flinched at the touch.

"So melodramatic," he said, his short tongue styling *so* as *tho*. "Do sit *down*, Winston. I'm not leaving, not until you've done whatever it is you need to do to restore this lovely lady to her former glory. And you're not going to *make* me leave, whatever opinion you might have on the subject. Not unless you want to spend every fortnight of the next ten years visiting *your* lovely lady down in Holloway."

∽

"He'd done his homework, the bastard," Ruby said, uncharacteristically flat. "Must have been keeping tabs on me for months, me and Sita both, in case he ever needed a favour and we weren't inclined to give it to him. He were like that, you know what I mean? The blackmailing sort. Always had one ear out for something he could use to get one over on you. Sort that'd salt away every detail, every bit of information for his little black book."

"As it happened, he weren't clued up on the job we were running *right* then - it were too recent, even for him. We'd only just started. But he had all the details on what we'd been up to before: names, dates, everything. And he'd have used it an' all, if he hadn't got his way - Win were sure of it."

∽

And so, with something worse than a gun to his head, Winston set to it: cleaning the girl's wounds with water and then an antibiotic ointment he kept under the sink; sterilising the flesh around and inside them, stitching and bandaging where he had to.

Nausea rippled through his guts at the sight of them - the acid burn of swallowed vomit kissing his windpipe as his hands threaded the needle to sew the ragged ends of her skin together, Soames watching him as he worked.

Watching, and smiling.

∽

None of the others spoke. Only Sita, whom El guessed must have heard the story before – might have known it well, even - seemed unaffected by the telling.

"Soames tried to pay him, when Win finished up with the girl," she continued, still sounding distant, her mind tuned to another place and time. "Not a lot, probably just what he had in his pockets, but still. *Pay* him, like Win had done him a service. If it'd been me, I think I might've decked him, bunged the girl a few hundred quid and a train ticket to Scotland and drove her to the station before he came to – and hang the consequences. But Win weren't like that - weren't impulsive like I am. He'd never have done nothing to put me in danger."

Her face sagged, the effort of recollection apparently taking its toll.

Karen cleared her throat.

"That's horrible," she said. "It is, really. But what's it got to do with this Soames coming after *you*, now?"

Ruby rubbed at her eyes and sighed.

"Like I said," she answered. "Win weren't impulsive. But

it gnawed away at him, thinking about Soames and that girl and what she'd likely gone back to, what he'd *let* her go back to. Thinking his hands were tied, that he couldn't help - that Soames'd trace it back to him if he said anything, tried to *do* anything for the girl. Trace it back to him, then pick up the phone to the Old Bill and tip 'em off about some of the things me and Sita here'd been up to."

"He had himself convinced we were helpless, is what I'm saying - that Soames had us over a barrel, and that was all there was to it."

"Me, though... I had other ideas."

CHAPTER 10

EDGWARE, LONDON
MAY 1972

She couldn't get it off her mind, once Winston had told her. It kept her awake at night.

It was like a virus; a sickness. As if the knowledge of Soames and his young girlfriend and those crescent-shaped tears on her breasts, her neck, her hips was a disease her husband had contracted and then passed on to her.

And then there was the other part of it - the knowing that Soames *had* her. That he'd kept tabs on her, made notes and gathered evidence - evidence he could use at any time he fancied, any time he wanted a favour. Could *keep* using.

Because it was true, what they said about blackmail: you paid, and you paid, and you never stopped paying.

On the third, sleepless night, a solution came to her.

It wasn't elegant; wasn't particularly fair, if you believed in the dispensation of justice. But she wasn't sure she could do better, especially not with Sita temporarily out of the picture, and the longer she waited, the worse things would be for the girl, and possibly for Ruby too.

The following morning, with the boys at school and Win at

the allotment - the place he went to get away from himself, to perform his godless variation on a prayer - she took the bus to her lock-up, a ten-car storage bay in Colindale she'd been renting in cash since the '60s from a property developer who, as far as she could make out, had her pegged as either a wealthy housewife with a spending problem she'd been hiding from her husband or a second-tier film star with a very forgettable face. She made a point of wearing her biggest, most elaborate sunglasses whenever they met, to keep him guessing.

She chose the Corvette for the journey: a vintage cherry red C1 she'd had shipped over from a dealer in Los Angeles the previous month. It was a lovely car; a great shiny slice of Americana, big and bold and impressive. It lifted her mood, driving it - sliding into the soft leather seats, running her hands over the steering wheel, hearing the engine come roaring into life like a jungle cat. It gave her a spring in her step; a bit of extra confidence.

She'd need them both, where she was going.

In the Corvette, she crossed the upper reaches of north London, zig-zagging the suburbs of Finchley and Southgate, the grey estates and half-built tower blocks of Tottenham and Walthamstow until she hit the cluster of Palladian architecture and well-tended greenery on the peripheries of Epping Forest that she still thought of as Essex, whatever the government said.

The place she was looking for was hard to find, necessitating a handful of detours through the eerily quiet streets of Ilford and Harold Wood and more than a couple of glances at the A to Z in the glovebox. The Corvette was more conspicuous there, the look and feel of the area more threadbare - the older money of Barnet and Brent and Harrow seeming to stretch not quite far enough east to touch the newer money flowing west from the Essex boroughs.

When she finally *did* see the house, separated from its neighbours by a long, wide driveway and a line of densely planted fir trees, she couldn't believe she'd managed to miss it, even from a distance.

It was strangely proportioned, for one thing - both its bright white walls and the many windows dotted around them curved rather than angular, cast in rounds and not the squares and rectangles she'd come to expect of a conventional dwelling. There were three storeys, one layered on top of the other in circles of decreasing size, the final storey topped by a small open balcony surrounded - *penned in* - on all sides by high metal railings. The overarching impression was of a nautical wedding cake, or an artistically inclined baker set loose on the early sketches of a luxury cruise liner.

She left the Corvette at the top of the driveway, wanting to maintain the element of surprise as long as was possible, and walked the path to the front door - an old-fashioned hardwood number that wouldn't have been out of place on the top deck of a tea clipper, crowned by a bulky brass knocker in the shape of an anchor.

The man who answered the door had aged ten years in the eighteen months since she'd seen him last: his pot belly now bloomed to full fat, his black hair and moustache streaked with grey and slivers of white, the smoker's lines at the corners of his mouth deepened to scar-like grooves and the circles under his eyes turned to sagging purple pouches.

The cigarette he'd been preparing to light before he registered who he was looking at fell from his lips to the ground as he took her in.

She seized the advantage his surprise gave her; it might be the only one she'd get.

"Alright, Des?" she asked him. "Mind if I come in? I got a proposition for you."

~

"Desmond King," said Sita, jumping in to fill the pause left by the parched throat and dry tongue that had caused Ruby to lapse into silence.

"Where have I heard that name?" asked Karen.

"Your Mum knew him," Ruby answered, sipping at a glass of water Dexter had conveyed to her from some unseen region of the apartment. "Your old man too, I shouldn't wonder."

"*Knew* him?" asked El.

"I'm afraid he's no longer with us," said Sita.

"Liver failure," Ruby added. "1983, must have been. Can't say I was surprised, neither - not with what he used to put away."

"Who was he, then?" said Karen.

"He was a lot of things, Des King," said Ruby. "But what he really *liked* was crossing the pavement. Him and his gang must've done over two dozen banks in the '60s. Never got caught for one of them, neither. Always managed to get away clean."

She took another long drink of her water.

"Well," she continued, "I say *always*..."

~

He hadn't wanted her there; that much was clear. But he'd known better than to insult her outright, so he held the door open to let her inside; walked her through the house with its decking floors and portholes and sat her down in the garden with a glass of lemonade. He'd poured himself three fingers of Scotch in a coffee mug, she noticed, but she couldn't begrudge it - not after she saw how badly his hands shook as he unstacked the chairs.

"What can I do for you, Ruby?" he asked, when he'd taken a drink - coughing to clear the morning phlegm from his throat.

Go careful, she told herself. He's polite enough now, but you don't know how he'll turn if you push him too hard.

"You got a problem," she said, slowly.

"Do I?" he answered, equally wary.

"Yeah."

"You gonna tell me what it is, then?"

She ran a finger across the rim of her lemonade glass.

"I know you done that building society job over in Woolwich last month, you and your lads," she said. "The one that got that old bloke killed."

It was a nasty way of putting it - she knew that. As she'd heard it, neither Des King nor his gang had gone in intending to hurt anyone, much less put a hole in the chest of a pensioner queuing up to deposit a bagful of loose change. But one of the young ones had been green, jittery, not used to handling a shotgun, and when it went off accidentally in his hands, he hadn't had the sense to point it up to the ceiling before it hit someone.

And now it wasn't just an armed robbery charge King and the rest of them would be looking at, if they got picked up for it. It'd be manslaughter. Murder, even.

"Thing of it is," she continued, when he didn't respond, "if *I* know, then it won't be long before the Bill know, too. Because I might have a bit more of an ear to the ground than your average plod, but they ain't *all* stupid. And sooner or later, one of them'll hear some of what I've been hearing. And then... well, like I said: you got a problem."

"What do you want?" he said, not looking her way. He was shaking again, she saw; the remains of the Scotch spilling out of the mug and onto the green cast iron of the table.

Go careful, she told herself again.

"Believe it or not," she said, "I want to help. Turns out, I got a bit of a problem of my own that needs sorting. And it seems to me that, if you're amenable, there might be a way to get rid of *both* our problems. Sort 'em both out, all in one go."

～

"He might've dumped the guns," she told them. "Chucked 'em in the river or buried 'em somewhere. In which case, I'd have been snookered. But I didn't think he would've done, somehow. He weren't stupid, neither. And the trouble with chucking things in the river or burying 'em in a field is that all it takes, *all* it takes, is for one of them things to wash up on a mudbank or get dug up by some bright spark with a metal detector, and suddenly you're right back where you started - only worse off, because now other people've got their hands on what it was you wanted hidden in the first place, and they're asking themselves, and maybe *more* than just themselves, how it is that a shedload of serious ammunition happened to find its way to that field or that mudbank unaided."

"He'd kept 'em - that was what I reckoned. Kept 'em close."

～

"*My* problem," she said, moistening her suddenly dry mouth with the lemonade and pushing on before he could deny it all or lose his rag, "ain't quite the same as yours, I'll grant you. I ain't going into details, 'cause you don't need to know 'em, but the fact of the matter is, there's someone I need out the picture, sharpish. And soft touch that I am, I'd rather see him inside than six feet under."

"So what I'm proposing is a bit of a quid pro quo. You help me get shot of him - and I'll see to it that the Bill don't so much as look your way about that Woolwich business."

"Sound good?"

⁓

"I see where this is going," said Karen. "Des King gives you the guns and whatever else incriminating he's got from his bank job, and you use it to set up Charlie Soames. That about right?"

Ruby nodded.

"Spot on," she said.

"And you weren't at all worried that Soames might have given you up to the police anyway?" asked Dexter, ever the lawyer. "Especially if he made the connection between the setup and the threats he made to Dad?"

"'Course I bleedin' was!" Ruby replied. "Worried myself sick about it, morning and night. But was else was I supposed to do? Didn't have a lot of other options, did I? At least if he was banged up, I'd have a bit of time to have a rummage round his gaff and see if I could find whatever it was he had on me. And he'd have a hell of a lot less credibility throwing accusations 'round from the inside of a cell than he would've done from some rich bird's house off Park Lane."

~

King pulled another cigarette from the box in his top pocket, clamped it between his stained front teeth and lit it, his hands steadying as he inhaled.

"Alright," he said, "you got my attention. I'm not saying any of it's *true*, what you just said. But let's say for argument's sake that it was, and I *had* found myself with a problem like that one you just mentioned. How exactly would you go about fixing it? And what would I have to do for you, if you did?"

"That," she replied, with more confidence than she felt, "is a bloody good question. And I think you're gonna like the answer. Because what I got in mind, it don't need much more from you than your blessing."

~

She recounted what she thought it would take - the shopping list of ingredients that, together, would bring about the right result.

First, the van. It would have to be new - that was a given. She couldn't risk there being any previous owners waiting in the wings for the Bill to talk to, when the time came. But it would have to be unremarkable, too - something completely innocuous, drab even, a Transit or a Morris Minor in grey or brown. Something you wouldn't look twice at, if you passed it in the street.

She was confident enough that she could lay her hands on one without much trouble.

Next, the certificates - the legal-looking bits of ownership paperwork that, when strategically placed in the glove compartment, would tie Soames irrefutably to the van.

These, too, she could take care of, or so she told Des King - though here (and this part she kept to herself) she'd likely need to pull a bit on Sita, who had of the two of them both the keener nose for forgery and the more cordial relationship with Ralph Anderson, a wizened little pixie of a man over in Wood Green who was widely considered the Michelangelo of the counterfeit document world.

Then something belonging to Soames, something that anyone who knew him knew was his. Not the knife; he'd never let that out of his sight. But a piece of jewellery, perhaps. The little gold pendant he wore round his neck, the chain so cheap and thin that a halfway decent pickpocket could sidle up to him in the pub or the paper shop and have the clasp untied before he'd even noticed they were there.

(She'd need Sita for that too, once she was back, Ruby thought - not because Sita was the better dip, but because she'd always been marginally better at disguising herself of the two of them, and keeping Soames in the dark for as long as possible was a definite necessity. Doing it herself would be too risky, too risky by far).

And finally, assuming King still had them - the shotguns.

∿

"And anything else you might have left over from the job," she added. "Anything the Bill can trace back to that bank. Don't matter what it is, so long as it's evidence."

∿

Soames, she happened to know, kept a garage in Cricklewood - an unwanted bequest from his old man, who'd been high up in the motor trade. It was empty, disused; visited once a month, if that, so Soames could check it was still standing.

She'd take the van there herself, late at night when there was no-one about; drive it inside, leave the pendant and the guns - the latter wiped clean of any incriminating fingerprints - in the cab, then lock the place back up and make her exit, heading back to Edgware by way of a phone box from which she'd dial the number of the Mapesbury Police Station switchboard.

That robbery in Woolwich, she'd tell the operator in a breathless voice that sounded nothing at all like her own - the one where that poor old gentleman was shot. I know who did it. Not all of them, not the whole gang, but the main one, the ringleader. And I know where you can find him.

∽

"He's known to the Bill, this bloke I want rid of," she told King. "They've had eyes on him for a while, on what he gets up to, but they've never had much to pin on him, so they've had to stick to watching. They'd bloody *love* an excuse to take him in."

This, she'd heard from Sita - who'd heard it, in turn, from a friend of hers, an Assistant Commissioner with the Met - was the gospel truth. Most of Soames' marks, it was true, stayed quiet after the fact; kept their own, embarrassed counsel. But not all. And those ones who *had* spoken up had been convincing enough to induce at least one department to begin an informal investigation - an investigation, Sita had assured her, that was very much ongoing.

Des King lit another cigarette - his third of the morning, on Ruby's count.

"*If* you were right about that job in Woolwich," he said, cirrus clouds of smoke rising up from his palate as he spoke, "and it's still an *if*: how would I know I could trust you with that hardware you seem to think I've got - that hardware you say could put me and my lads away for a very long time? Seems to me you'd be asking me to take a hell of a leap of faith. And that's before I've even asked about whatever poor bastard it is you want sending down instead."

"Him?" she said derisively. "You don't want to worry about him. He ain't worth your tears, I'll tell you that. And as for the other thing... like I said, if *I've* heard about that Woolwich job, then other people will have an' all. Word travels, don't it? Whether you want it to or not. And I can see from your face that you know that as well as I do, that you been wondering yourself how long it'll be before the hammer falls and there's a knock at the door you don't want to answer. So here's a question for you instead, and I'm thinking it's a better one for you to be asking yourself: other than packing your bags and taking your missus to the Costa Del Sol for a very long holiday... what choice have you got, except trusting me?"

∽

El took a breath she didn't realise she'd been holding while she'd been listening to Ruby talk.

"It worked, didn't it?" she said, knowing the answer. "You did it, and it worked. Soames went down."

Ruby nodded again.

"Even better than I thought it were going to," she said. "The Bill turned up to his garage about an hour after I called 'em. Arrested him at home the very next morning, bright and early."

"It was the opportunity they'd been waiting for," said Sita. "No-one cares for a vulture, not even the police. And I won't pretend I'm sorry that those women he tricked were spared the ignominy of a trial, however foolishly they might have behaved."

"How long did he get?" Karen asked.

"How long did he *do*, you mean?" Ruby replied.

"Isn't that what she asked?" said Rose.

This time Ruby shook her head.

"He *got* life," she said. "Twenty year minimum tariff. The Bill never found no-one else to charge with him, and what with the robbery and that bloke in the building society pegging it, it stood to reason he'd be looking at a long stretch if he got convicted. Which he did, I should say. The jury didn't take to him any more than the Bill did. But as for how long of that he *did*..."

"He *was* at Hendon, as of the year before last," Sita said. "We'd been doing what we could before then to monitor his movements, inasmuch as there were any movements to monitor, but I'm afraid he rather dropped off our radar lately, what with one thing and another."

One thing and another, El thought, marvelling at Sita's knack for euphemism. Then: twenty years. *Twenty* years, for a job you didn't do. That's a lot of time to nurse a grudge.

"And you think he's out now?" said Dexter.

Ruby shrugged.

"It's been more than twenty years, ain't it?" she said. "And seeing as it were pretty obvious to begin with who had reason to stitch him up, and seeing as he's had a quarter of a century to work it out if he hadn't done to begin with, *and* seeing as someone's been after your brother and your Auntie Sita with a knife I'd swear on your Dad's life was *his* knife... I'd say the odds of it were good, wouldn't you?"

CHAPTER 11
HERNE BAY, KENT
JULY 1997

Satis House - that was El's first thought, on seeing the derelict seaside mansion that, according to Dexter's contact at the Home Office, had quartered Charlie Soames since his release from HMP Hendon. Satis House, and Miss Havisham inside, stalking the hallways in her moth-eaten wedding dress, a train of mice and rats and spiders dancing at her feet.

"It's a little run-down, isn't it?" said Rose, taking in the boarded windows, the crumbling brickwork, the tangles of weeds and rushes springing up to shoulder height on every side.

Karen's preliminary digging had identified the house as an inheritance rather than a purchase, passed down to Soames in his father's will along with the Cricklewood garage. Which made sense to El: it was big, and it was old - 17th century or earlier, on first glance - but she struggled to imagine anyone choosing to live in it, much less paying for the pleasure.

The narrow path that led from the road to the house was winding, the overgrown grass and nettles growing alongside and across it suggesting years, if not decades of neglect. They took it slowly, cautiously - El relieved that DI Gwen Sandhu's work, unlike Angela Di Salvo's, necessitated sensible shoes, a thick coat and a high street trouser suit that kept the mud from her legs.

Rose - DS Helen Layton, for today at least - was similarly dressed, but altogether more nervous. And as far as El was concerned, for good reason: she'd never played the inside before, not really. Not when there was anything much at stake.

∼

"She'll be absolutely fine," Sita had assured her. "*Better* than fine, I would think. You forget, darling - she's spent most of her life pretending to be somebody she isn't. I doubt another half hour will tax her."

El had her doubts. Had her doubts, in fact, about the entire undertaking, about the wisdom of going to see Soames at all, when so much of the information they needed to protect themselves - how long he'd been out of prison, whether he really *was* behind the attacks on Michael and Sita and what other surprises he might have in store for the rest of Ruby's extended family if he was - could have been gleaned through safer, more covert channels. But Ruby had insisted.

"You'll get more out of him face to face," she'd said. "Especially you," she'd added to El. "You pitch it right, push his buttons, and he'll tell you a bleedin' sight more than you'll get from looking him up on a computer."

Karen, receiving the observation as a personal affront, had muttered something indecipherable but vexed and stalked away to Sita's bathroom.

Maybe this is what I deserve for thinking I could retire, El had thought, already weary at the prospect of what lay ahead.

"Do I at least get to take Karen with me?" she'd asked. "Nothing you've said makes me want to drop in on him solo."

Ruby and Sita had traded one of the coded looks that she found so persistently infuriating - Ruby tilting her chin questioningly, and Sita replying with an almost-imperceptible shake of the head.

"I ain't sure she's right for this one," said Ruby cagily.

"And why is that?" asked El, well on her way to irritated.

Ruby had started to answer, but Sita - sensing El's mood - had intervened instead.

"You won't remember Leon Baxter," she'd said, in the same even tone El had heard her use to mollify disgruntled marks, before they caught on that they were being conned. "He was long before your time, of course. But I wonder, have you ever *seen* him? In a photograph, perhaps, or a newspaper article?"

El tried to visualise Karen's father's face, the smile or the frown that might have briefly graced the inside pages of a local paper after his disappearance twenty years ago or more, and failed.

"No," she said. "No, I don't think so."

"Ah," Sita replied. Then: "In that case, you may have to take me and Auntie Ruby at our word. The issue, you see, is one of familial resemblance. Leon Baxter was rather well-known in our corner of the world, and Karen…"

"Is the spitting image of her old man," finished Ruby. "Put her in front of Soames, even in a policewoman's get-up or what have you, and he'll smell a rat straight off, even if he can't put his finger on why."

"I'm not going on my own," El had protested.

"Please don't look at me," Dexter said, before she could ask him. "We know he knows what *I* look like, and while I would share many things with Michael, I'd prefer that we didn't end up with matching stab-wounds."

Ruby and Sita exchanged another furtive look.

She'll need someone with her, El imagined she could read in Sita's pursed lips and raised eyebrow. *Who knows what she'll find there?*

Who do you suggest? Ruby's wrinkled forehead seemed to say in response. *We ain't exactly rolling in candidates here.*

There was absolute silence for a beat or two. And then the eyes of both women fell, almost in unison, on Rose.

∽

The young white man who answered the door was camp, slightly built and as friendly-looking as a cartoon piglet - nothing like the bent-backed butler El might have expected to usher them into a house so monstrously gothic. He wore the purple scrubs, blue plastic apron and disposable gloves of a home care assistant, and smelled strongly of lanolin and antiseptic.

He introduced himself as Jared, no surname.

"What can I do for you today?" he asked, his friendliness undimmed by the warrant cards they presented.

"We need to have a word with Mr Soames, if he's in," said El.

Jared's open face looked momentarily conflicted.

"He's *in*," he said. "But I've only just got him out the bath. Is it urgent?"

"It is, I'm afraid," El said.

Jared nodded understandingly, one overstretched key worker to another.

"You'd best come on through, then," he told them.

Inside, the house was less dilapidated - dated but clean, its threadbare carpets vacuumed and its walls and ceiling surprisingly free of cobwebs.

"The cleaner comes in in the mornings," Jared said, when he saw them looking. "Does all the surfaces, has a bit of a hoover round. There's not much he can do with the garden, though - you must have seen for yourselves how wild things have got out there. And I don't know one end of a lawnmower from the other, just between us, so I wouldn't be much use even if I *didn't* have my hands full with Charlie."

"What is it you do for Mr Soames?" El asked.

"Oh, I do everything," he answered. "His meals, his medication, his personal care... you name it. I'm not live-in, he's not quite there yet, not while he can get himself in and out of bed, but I'm here every day but Sunday, 8 'til 4."

"Does he need a lot of care?" asked Rose - communicating, to El's relief, no more interest than the bathing, dressing and toileting requirements of an elderly man would usually pique in the course of routine questioning.

"Not as much as some I've worked with. But he can't walk very far, with his emphysema, and gets very out of breath when he doesn't have his oxygen, so it can all get a bit hands-on. He's still all there, though," he added quickly. "No dementia or anything like that. He had a stroke two years ago, which means his speech gets a bit slurred when he's tired or excited, but he's as sharp as you or me when he has to be."

Oxygen and late-stage emphysema, El thought - not exactly a winning formula for an attempted murderer. If it *is* him going after Ruby, then he's got someone doing the legwork for him.

Jared seemed an unlikely candidate, on first impressions, though she wasn't entirely willing to discount him as a possibility quite yet.

"Does Mr Soames get many visitors?" she asked.

"Just me and the cleaner, that I know of," he said. "There's a social worker who comes to check on him – not often though, maybe once a month or so? I can count on one hand the number of times I've seen her. He can't really get out and about without lugging the oxygen tank around with him. I suppose it can't be easy trying to keep in touch with people when you're..."

He stopped himself, mid-indiscretion.

You know he was inside, then, El thought. How did you find out, I wonder? Did he tell you himself?

"Anyway," he said, "no, is the answer. No visitors. I can ask the cleaner if he knows of anyone, if you want? He might have seen something I've missed."

"Thank you," said Rose. "That would be very helpful."

They walked together to the back of the house, through a long oblong dining room and into the conservatory, its dirty glass walls opening out onto the untended grounds beyond. There, in a wicker armchair, a tartan blanket draped over his knees and an oxygen mask clamped to his nose and mouth by an elasticated strap sat an old man, scrawny and jaundiced in his pyjamas.

Jesus, El thought. If he was thirty five in '72...

She'd heard that prison aged people; had seen the phenomenon close up in one or two acquaintances. But never quite this dramatically.

The man in the wicker chair, with his paper skin and drooping mouth, could have passed for eighty - but must, she realised, have been barely into his sixties. Younger than Ruby and Sita.

"Visitors for you, Charlie," said Jared, in a loud, cheerful voice.

Slowly, the man reached a hand to the mask and prised it away from his jaw, letting it fall onto his chest.

"Visitors?" he wheezed. The lisp Ruby had described was there - *vithitorth*, the question had sounded like - but was subordinate to the gasp and whistle of his breath.

"Detective Inspector Sandhu, Mr Soames," El said, flashing the warrant card a second time. "And this is Detective Sergeant Layton. We were hoping to have a word with you about an incident in Kensington last week."

"In *Kensington?*" said Jared, with the same wide-eyed surprise he might have applied to *Ulaanbaatar?* or *the Mississippi Delta?* "You're not local?"

"Can we have a few minutes, Jared?" said Soames. "In private?"

Jared looked from Soames to El and Rose, concerned but powerless to refuse.

"I'll be cleaning up in the bathroom," he told Soames. "You just call me if you need me, okay?"

He stepped back out into the hallway, leaving the door to the conservatory ajar.

"Would you mind closing that?" Soames asked Rose, when he'd left. "Sound travels everywhere in this place, and he's got very big ears for such a little poof."

Anger, then disgust passed over Rose's face at the slur - not obvious but there, all the same.

Keep it in, El willed her. For God's sake, keep it in.

"We won't take up too much of your time, Mr Soames," she said, when the door was shut. "But we were hoping to ask you a few questions about your whereabouts in the early hours of last Tuesday."

It was a faintly absurd opening gambit, she thought - the most cursory look at him suggested that he hadn't left the house in weeks, let alone the county. But she had to start somewhere.

Soames smiled - an unpleasantly rapacious peeling back of the lips and revealing of the sharp yellow-brown points of his teeth that El would have found unsettling even without knowing his history, what those teeth had done.

"You can drop all that, now Jared's gone," he said, every other word punctuated by the wheezing rattle of air dredged deep from his failing lungs. "I know who you are, Miss Gardener. And *you*, Lady Winchester. To be perfectly frank, I expected to hear from one or other of you before now. But I won't hold it against you. Age takes its toll on all of our faculties, even your Mrs Redfearn's. I suppose I should be grateful that two visits from my friend with the knife were enough to grab her attention, at her time of life."

He put the mask to his face and took a long, slow pull of air before continuing.

"Now," he said, "I know you *thought* you were here on some sort of reconnaissance mission. But as I'm sure you're fast beginning to realise, you were wrong. In fact, you're here to listen. So I invite you both to close your mouths and take a seat. Because I have a lot to say, and I'm going to need you to keep up."

PART II
SEPTEMBER

FROM THE EVENING REVIEW
8TH MARCH 1991

Wainwright, Guilty Of Perjury, Jailed For 18 Months

Edward Wainwright, chief executive of clothing giant Fine Cloth and presenter of the Channel 4 series MD SOS, was convicted at the Old Bailey today on perjury charges and jailed for 18 months.

Wainwright, 63, showed no reaction as he stood in the dock to hear the verdict against him.

"These charges represent a very serious set of offences," Mr Justice Eddington told the court, as Wainwright was sentenced.

Wainwright was convinced of perjuring himself in an affidavit to the high court during a libel case brought against The Clarion newspaper and his own biographer, Henry Dashwood, last year, following the publication of a story detailing an extramarital affair between Wainwright and a hairdresser, Vivian Jelson. He was also found to have perjured himself during the libel trial.

He was sentenced to 18 months for the first count of

perjury, and a further 18 months for the second. The sentences will run concurrently.

Additionally, he was ordered to pay £150,000 costs and was told that he would serve at least one year of his sentence.

Following sentencing, Wainwright was taken to HMP Hendon, north west London, to begin his prison stay.

He plans to appeal the verdict, his solicitor, Anne Marsden, said after the hearing.

Continued on page 2.

FROM THE OAKLAND GIRLFRIEND
SEPTEMBER 1997

Yes I Am, Says English Aristo

Reclusive English aristocrat and art connoisseur Lady Rose Winchester, widow of deceased Fairlight Media CEO Sir Sebastian Winchester and rumoured owner of the world's largest collection of Roy Lichtenstein paintings, confirmed this week what some of us have suspected for a while: she's one of us.

At a benefit for the Bay Area Children's Society held Friday night at San Francisco's Museo de los Arroyos, Lady Rose and her date - a woman she named only as "Kate" - cuddled up and smiled for the cameras and seemed delighted to be spending the evening in each other's company.

Asked directly whether this public appearance constituted an official coming out, she answered: "Absolutely. Let all your readers know - I'm gay, and I've never been happier."

CHAPTER 12
COW HOLLOW, SAN FRANCISCO
SEPTEMBER 1997

Bulldog's was an embarrassment of Anglophilia - its tightly stacked shelves awash with boxes of PG Tips, family-size bars of Dairy Milk and, to El's mild horror, jar upon jar of potted beef. Strings of Union Jack bunting hung low from the strip-lit ceiling, the little flags dancing in the breeze blowing in from the marina with every swing of the entrance door. An elaborate shrine to the Princess of Wales had been erected by the checkout, a ten inch framed photograph at its centre - testament to the grief still keenly felt at the loss of Diana by the eponymous Bulldog, an expat Mancunian marketing manager turned grocery store proprietor and, since settling in the Bay Area, proudly out leather queen.

There was nothing there that El couldn't have picked up at a third of the price from her local supermarket or the Departures lounge at Heathrow, but she browsed the aisles avidly regardless, studying the labels on every tin of baked beans and packet of chocolate Hobnobs with the ferocity of purpose of a mystery shopper on the lookout for points to deduct from the final tally. There were, she noted as she made her rounds, mercifully few other customers in the store to block her path or disrupt her line of sight; partly, she imagined, because it was the middle of the day, and partly because - as Rose, who knew the city best of all of them, had suggested - Bulldog's had at least two rival, but more recently established British-themed food retailers snapping at its heels and eating into its profit margins.

("I don't rate them, though," Rose had added of the newcomers. "They're American-owned, both of them. I nipped in to get a few things from the one on Chestnut Street when I was last over here, and the woman behind the counter handed me a *pumpkin* when I asked her where she kept the orange squash").

She was on her third lap of the chilled section when she saw him, loading smoked back bacon and thick-veined Stilton into a shopping cart: a stocky, grey-haired walrus of a man, all luxuriant eyebrows and well-cultivated moustaches, his wide chest and substantial gut covered by a brown short-sleeved shirt open at the neck and, incongruously, the tight-fitting khaki trousers of a teenage undergraduate. His fair skin was pink and his nose peeling, a casualty of the hot late-summer sun and what she guessed was his own refusal to capitulate to sunscreen. He was, to her at least, as screamingly English to the naked eye as the contents of his trolley.

She accelerated, making a beeline for his fridge, stopping just short of his broad back.

"Sorry," she said, reaching around him for a block of Red Leicester, "can I just squeeze past you there, love?"

He spun around to look at her, his attention captured.

It was the voice, she thought; the echoes of Halifax, or possibly Wakefield, in her short vowels and affectionate colloquialism. It would have fallen on him, in this place, like the opening chords of a song half-remembered from childhood; would have sounded, more than anything he'd heard recently, like home.

"You don't get many of you 'round here," he said, his accent a gruffer variation on the one she'd offered him. He smiled at her as he spoke, the action drawing his moustaches up into his nostrils.

"Many of me?" she asked.

"Yorkshiremen," he answered. "Or women, I should say. Where are you from, lass?"

"Leeds," she told him, deciding as she said it that it was a better choice than the smaller towns she'd been debating - that a big city might afford her that bit more wiggle room to fudge the cultural and geographic specifics, should she need to. "Though I'm surprised you can tell, I've lived in London so long."

He chuckled knowingly.

"You and me both," he said.

She dropped the cheese into her basket and took a step to the right, moving as if to extricate herself politely from the conversation.

("You sure about this?" she'd asked Ruby and Sita, when they'd proposed Bulldog's as a likely place to engineer the first, accidental meeting - finding it difficult to believe that a man in his position would stoop to doing his own shopping at all, when an assistant could be dispatched to any shop from Oakland to San Mateo at the drop of a hat.

"Totally," Ruby had said. "He does everything himself, always has. Does the shopping, mows the lawn, changes the lightbulbs... you name it. You know the sort - rich as Croesus, but prides himself on being just like the rest of us commoners. Typical Northerner, if you ask me. Like one of them mill owners out of Elizabeth Gaskell."

El, knowing Ruby considered El's Midlands hometown Up North and El herself as Northern as a Gateshead miner, had bitten her tongue).

"What brings you all the way out here?" he asked her, prolonging the dialogue exactly as she'd hoped he would.

He was lonely, she thought. Lonely and homesick.

"Oh, you know," she said vaguely, "work stuff. Thought I might get a bit of time off to go and have a look around, maybe rent a car and drive up to Wine Country, but it hasn't happened yet."

"What is it you do for a living, then?"

She let herself look nervous - reluctant to give away personal details to the strange old man who'd cornered her in the dairy section.

He saw her unease; seemed to understand he'd have to assuage it somehow, if he was going to persuade her to keep talking.

"Don't look so nervous," he said, smiling again. "I'm old enough to be your dad. It's just nice to talk to someone who doesn't sound like they just walked off the set of Baywatch. You'll see what I mean, if you stop here long enough."

She relaxed her shoulders; rearranged her body into a less defensive posture.

"I'm a programmer," she said, tucking a loose handful of her newly pink hair behind one ear. A strand of it caught, painfully, on the trail of silver earrings Sita had set into the lobe and cartilage.

("Better verisimilitude than comfort, darling," Sita had told her, as she'd approached her with the piercing gun. "These are the sacrifices we make for our art").

"One of them Silicon Valley types, eh?" he asked.

"Hardly," she said. "But I'll happily take a cheque off

them, if they make me an offer. I just need to persuade them that what I've got is worth their money."

His pupils widened slightly, his professional interest stirring. There was nothing in the background research Ruby had compiled to suggest he'd ever invested in technology - but she supposed you could only stay in San Francisco for so long before the Gold Rush called to you, the smell of newly-minted tech cash drawing you in as irresistibly as a Looney Tunes rabbit lured to an open window by a blueberry pie.

"Selling something, are you?" he said.

She shrugged, bashful.

"Just some software," she said. "Nothing very exciting."

"What's it do, then, this software?"

She eyed him up, suddenly wary again.

He realised his mistake - that he'd pushed too hard, asked too many questions - and backtracked.

"Sorry," he said, his moustaches drooping. "Never know when to stop talking, me."

"You're alright," she said - warming to him in his moment of what seemed like genuine remorse, and ignoring the lightning-flash of guilt that shuddered through her as a consequence.

He looked down at his trolley, the blue cheese and bacon he'd layered on to an already substantial mound of Jaffa Cakes, Walkers Crisps and salad cream.

"Listen," he said. "There's a cafe up the road, a proper one. Let me get them to put this behind the counter, and then what do you say I buy you a cup of tea, if you've not got owt else on this morning?"

She bit her lip, showing him she was considering the offer - the small reward of a friendly face and a familiar accent in an alien place competing with the more significant risk of agreeing to a drink with a perfect stranger who might well be interested in more than just her software.

"That's very kind of you," she said, "but..."

"No funny business," he added quickly. "Just a sit down and a natter, one weary traveller to another. Go on."

She studied him again, weighing up the threat and the promise.

"I don't even know your name," she said.

This time he beamed, the moustaches curling at the edges.

"That's easily remedied," he said. "It's Ted. Ted Wainwright."

She allowed herself a second's pause, then inhaled sharply - her wariness turning to shock, then mortification.

"Oh my God," she said slowly. "I should have known. I *thought* I recognised your face. You're *that* Ted Wainwright, aren't you? You were on that show on Channel 4, that business rescue thing. MD SOS?"

"That were me," he said, with no trace of ego. "Though it feels like a hell of a long time ago now, that does."

You're wondering if I know the rest of the story, aren't you? she thought. If I read about you in the papers. Or saw you on the news, when they took you down in handcuffs.

"Well, it's nice to meet you," she said weakly - more trusting now, her guard more obviously down. A little bit starstruck, even.

"And you," he replied. "But fair's fair. Now you know *my* name, shouldn't I get to hear yours?"

She willed herself to blush; concentrated, and felt the creep of embarrassment travel up her neck and onto her cheeks.

"Right," she said haltingly. "Yeah, of course. Sorry, yeah. I'm Angela. Angela Di Salvo."

Over three cups of weak black tea and a plate of heavy buttermilk scones, she told him her story - what it was that had brought her to the city.

She wasn't just a programmer, she said; she was a *computer games* programmer, one of a handful of in-house developers at a twelve-strong studio on the Isle of Dogs. They specialised in puzzles and point-and-click adventures, their most lucrative output the multi-title Gerbils! franchise, wherein players were tasked with guiding a pair of brainless pet rodents from their owners' garden to the safety of their indoor cage while navigating a succession of ever-more-deadly domestic booby traps. It was fun, satisfying and generally well-paid work, made more satisfying still when the founder of the studio, inspired by the actions of his larger US competitors, had encouraged his team to spend one day of every working week developing their own side-projects - and, bucking the current trends of the industry, had allowed them to retain the rights to any intellectual property these side-projects generated.

She'd always been interested in graphics editing and image-manipulation - it was one of the interests that had led her to game design in the first place. And when, flicking through a magazine in the staffroom on her lunch break, she came across an article about life on the run for long-term fugitives, an idea for a side-project occurred to her.

Existing age-progression software, she knew - the kind the police used to predict how criminals might look, twenty or thirty years after they'd disappeared from public view - commonly relied on a degree of artistic interpretation: on the image creator making predictions about the way the suspect's appearance would evolve over time, based on anything from a single photograph to a lifetime's worth of photo albums and the faces of the suspect's immediate family, and then drawing on these predictions to sketch out a line or wrinkle here, a receding hairline there, a thickening of the nose or a softening of the jawline.

Other, newer alternatives drew on larger-scale data - the photographs of a hundred people, or a thousand, or a hundred thousand of the same sex and ethnic group - to estimate how the individual's face might change over a similar time-frame; an algorithm here replacing the human touch in divining the relevant changes, but the look of the aged-up image still, ultimately, a matter of guesswork and prognostication.

But what if, she wondered, there were a way to remove the guesswork? To *guarantee* the accuracy of the final outcome?

"It got me thinking about forensic anthropologists," she told Wainwright, "and the way they do facial construction when they've got nothing but a skull to work with. They use software - but they also use modelling clay, stuff like that. They work out which bits of bone fragments go where, and then fill in the gaps, until they've got something that looks like a real person. It's not always 100% accurate, what they end up with - it doesn't always stand up in court, for example - but a lot of what I've seen looks pretty good to me. So I asked myself: how would you go about writing the code for a piece of software that reconstructed a *living* face the same way?"

("You do *know* there's already people starting to do this sort of thing in the States, don't you?" Karen had said, when Ruby had first floated the idea for the rope. "At the Smithsonian, places like that? It's not exactly an established field, but it's getting a bit of traction. It's not *new* new, is what I'm saying."

"And how well do you think a bloke like Wainwright knows the ins and outs of the Smithsonian?" Ruby had answered, half-rhetorically. "Reckon he subscribes to Forensic Anthropology Today, do you?")

Writing and testing the code took months; far longer than it would have done, had she been able to dedicate a solid block of time to the task. Six months in, she was sleep deprived, exhausted - her every waking moment spent darting back and forth between Gerbils Unbound!, the latest entry in the series (scheduled for release in early January 1998) and the project she'd come to think of, privately, as Dorian Gray.

And then, finally, it was finished.

"Did it work?" Wainwright asked her. He was on the edge of his seat, she noticed; hanging on her every word.

"There's still a small error margin," she conceded. "But we're looking at an overall accuracy rate of something like 98%. I've run over four thousand historical face-shots through it so far, and nearly every one has been a nigh-on perfect match for the person as they look now."

"*Historical* face-shots?"

"You know... baby photos, pictures from birthday parties, that sort of thing. You run them through the program, and digitally compare what it generates with the person as they look today. It's dead easy to use, now it's up and running. Though it's still in beta, obviously. It'll need more work doing to it before it's ready to go to market."

His eyes were saucers now, his mouth virtually hanging open.

It was the baby photos, she thought - disgusted with herself, with how well she'd played him. The baby photos sealed it. Got him on the hook, just like you knew they would.

"You said you were selling it, this bit of software?" he said, trying to play it cool, to keep his excitement – and his burgeoning hope - in check.

"It's what I'm here for," she said. "I'm back to back with meetings all week."

"Potential buyers?"

She nodded.

"Investors too. Thought I'd best hedge my bets in case none of the buyers bite, so I've got a couple of venture capitalists lined up tomorrow and Friday. You don't know 'til you try, do you?"

He took a small, reluctant bite of his scone, almost certainly for the show of it; swallowed it down before he could possibly have tasted it.

"How does it work, then?" he asked.

She laughed.

"Give me a hundred thousand for it, and I'll tell you anything you want," she said, smiling to soften the blow of the rebuff. "Pounds, not dollars. Otherwise that's a trade secret you're asking me to give away."

"That's how much it's worth? A hundred grand?"

She looked down at her plate self-consciously.

"Could be," she said quietly. "Let's see what the VC says tomorrow. I might have got it all wrong."

She could *feel* it these days - that gossamer-fine heartbeat of a moment, right before the mark tipped from *almost* to *all in*. She felt it now; could see it in his tapping fingers, the infinitesimal twitch of his eyelid.

"And what if I did?" he said.

"Did what?" she answered, feigning confusion.

"Make you an offer. Or express an interest in making one, let's say. Would you tell me then?"

∼

Don't be daft, she told him. It's a program - a piece of code. The sort of buyers I'm talking to are in tech, security, law enforcement. They'll be selling it on to the police and the government. What could *you* possibly want with it?

I've got my reasons, he said. And you know who I am, so you know I can afford it. It's not a wind-up; I'm not pulling your leg.

But *why*? she asked, nonplussed at the turn the conversation seemed to be taking.

He mulled the question over.

How about this? he said. You come and see me at the office before you fly back home and show me how it does what it does, or as much as you *can* show me without giving the game and all your IP away, and I'll tell you why I might want it. Quid pro quo.

She stared at him, radiating puzzlement. But when he reached into his wallet for a business card and held it out to her across the table, she took it with no objection at all.

∼

Three blocks from the cafe and heading west on foot towards Presidio Heights, she took a brand-new, American-issue mobile phone from her pocket and dialled one of only seven numbers saved in the phone's address book.

"We're on," she said, before the woman on the other end could answer. "Tell Karen to get ready."

∼

Twenty feet behind her, innocuous in Bermuda shorts and a Giants cap and lost among a moving procession of tourists just arrived in the city from Milwaukee, a man she'd never seen before watched her go. When he judged she was distracted, preoccupied by her phone call, he pulled the camera dangling around his neck to his eye, pointed the lens at her face in profile and took his shot: once; twice; three times. Then replaced the lid, and walked on.

CHAPTER 13
HERNE BAY, KENT
JULY 1997

Hunched over in his chair, his hands clawed and his cheeks sunken, Soames could have been a gargoyle - a chimeric grotesque, scaring away intruders from the shingles of his decaying country house.

"It *was* you who went after Michael and Sita, then?" El said, not doing him the courtesy of sitting.

"Indirectly, indirectly," Soames replied. The admission seemed to leave him breathless, forcing him to take another pull on the oxygen mask.

"Who did you send?" demanded Rose, the new note of raw, cold anger in her voice reminding El of the woman she'd got to know in a townhouse in Notting Hill what felt like a decade ago now - the one who'd masterminded a hit on her own father as payback for the sins of his past. "I'd be interested to know what kind of person could be persuaded to ambush a senior citizen on her doorstep in the middle of the night. And how much they'd ask to be paid for the privilege."

Soames rested his withered head against the back of his

chair and closed his eyes. For a second, El wondered if he'd fallen asleep.

"I don't have much air left in me, Lady Winchester," he said after a moment, his eyes still shut. "And I don't intend to use it to answer that question. So if I were you, I'd try another. You might ask me, for example, what I want with our Mrs Redfearn. Or with any of you."

"You know it was Ruby who set you up," El said flatly. "That she had you put away."

There was no sense pretending he didn't; she'd known that almost as soon as Jared had left the room, as soon as Soames had spoken.

"Not at first," he said, sounding strained, the words like gravel in his throat. "But I've had a lot of time to think about it, Miss Gardener. A *lot* of time. And people talk. You might want to remind Mrs Redfearn of that, when you see her."

And the first thing *she'll* want to know, El thought, is *who*. *Which* people talked - which *person*.

Because you're not going to tell us, are you? Not here, not now.

"What is it you want?" said Rose. "You've obviously expended some effort to bring us here. I assume it was for a purpose?"

Soames' eyelids fluttered open.

"I have to admit," he said quietly, "I had hopes it would be Mrs Redfearn I'd be speaking to today. That she and Mrs Acharya would have put on their wigs and greasepaint and driven out here themselves. What I have to say is really more for the sorcerer than the dancing broomsticks."

He means Sita, El thought. Mrs Acharya is Sita. That must have been what she was calling herself, when he knew her.

"Well, we're the ones you have," said Rose, with some of

the arrogance, the haughty aristocratic disdain that El remembered from their early meetings. "So whatever you have to say - say it."

Soames smiled again - the grin of a vulture on a hilltop, surveying a carcass so large and so fresh it would eat for a week.

"As I said," he replied, "I don't have much air in me. So I'll get straight to the point. I know about you - about *all* of you. Not the cons, before you ask - I've no interest in them, and I can't imagine the police do either, or they'd have come for at least one of you before now."

"What, then?" El said, sudden apprehension coiling in her stomach.

The smile widened.

"About your father, Lady Winchester," he said. "Mr Marchant. The *late* Mr Marchant, I should say. I understand you did away with him last summer, you two and Mrs Acharya and Mrs Redfearn and some of your friends. Miss Baxter and that unfortunate girl with the head injury - Miss Morgan? And that those boys of Mrs Redfearn's helped remove the body."

El might have expected Rose to crumble, then. But she didn't. If anything, the statement - the barely veiled threat of it - seemed to galvanise her, to stoke her anger.

Maybe she's been expecting this, El thought. This, or something like it, since it happened. Ever since Ruby stuck that knife in Marchant's neck and left him bleeding to death on her kitchen floor.

"I'm going to ask you again," Rose said, levelly. "What is it that you want?"

Soames took another, lingering pull on his oxygen - this time, El surmised, for dramatic effect; to keep them hanging.

"I have a job for you," he said when he'd finished. "For

all of you - the whole gang. But *want* isn't quite the right word. I wouldn't want you to think that it's a *suggestion*. The job I'm envisioning for you isn't optional - it isn't a question of agreement, of *yes* or *no*. You *will* do it for me. Because if you don't, I'll have no hesitation in sending every one of you to prison for the rest of your lives. And I can tell you from experience, you won't enjoy it."

∽

It was power, it struck El afterwards. The pure, white-hot thrill of tugging people's strings, and knowing they had no choice except to caper for you, for as long as you wanted them to - a malign inverse of her own modus operandi, of the cons she worked herself. The cons she *used* to work.

The string-tugging theory measured up with the little she knew of Soames already: the blackmail, the calculated fleecing of the lonely and bereaved, the girlfriend so young and so vulnerable that she'd never leave him, no matter what he did to her.

He probably *did* want the job done, and done the way he'd told them - he'd been planning it long enough that there couldn't be much doubt of that. And there was even less doubt in her mind that he wanted Ruby to suffer, that he wanted to punish her for the nearly quarter century he'd spent inside. But there was more to it than just that, she was sure of it.

The pleasure for him, she suspected, came not just in making her pay, but in knowing that he could *keep* her paying, over and over, for as long as he wanted. And that her compliance could be guaranteed now, as he'd thought in the '70s that it could be, through explicit threats against the people she loved.

He'd been wrong then, of course; had misjudged her, and badly. Underestimated what she was capable of when she was backed into a corner. But as he said himself: he'd had a lot of years to reflect on his mistake. It wouldn't be one he'd make again.

He'd have more on Ruby this time around. And not just on Ruby - on all of them, Dexter and Michael included. However he'd come by it - and El had her own ideas about that - he'd have evidence, solid and irrefutable; enough that, if push came to shove, he'd have something to offer the CPS beyond his own sworn testimony.

The *kind* of job it was would also delight him - she was sure of that, too. For women like them - women who believed, even if they were kidding themselves, that they had scruples, and that a job designed to capitalise on other people's grief and pain wasn't a job that ought to be done, by them or by anyone - it would seem obscene, unconscionable. Doing it at all would hurt them. And if they pulled it off, made it work, then the very success of it would torment them for a long time after. Which seemed to her exactly the outcome that he wanted.

~

"What's the job?" she'd asked eventually, once it was clear that there *wasn't* a choice, that he really *did* have them over a barrel, and that the best she could hope for was that Ruby or Sita or Karen would find a way to think them out of the hole they'd landed in, once she and Rose were back in London.

"I think you'll like it," he'd said, still wearing his carrion smile. "It's one of the classics."

~

"An old friend" - that was how Soames described the mark, though she understood later that *former cellmate* would have been the more accurate designation.

They'd met in Hendon, nineteen years into Soames' sentence. Ted Wainwright was older, like him - Soames guessed it was one of the reasons they'd been thrown together - but his health was better, and Soames had found him a useful companion, one not averse to pushing him around the block in his wheelchair or hoisting him full-body out of his bunk when he woke up struggling for breath.

"He'd got eighteen months, I believe," Soames told them. "Out in a year was the expectation. So quite different from an all-dayer like me, and terribly green. But we muddled along."

Wainwright's sentence, Soames had learned from the news, was for perjury. An occasional TV presenter and owner of a global chain of American-style jeans-and-t-shirt stores that were both too new and too casual for Soames to ever have cause to patronise before his wrongful conviction had claimed him, Wainwright was a semi-public figure on both sides of the Atlantic – well known enough for an unofficial biographer to have set about writing his life story, a big name publisher to have offered a significant advance *for* that story and a Sunday tabloid to have secured the pre-publication serialisation rights. Among the personal tragedies and professional triumphs the serialised book detailed was the revelation of Wainwright's infidelity - of a year-long affair he'd ostensibly enjoyed with a former hairdresser who was, to the horror of tabloid and biographer alike, both the same age as Wainwright and markedly less well-maintained than his then-current wife.

Wainwright, not unexpectedly, had denied the accusation - and then, girded by his own hubris, had gone one step further, suing both newspaper and publisher for libel. He lost the case; was subsequently prosecuted in turn for the apparently false testimony he'd provided at the trial and before it and, thereafter - despite the best efforts of his legal team - convicted. Learning that he'd be spending the bulk of his sentence not in the open Category D prison he'd been expecting but in the altogether harsher environs of Her Majesty's Prison Hendon had come as a particular shock.

He was a talker, Soames had discovered early on in their acquaintance; a talker and a pontificator, given to long midnight monologues about whatever was on his mind in the moment. It had irritated Soames at first, this incessant gabbling. Until, one night, something Wainwright said captured his interest.

"He was talking about his daughter," Soames said. "His *little Ingrid*, as he called her. The name, or perhaps I should say the name in conjunction with *his* name... there was something familiar about it, though I couldn't think what immediately."

On and on Wainwright had droned about this Ingrid: what a beautiful baby she'd been, how funny and affectionate. There was a melancholic note to the rhapsodising, one that made Soames wonder if this child, this Ingrid, was estranged from Wainwright somehow, if a rift had opened between father and daughter since the halcyon days of her babyhood, however many years ago they might have been.

"You'll see her when you get out," Soames had said, as much to shut him up as to soothe him. "And you can always send her a V.O., if she can bear to come here for a visit."

"She's gone," was all Wainwright had said in response.

"Gone?" Soames had asked - that same bell ringing

again; another recollection stirring, unformed and nameless, in the dusty archives of his memory.

"Taken," Wainwright had replied, the word catching in his throat.

And somewhere in the archives, a cabinet had sprung open.

Little Ingrid, he'd thought. The Yorkshire Lindbergh Baby.

The story came back to him then, almost wholesale - the same story Wainwright would eventually tell, in fractured and emotionally charged instalments, over the course of the weeks and months they bunked together.

In the spring of 1955, when Ted Wainwright was barely halfway into his twenties and still better known as the son of a decently successful textiles manufacturer than the international businessman and philanthropist he'd become, a group of masked men had forced their way into the home he shared with his wife (his *first* wife, Soames had mentally corrected himself) and their baby and, after tying the hands of both husband and wife to the bannisters with a length of cable and giving the husband a battering around the head, had grabbed the sleeping child from her bed and run off with her into the night, never to be seen again.

It was a kidnapping, the police had said at the time: a gang of chancers, albeit very *well prepared* chancers, looking to extort a pay-out from a local boy made good. But, though the Wainwrights waited, no demand for money was ever made, no ransom note delivered promising the safe return of Little Ingrid in exchange for a briefcase stuffed with £5 notes. And Ingrid herself remained missing.

Weeks came and went, then months, and eventually years. For the Wainwrights, suspended in time, the passage of these milestones meant nothing; Ingrid, they knew, was still alive, and would eventually return. Other possibilities were inconceivable; no God or just universe would allow them.

For the local police and the regional press, though - those few men and fewer women who kept half an eye on the now-cold case long after national interest had waned - the reality seemed clear: body or no body, Ingrid was dead. Murdered, quite possibly, on the very same night she was taken.

And when, two years on from the crime, Mrs Wainwright sank down into the River Ouse with a heavy stone in each of the pockets of her peacoat and the coroner, a good and trusted friend of Mr Wainwright's late father Bill, had proven tender-hearted enough to rule her death an accident, it seemed to these onlookers like nothing so much as the coda to a tragedy - an ending, of sorts, albeit one that would bring *Ted* Wainwright no solace at all.

"They got it wrong, though, about Ingrid," Wainwright told Soames from the upper bunk, through what could have been tears. "I can see how it must have looked to them, the detectives and that, but you'd *feel* it, wouldn't you, if something like that'd happened to one of your own? You'd feel it. And I'm telling you now, same as I told them then: I never felt anything at all. So I *know* she's alive, do you see? I know it."

In the dark, Soames had nodded, and uttered suitably sympathetic sounds, while behind his rheumy eyes, the earliest beginnings of a plan began to coalesce.

∽

"He's spent a fortune trying to track her down," Soames said. "Tens of thousands. *Hundreds* of thousands. All for a child that anyone with any deductive reasoning at all could tell him is buried under six feet of earth on the top of a moor somewhere..."

He trailed off, his breath lost, and reached for his mask.

"That's what you want us to do?" Rose asked, disgusted. "Trick a grieving old man into emptying his bank account by pretending to be... what? Private detectives who can help him find his missing child? It's repugnant, absolutely repugnant."

Not just detectives, El thought. *Psychic* detectives. It would have to be.

I'm not doing this, *none* of us are doing this - whatever bear-trap Soames has got us in, we'll get out of it, we always do. But if we *were* doing it ... a private detective con on its own wouldn't cut it. This Wainwright - he'll have seen enough investigators and missing person specialists and ex-Scotland Yard consultants to last a lifetime. We'd have to go bigger, better. More ethereal. And we'd need to give him a *hell* of a convincer.

She grimaced, appalled at herself for considering the possibility, even hypothetically.

Soames released the mask; pushed it, this time, up and onto his temples, where it sat, absurdly, like a pair of superannuated racing goggles.

"If *that's* what you thought I intended you to take from the story," he said, "then I have some good news for you, Lady Winchester. Because *finding* the child isn't quite what I have in mind."

CHAPTER 14
PRESIDIO HEIGHTS, SAN FRANCISCO
SEPTEMBER 1997

At first, El had resisted the idea of the five of them renting a house together. It was too risky, she argued, for the whole team to be concentrated in one place; would be more sensible by far to book separate suites in separate hotels scattered across the city, in Chinatown and Hayes Valley, Pacific Heights and Russian Hill. But then Rose had been reluctant to leave Sophie behind at home, even in the care of her sister-in-law, and Sita had lodged her usual complaints against the impersonality and sterility of chain hotels, even those at the five star end, and a short term rental that was both big enough and luxurious enough to accommodate the needs of all concerned had seemed the obvious solution.

Now, stepping through the door of the sprawling Spanish Colonial property on Jackson Street that Rose's US realtor had found for them, she had to concede that maybe Sita had been right, and that if they really *were* going to be staying in the city until the job was done, they'd be more comfortable living and working in the same shared but fundamentally private space - a space where they could talk freely about the logistics of the con without worrying they'd be overheard, where Ruby could leave her reams of background research spread out across the kitchen table with impunity and Karen could set up camp in the basement with her PowerBook and her packing crates of wires and computer equipment.

For much of the fortnight they'd been there, El had joined her in the basement, assimilating as much information as she possibly could about artificial intelligence, facial recognition technology and the practical applications of age-progression software in the US - a decision that had nothing at all to do, despite Karen's assertions to the contrary, with Rose.

"You're avoiding her," she'd said, the third morning they were down there - telling El, as much as asking her.

"Avoiding who?" El had answered, knowing exactly who Karen meant but refusing to acknowledge it aloud.

"You know who. Did something happen?"

"I don't know what you're talking about. Nothing's happened. Everything's fine."

"Bollocks is it. One minute there's stars in your eyes whenever you look her way and you've got everyone thinking you're about to pop the question, the next you're so scared of getting caught on your own with her you spend all day every day hiding out in here with me, pretending to care about Boolean conditions and DNA profiles. I don't get it."

"Everyone? Who's everyone?"

Karen, exasperated, had shaken her head, delivered an admonishing click of her tongue and spun around in her chair to face her laptop, away from El and her apparently preposterous denials.

To El's surprise, all four of the women were gathered together in the sunroom - a large, airy construction dominated by marshmallow-soft chairs and throw cushions that led out onto a wooden veranda and, beyond it, a backyard lined with blue gum eucalyptus trees dense and high enough to shield them from the prying eyes of neighbours. They were working, she saw - Karen typing frenetically into her keyboard at the coffee table, Ruby scrutinising the pages of what El inferred from the rainbow palette and portrait shot of kd lang on the cover to be a lesbian newspaper, Rose and Sita poring over the faded pen and ink letters scrawled across a creased, yellowing document that was either decades old or deliberately stained to suggest so.

On one of the marshmallow chairs, the flared ankles of her jeans dangling from one armrest, sat Sophie, her eyes darting back and forth between Sita and her mother and the graphic novel on her lap.

("She knows," Ruby had said, early on, when El had expressed discomfort at Sophie's presence in the house for the duration of their stay; at the likely difficulties of pulling off a job while keeping that job hidden from an inquisitive, ever-present teenager with nothing to do all day but snoop. "Rose told her."

"What does she know?" El had asked.

"About the job. About Wainwright."

El had been speechless; had struggled to imagine how such a mother-daughter conversation might possibly have played out.

"Rose just... *told* her?" she'd said eventually.

"That's the way I heard it. Seems she don't want no more secrets between 'em, after what happened with Marchant. After what *nearly* happened with the little 'un. Can hardly blame her, can you?"

"And Sophie knows what we do? Who we are?"

"I should think so."

"Hold on," El had said, growing more flummoxed by the second. "Hold on. I want to make sure I've got this right: Rose's daughter, Rose's *thirteen year old daughter*, knows we're cons? That her *mum's* a con? And that we're talking about flying out to America specifically in order to *run* a con on Wainwright?"

Ruby had found this reaction hysterical.

"What?" El had said. "What's funny?"

"You are, girl!" Ruby had laughed, the grin on her face causing spiderwebs of wrinkles to break out along the faultlines of her mouth and cheeks. "You should hear yourself, getting your knickers in a twist about young Sophie knowing what you get up to! It's bleedin' *hilarious*."

"I don't see why," El had muttered.

"Tell me," Ruby had said, still grinning. "How old were *you* again, when you started this game? When I started *showing* you this game?"

And El had flashed back, of course she had, to the night she and Ruby had met; to the angry, swaggering kid she'd been, the one with twenty quid of a mark's money in her pocket and no real clue at all about the job or how to do it. To the first lesson Ruby had taught her, had *let her learn*, in a greasy spoon in Marylebone the year she turned fourteen.

"Okay," she'd conceded, not meeting Ruby's eye. "Point taken").

"Go alright, did it?" Ruby asked her, not looking up from her newspaper.

"He's on the hook," El replied, kicking off her skate shoes and throwing herself down into another of the chairs. "Can't say it was my finest hour, but he's on the hook."

"What's on the hook?" Sophie asked, with an innocence that El thought was probably feigned.

Because she wants you to say *it,* she added to herself. *She wants to* hear *you say it.*

"We'll talk about it later," Rose said, shooting her daughter a look that suggested she shared El's suspicions.

"It means we've whetted his appetite, darling," said Sita, more gently. "It's a kind of sales technique. Before a... let's call them a *customer*, shall we? Before a customer can be persuaded to buy into a product, they need first to come to the realisation that they *want* that product. Or better yet, that they *need* it - that they couldn't bear to be without it, whatever *it* might be. That's what El's been doing this morning with Mr Wainwright - cultivating that need."

"It's called the rope," Ruby added, still studying the newspaper as if her life depended on it.

"And I'm not a roper," said El. "So remind me again why it's *me* doing this bit?"

"Think he'd buy one of them two as up-and-coming game developers, do you?" Karen piped up from the table, pointing first at Ruby, then at Sita. "I'm not saying they're the wrong age bracket, but their idea of a console is a bit more Enigma machine than Super Nintendo."

"Didn't see you queuing up to reel him in, Little Miss Microchip," said Ruby.

"Gonna find someone else to do all this for you, are you?" Karen replied, holding up the laptop.

"On which note," said Sita, rerouting their verbal sparring with a deftness El wasn't sure she'd manage herself, in her current frame of mind. "Were you able to track down the invitation?"

"Top of the cabinet," Karen said, gesturing with her thumb to a heavy cream envelope resting on the marble sideboard behind her and turning her attention back to her screen. "By all means be yourself once you're through the door," she added to Rose, "but if anyone asks you when they check your ticket, you're a movie producer named Linda Harrigan, and you've just ploughed all your money into a dinosaur film you're hoping is gonna be the next Jurassic Park. Heads up: it won't be. I read the last draft of the script she had saved on her computer, and it's shit. You don't even *see* a dinosaur 'til the second act."

"And you didn't have no trouble getting hold of it?" asked Ruby. "The invite, I mean."

"Nah. Waited for the postman to come then took it straight out of Harrigan's mailbox, easy as. If I were her, I'd be getting someone to keep a better eye on my post, next time I had to rush off to Auckland in a hurry to sort out an animatronic triceratops."

El didn't know what, exactly, Karen had done - or what tech-community favours she'd called in - to precipitate whatever on-set crisis had dispatched the real Linda Harrigan from her San Francisco base to the other side of the world. But she was, as always, thankful to have her *inside* their tent and pissing out, and not the other way around.

"And you're certain there are *two* names on there?" said Sita, unsealing the envelope inch by careful inch.

"Have a look for yourself," said Karen. "It's Linda Harrigan *and guest*, see? She gets a plus-one. So you might want to give your mate Kate a bell and ask if she's got a ball-gown lying around. Or a tuxedo."

∼

A snake-oil salesman: that was what Ruby had called Kate Zhou, when her name had first come up in conversation.

"I ain't criticising," Ruby had added, lest El misunderstand the description. "She's a nice girl. Smart, an' all. It's just a bit... *American* for my tastes, what she does. A bit PT Barnum."

Kate Zhou's speciality, El gathered, was the Magical Elixir - selling miracle cures for baldness, weight gain and erectile dysfunction to a diligently-curated portfolio of mostly older men who'd chosen, for their own reasons, to forgo the benefits of conventional medicine in the war they continued to wage against the ageing process.

"She don't just con 'em once, neither," Ruby said. "She *milks* 'em. Like I said: she's a smart one. Chooses just the right marks - the ones who really *believe*, or the ones wanting a quick fix and who don't care if they have to keep paying until they find the one that actually works for 'em. So when she's got 'em on the hook, she can *keep* taking ' em - selling 'em pill and potion after pill and potion until she's ready to pack up shop and get out of Dodge."

Like Barnum, she was a fast talker - confident, charismatic, articulate. A Bay Area native who kept a condo in North Beach but spent ten months out of twelve on the road, trawling hotel bars and the business lounges of Midwestern airports for new catches who might be amenable to spilling the details of their impotence or midnight hamburger habit after a drink or five, she was single, childfree, somewhere between thirty five and forty and - or so Sita, who had known her the longest, speculated - either a former attorney or a one-time jailhouse lawyer with a formidable knowledge of state and federal statute.

She was also, if El had understood correctly, set to be Rose's date for what Ruby and Sita hoped would be remembered in the fullness of time as a very eventful evening.

∽

The woman who landed on their doorstep just after six o'clock that night had on neither a ballgown nor a tuxedo, but a tailored black trouser suit, a pair of thick-heeled sandals that added three inches to her height and a tortoiseshell clip that kept her short dark hair out of her eyes. She was fine boned, louche and androgynously beautiful, and seemed entirely unfazed to discover El on the other side of the door, and not the older women who'd sought her help.

"You're El, right?" she said, in a lazy Californian drawl that was friendly enough, but which El found immediately irritating, for reasons she elected not to analyse. "Or, wait... Karen? You're not exactly dressed for a benefit, so I'm thinking you're not Rose, and no offence, but you look a little older than thirteen, so I'm guessing you're not her rugrat either."

"Sophie," El replied, sounding - even to her own ears - irrationally hostile, and unexpectedly protective of the child. "Her name's Sophie."

"Sophie, right. Sure. But since I'd put money on you *not* being her... which one *are* you? The grifter or the techhead?"

"Grifter all the way, this one," Ruby answered, coming up behind El. "Wouldn't trust her anywhere *near* a computer. How you doin', darlin'? You alright?"

She sidled through the narrow doorway, past El, and wrapped the interloper in an embrace - a move that, against all reason, exacerbated El's irritation.

"Pretty good," the woman said. "Getting a little chilly out here on the porch, though."

She shot El a smile that was as lazy and infuriating as her accent.

"Can't have that, can we?" said Ruby. "Come on in, love. She's nearly ready for you."

Ruby led her through to the sunroom, El trailing behind them. Neither Sita nor Karen were in there; just Sophie, stretched out across the same chair she'd been occupying since the morning, the graphic novel she'd been reading now traded for a paperback with a grimacing, red-mouthed clown on the cover.

She looked up from the book as they entered; took in the stranger who'd infiltrated their space.

"Are you here for my Mum?" she asked, without preamble.

The woman seemed thrown, for a moment, but recovered swiftly.

"I guess I am," she said. "I'm Kate. And you must be Sophie?"

Sophie nodded, sombrely.

"Are you gay?" she asked.

"Here," Ruby said, brows furrowing, "you can't just go 'round asking people that. Didn't your mother never teach you no manners?"

Kate, though, seemed not to mind the question.

"I date women," she answered, as casually as Sophie had asked. "Men too, sometimes. That okay with you?"

Sophie seemed to consider this, then nodded again.

"Mum's gay, but she doesn't date anyone," she said. "I don't know why. I asked her if she wanted a girlfriend, and she said no. I think she might have been lying, though."

This peeling onion of revelations - that Rose had come out to her daughter in the months since Marchant; that she didn't *date*, whatever that meant; that she *said* she wasn't looking for a relationship but actually *was*, possibly - caused of bubble of anxiety to rise, unexpectedly, in El's stomach; an echo of the awkwardness she'd felt the night that she and

Rose had gone for dinner back in London, before Soames had made his malign presence known.

She swallowed it down; focused instead on the strange intergenerational exchange she was apparently witnessing.

"I'll keep that in mind," said Kate, bemused.

"I know it's not a *real* date you're going on," Sophie told her. "But she still might not be very good at it, if she's out of practice. So you should to be kind to her, even if she says the wrong thing or spills something on your trousers."

"I'll do my best," Kate said, with a poker face that El thought was probably to her credit. "Besides, how do you know it won't be *me* who spills something on your Mom? Could be I'm a lousy date myself."

"Consider me forewarned," said Rose, sweeping into the sunroom in a cloud of citrus perfume, a silver evening dress the texture of a mermaid's scales covering her from calf to shoulder.

"I'll play it safe," said Kate. "Stick to mineral water."

"Perhaps I'll do the same," Rose told her. "Spare us both the blushes, should any glassware go flying. My daughter has been interrogating you, I take it?"

"You told me to ask, if I had any questions," said Sophie defensively.

"Ask *me*," said Rose. "Not our guests."

"I didn't mind," said Kate. "Besides, I got some useful information out of it. Right, Sophie?"

"See?" Sophie protested. "She didn't mind!"

"Nevertheless," said Rose, "there's such a thing as politeness, as I'm sure El and Ruby would agree."

She smiled at El conspiratorially, and El's stomach dipped and rose again, entirely against her will.

"Should we get going?" Kate asked. "I don't make it to a

lot of these things - is it better to be early, or fashionably late?"

"Earlier the better, I reckon," said Ruby, before Rose could answer. "Give everyone a chance to get a good look at you, before they kick off the auction."

"There's an Edward Hopper retrospective in the adjoining gallery," Rose suggested. "We could kill a little time in there?"

"Why not?" said Kate. "I could go some urban realism ahead of watching you try to buy a yacht."

"Operative word, *try*," said Ruby. "I ain't interested in spending the rest of this trip working out how to transport some bloody great sailboat across the Atlantic. You want to be *seen*, that's all. You want people to remember you."

Kate made a show of looking Rose up and down appreciatively.

"Can't see anyone forgetting her, in a dress like that," she said.

El's throat tightened, her fingers flexing involuntarily into fists.

"Let's hope so," said Ruby, throwing a quizzical glance El's way. "Just make sure you swan about a bit, once you're in there. And whatever you do: keep smiling for the cameras."

CHAPTER 15
SOUTH OF MARKET, SAN FRANCISCO
SEPTEMBER 1997

The US head office of The Fine Cloth Company was tall - not quite on a par with the Coit Tower or the Transamerica Pyramid or the other concrete spears and rectangles that punctured the curving skyline of the city, but high enough for El to have to crane her neck to see the top. Like its neighbours, it seemed to her faintly unreal - separated from the drugstores, coffee shops and animated foot-traffic of Market Street by a pedestrianised walkway, and dotted with Narnian lamp-posts that gave the whole enclosure the look of a film lot recreation, an artificial replica of a working office block.

She adjusted the laptop case that bisected her chest, ran a palm through the neon pink of her hair and pushed through the revolving doors and into the lobby, fortifying herself against the truculent receptionists and gatekeeping personal assistants whose jobs depended on their ability to deter walk-in visitors, to *keep out* people like her - and saw Wainwright himself, now in suit and tie, perched on one of the irregularly shaped stone slabs opposite the front desk that might have been benches, but might equally have been a stab at rough-hewn corporate sculpture.

His head turned towards her as she approached him, and there was relief as well as anticipation in the smile he gave her.

He wasn't sure I'd turn up, she thought. And he's nervous, nervous as hell. He could've stayed in his office, had someone send me up to him when he was ready - but he didn't. He came down here, all the way down from the top, and he *waited* for me.

He shifted position; pulled himself to standing, slow as an iceberg despite his excitement.

No, she corrected herself, feeling the low-level guilt she'd lived with since leaving London wrap tighter around her guts. Not excitement. Hope.

∼

"Who told him?" Karen had demanded back at Ruby's new flat in West Hampstead, when El and Rose had laid out Soames' plan and the dirt he had on all of them - the hold he had over them. "If he knows about what happened with Marchant, *who fucking told him?*"

Ruby, who'd sat stock-still and uncharacteristically silent through El's enumeration of the trip to Herne Bay - what she and Rose had found there, the trap that Soames had laid for them - broke into dry, hollow laughter.

"You ain't figured it out?" she said. "All them brains of yours, and you're telling me you ain't got even an inkling?"

Hannah, El thought - forcing herself to *think* the name, even if she wasn't quite ready to say it aloud. She thinks Hannah's the one feeding Soames his information.

"*Her?*" said Karen, apparently drawing the same inference but sharing El's reluctance to give voice to it.

"Makes sense, don't it?" Ruby replied. She sounded... not beaten, exactly, but pensive: a tired boxer with a haematoma and a bloody lip, weighing up a strategy for the seventh round. "We knew she'd come out of the woodwork eventually."

"Say that's true," said Rose. "How would *she* know to reach out to Soames? She'd have been a teenager when he was sentenced. And they're hardly obvious bedfellows."

Ruby shrugged.

"I don't know, do I?" she answered. "Could be they had someone in common - a mate in Hendon, or what have you. Could be he heard she were sniffing around for something on us, and *he* reached out to *her*."

"'People talk,'" El said, remembering Soames hunched over in his chair, the gleeful clasping of his hands. "That was what he kept saying. 'People talk.'"

"Bleedin' right they do," said Ruby. "'Specially in the nick. It's wall-to-wall gossip in them cells."

"Fuck all else to do inside, is there?" Karen added. "My Uncle Perce did eighteen months in Gartree. Said his ears never stopped ringing from people trying to tell him shit he didn't want to hear."

"Regardless of *how* he knows," said Sita, the brittle edge to her tone suggesting that her normally elastic patience was stretching to its limits, "we can be sure that he *does know*, and that he's intent on *using* what he knows. Which leaves us, I'm afraid, in rather a difficult position. Because I can't, from all that El has told us, conceive of a single way forward beyond our doing exactly what he asks of us."

∽

Wainwright took her, not to his office, but to an empty conference room on the ground floor - a sparse, impersonal space decorated with posters of young adults, male and female, modelling bootcut jeans, vest tops, denim shirts and polka dot blouses in a range of wholesome Alpine settings for which, in her opinion, not one item of the clothing would be practical.

"They're from the summer catalogue," Wainwright said, catching her staring. "Can't say much of it's to my tastes, but the girls in Merchandising seem to know what they're doing, so I let them get on with it, mostly."

He pulled out a chair for her from the conference table, and another for himself directly across from hers. She took his lead and sat, unzipped the laptop case and placed the computer on top of it - gently, reverently.

"Your program on there, is it?" he asked, gesturing to the laptop. There was sweat on his upper lip, she noticed; three small beads of it, nestled in the dense grey hair of his moustaches.

"Do you want me to run you through the demo?" she offered. "I've got it down to a fine art now, with all the meetings I've had this week."

"If you don't mind?" he said.

She shrugged, diffidently - this *other* Angela Di Salvo still a little confused, or so the shrug said, by what interest a man who ran a chain of clothes shops could possibly have in age-progression software, especially when it was still technically at the testing stage, but willing to go along with that interest if it might lead, somewhere down the line, to a sale. Then opened the laptop, beaming blue light onto the white wall behind her.

"Give me a second to load it up," she said. Her screen shielded from him, at least temporarily, she double-clicked the program file on the desktop, exactly as Karen had instructed her to before she'd left the house in Presidio Heights that morning: a tiny, innocuous-looking digital square marked DORIANGRAY.EXE. It opened, filling the screen with a single image: a close-up, high-resolution shot of a blonde, blue-eyed child, perhaps ten years old, smiling happily at whoever had taken her picture.

("Who is she?" El had asked Karen, when she'd first seen the program in action.

"Fergus' sister Becky, about twenty years ago," Karen had answered with a grin. "I robbed it out of one of his photo albums before we left. It was her or a kid off an advert, and I thought Becky might be a bit more, you know... inconspicuous").

"Ready?" El asked Wainwright.

He nodded.

She turned the laptop around so that the screen faced him and pressed the Enter key. A scattering of green dots materialised on the child's digitised face - her cheeks, her chin and forehead, the bridge of her nose.

"Who is she?" Wainwright said, squinting at the image.

"My cousin Lila, when she was little," El lied. "I need permission to share the photographs of anyone I show to potential investors, and I knew she wouldn't sue me if I shared hers, so I've been using her as a guinea pig."

A connecting line appeared between two of the dots, then another line between two more, and another, until the girl's face was a mesh of intersecting stria.

"What's it doing?" asked Wainwright.

"Collecting information," El replied. "It analyses the position of specific facial features in relation to others, then calculates how those features are likely to change as the subject ages. Keep watching."

The lines vanished, then the dots, until the girl's face was perfectly clear again. Then it began to change - the jaw and chin narrowing, the ears appearing to grow very slightly, the forehead enlarging and the lips thinning.

"This is how the program thinks Lila would have looked at fourteen," El said.

On the screen the pixels blurred, and the face began to change for a second time - the cheeks filling back out, the hairline ebbing and flowing to a widow's peak, the tip of the nose sharpening.

"And this is how it thinks she'd look at eighteen," she continued.

The image shifted again, this time more subtly. Now the girl was well into adulthood – twenty-four or -five, her features still sharp but the smallest of lines beginning to develop around her eyes and mouth.

"And in her mid-twenties," El said.

The girl's nose began to thicken once again at the base as her hairline rose an eighth of an inch higher on her head and the earliest beginnings of a wrinkle darkened between her brows.

"And this is its best guess at how she'd look at thirty," she concluded, pressing the Space bar and freezing the girl in the least youthful of her iterations.

"Bloody incredible, that is," Wainwright said, his eyes glued to the screen. "And it's accurate? She really does look like this now, this Lila?"

"Oh, yeah," said El, a note of stage magician triumph creeping into Angela Di Salvo's voice. She'd sawn the girl in the box in half, it said, but don't worry – she knew *just* how to put her back together.

She pressed the Escape key, and the girl's face disappeared, replaced by the laptop's almost empty desktop. With a flick of the touchpad, she moved the cursor across the screen to hover over an image file, this one labelled LILA.JPEG.

She double-clicked, and another image took over the screen - a conventionally pretty thirtysomething woman in a wedding dress and veil, clutching a bouquet and beaming at the camera.

Her face was, undeniably, the face of the woman the program had created for them a moment before - the adult evolution of the blue-eyed, blonde-haired child.

"I don't believe it," said Wainwright breathlessly. "I don't bloody believe it."

("She spent nearly a grand on that dress," Karen had said, tapping a finger on the digitised version of the other photo of Becky she'd stolen from Fergus's album. "You gotta feel bad for her. Turns out he was shagging half the wedding party - the marriage only lasted six weeks").

"It's not bad, is it?" said El, Angela Di Salvo's pride in her work shining through.

Wainwright was awestruck, still seemingly unable to tear himself away from the second image - a dazed supplicant gazing up into the face of God.

"It's incredible," he said, in what was almost a whisper. "Absolutely bloody incredible."

∽

"It won't be easy," El had said to the rest of them, that night in West Hampstead, when the decision was made and they'd started, very tacitly, to make a plan. "Wainwright's not in London. He's not even in this country anymore. He's got a US passport and half his business is in the States - he was on licence for a bit when he was first released, but as soon as he could he hopped a flight to San Francisco and he hasn't been back since. He's not a big fan of the British press after what happened - Soames thinks getting away from them was part of what made him want to leave."

"San Francisco?" Sita had said, head cocked in a way that had strongly suggested to El that the seed of another idea had been planted, one that might very soon begin to germinate.

"Yeah," she'd replied.

"Silicon Valley?"

"Not that far out, I don't think," El had answered - not understanding where Sita was heading, not yet. "I can check. But the Fine Cloth HQ is right in the middle of the city, so he'll probably be near there, somewhere?"

"Still," Sita had said quietly, lost in thought, "close enough. Certainly close enough."

She'd turned her attention to Karen.

"How long," she'd asked, "would it take you, hypothetically, to write us one of those computer programs you're so good with?"

∼

"Does it work on anyone?" Wainwright said. "I mean, could it do this on any photo you give it?"

El appeared to give this some consideration.

"Not *any* photo," she told him, showing every indication of wanting to hedge her bets - of not wanting to oversell her creation, however revolutionary she might privately believe that creation to be. "You'd need a head shot, face-on, and reasonably close up ideally. There'd have to be enough identifying features for the algorithm to scan and build out from. And the lighting would have to be decent, too. You couldn't just upload, I don't know... a polaroid of someone dancing in a nightclub with their head down."

"Makes sense," Wainwright agreed.

"That's not a *huge* limitation, obviously, if you licensed it to, say, the police or the Marshals Service - people looking to catch criminals who were known to them already. Something like a mugshot would give you more than enough to work with. And of course," she added, almost as an afterthought, as if the point were barely worth making, "it'd have to be a digital file. Any photo you used, it'd have to be in a format the program would actually recognise."

("You tell him that," Karen had said, back at the house, "and things'll go one of two ways. Either he's got no fucking clue what a *digital file* is, and we're looking at a bit of a delay while he works out how to scan an old photo or take it to a print shop that can do it for him. Or he's a bit more on the ball, and he'll have whatever photo he wants to give you burned to CD or ready to go on a memory card. He's old, so that last one's less likely. But then, if he's been sending emails out to private detectives left, right and centre and he knows his way around the internet... well, you never know. You might get lucky").

Wainwright drew the knuckle of one finger across his moustaches, wiping away the sweat that had gathered there.

"If *I* had a picture," he asked, "and it were already on, say, a compact disc you could shove straight in the computer... would *that* do? Would that software of yours be able to do the business with it?"

"I don't see why not," El said - Angela Di Salvo still humouring him, still bemused but playing along. "What's the picture?"

He held up a hand to ward off further questions.

"Wait here," he said. "I won't be two minutes. There's something I need to get from upstairs."

He leapt up from his chair and out of the door faster than she thought his bowed legs could carry him. And he really *was* two minutes, bursting back into the room so soon after he'd departed it that she'd only half-finished loading up the software that she'd need for the convincer - the river of fresh sweat rolling down his collar and the heart attack-red of his complexion telling her he'd taken the stairs to his office at an Olympic sprint.

He thrust a damp hand out towards her. Around the middle finger, suspended in the air like a spinning plate, was an unmarked silver disc.

"This," he started breathlessly. "There's a photo on it. Only one. But it should be alright for what you're after. Can you do it? Make it change - make *her* change? Make her older?"

~

"Like Australia," said Ruby, when Sita had finished explaining the idea she'd begun to cultivate. "Perth, in '69 - the old bastard with the iron mine and the son he chucked out for getting hitched to that Greek girl. That's it, ain't it? That's what you're proposin'."

El had bitten her tongue, resigned by now to these conversational ellipses.

"After a fashion," Sita had replied. "Something a touch more modern than that one, of course. But a similar premise."

Ruby had thought this over.

"Wouldn't work," she'd said after a while. "You couldn't have El play the inside, not for that."

"What are you saying?" El had countered, annoyed by the dismissal even in the absence of the appropriate information. "You think I'm not up to it?"

"I *think*," Ruby had told her, "that Wainwright's about as pale as milk. You not seen him in the papers? And if it's the '50s we're talking when that little girl got took, then chances are his missus was an' all. I don't know what the hell she'd look like these days, if she were still with us, but she wouldn't have your colouring, I know that much. Besides," she'd added, "that kid'd be forty-odd now. And good as you might be, and convincing as you are in your corporate get-up, I happen to know you still have to get your passport out to buy a pack of them fags you never stop smoking."

El had begun to formulate a reply, still unsure of which part of Ruby's premise she ought to find the most offensive when Sita had spoken up - at first, El had thought, to defend her honour.

"I can't disagree," she'd said, to El's displeasure. "But rather fortunately, it wasn't *El* I had in mind..."

∽

The digital photograph that filled the screen was older by far than the one of Fergus' luckless, only briefly married sister - a black and white portrait, creased at the edges by time and handling. The subject was an infant: a baby girl, perhaps a year old, light curls falling down onto her chubby cheeks.

"Who's this?" El asked.

"My daughter," Wainwright answered.

The same green dots as before appeared on the screen, swirling around the child's face before settling on her eyes, chin, nose and cheekbones - then the lines, connecting eyes to cheeks, nose to chin in the same, seemingly random geometric pattern.

The dots vanished, as before, and the face began to change - cycling through childhood and early adolescence, the contours of the girl's features moving and reshaping as she aged.

Wainwright's breathing kept apace with the changes, every pixellated shift and slide of the image inciting a new intake of air, and then a longer pause as the breath was held.

"How old do you want to go?" El asked, pausing the image at, she judged, somewhere around twenty two.

"Forty four," Wainwright said, the words tumbling out of him. "Go to forty four."

El raised an eyebrow that conveyed - she hoped - at least some of Angela Di Salvo's perplexity, then nodded, and pressed the Enter key again.

On the face cycled, taking the girl on the screen further into her twenties, then her thirties - faint dark circles growing underneath her eyes, and small creases beginning to develop in the triangle between nose and mouth.

"Nearly there," El said, her hand hovering over the Enter key.

The face shifted again, propelling the girl - now firmly a woman - out of her thirties, and into her early forties.

El pressed the Enter key. The image stalled again.

And there, on the screen, her features frozen in black and white, was Rose.

CHAPTER 16
WEST HAMPSTEAD, LONDON
JULY 1997

"Rose?" Ruby had replied, as surprised as El had been by Sita's suggestion. "She ain't a grifter. Nothing personal, love," she'd added to Rose herself, "but a job like this... it needs a bit of experience. A bit of finesse, know what I mean? It ain't straightforward."

Rose, who'd worn a look of wide-eyed terror from the moment her playing the inside had been mooted, had nodded in vigorous agreement.

"It goes without saying that I'll do whatever I can to help, of course," she'd said. "But I really don't think I'm right for this. Could we call in Kat, perhaps? She's not so far off my age, and I don't doubt she could pull it off."

"You wouldn't get her on a plane," Karen had chimed in. "Not yet. She's still adapting."

Kat Morgan's mobility problems, yet another legacy of the Marchant affair, meant she now relied on a wheelchair to navigate any distance greater than a quarter-mile and a pair of walking sticks to get around the specially-modified house in Blackheath she now occupied. She had money these days, like the rest of them; could afford private physiotherapy, and a lot of it. But she was struggling, still, with the day-to-day limitations the head trauma she'd suffered in the course of their last job had imposed on her - and it was very likely she'd consider a twelve hour flight across the Atlantic, even in first class, too ambitious an undertaking in her present condition.

"Someone else, then," Ruby had insisted. "We ain't so short-handed we can't scare up *someone*."

"That won't be necessary," said Sita. "Rose is *perfect*, don't you see? She's exactly right."

"I'm not sure I understand," Rose said.

"Not sure *I* do, neither," said Ruby. "Think you might have to walk me through this one. Perfect *how*?"

Sita's already-broad smile had widened to a beam - the full-toothed grin of a card-sharp about to lay a straight flush on the table.

"She's perfect," she said, "because she won't *be* grifting. She won't *have* to grift. All she'll have to be is herself."

∽

Wainwright didn't move; didn't speak.

"Everything okay?" El asked him, when too much time had passed for the silence between them to be comfortably ignored - letting a little of Angela Di Salvo's nervous concern edge into her voice.

He didn't react, seeming aware of nothing at all but Rose's face on the screen in front of him.

"Mr Wainwright?" she tried again.

"98% accurate," he said, sounding dazed, distant. "That was what you said the other day. Is that right? You're not just saying it to get me or one of the tech blokes you're meeting to make you an offer?"

She hesitated, Angela Di Salvo thrown by the question.

"I don't think you understand," she said slowly. "You can't *fake* the results. If the software didn't work, it'd be obvious. All you'd need is two photos, a Before and an After. If the aged-up image it generated didn't match the real After photo, you'd know in about two seconds. Anyone has any doubts or any questions, they can just... test it. Do you want to try for yourself?"

It was a gamble, offering to let him play around with the program. If he said yes - if he wanted more proof, really *did* need more of a convincer - then the whole con would be blown. Over and done, in the time it took him to figure out that the only two adult faces Karen's hastily mocked-up program would ever give him belonged to Becky and Rose.

She didn't think he would, though. She'd seen enough marks on the cusp to know what she was seeing in his glazed eyes, the front teeth biting, probably unconsciously, into his knuckle. He *wanted* to believe what she was showing him.

"No," he answered after a beat. "No, don't worry. It's enough, what you've showed me."

Generally, it was a moment she let herself enjoy - the mark not just on the hook but reeled in, the magnesium flare of elation at having judged it all just right. But not here; not now.

"Does that mean you're interested?" she asked him.

He looked confused, momentarily - then remembered the pretext for her visit, the lie he'd spun her about his possible interest in buying the rights to the program.

"It means I might be," he said evasively. "I'll need to go away and have a think about it. It's a lot to take in, what you've just showed me."

"I understand," she said. "But just to be completely

transparent: one of the companies I've met this week has put in an offer already. So if it *is* of interest, it would be good if you could let me know fairly soon."

He was barely listening, she thought; his mind somewhere else altogether, debating an entirely different question.

"I'll let you know," he said, distractedly. Then: "The... what did you call it, the After image of the photo I gave you - can you make me a copy? Print it out for me?"

"I can do better than that," she answered, parroting what Karen had told her. "If you've got an email address, I can send it to you right now. Save you the paper."

"I've got one, but it's my secretary who deals with it," he said. "I'll get her to..."

The door to the conference room, hitherto closed, burst open, revealing a worried-looking young woman with eyebrows plucked almost to invisibility - and behind her, Sita, fearsome in a funereal navy suit, conservative jewellery and a mask of stern, bureaucratic displeasure.

"I'm *so, so* sorry, sir," spluttered the girl - an office temp, El guessed, and one unlikely to have her contract renewed after today's performance. "I explained you were in a meeting, but she insisted..."

"Mr Wainwright," Sita interrupted, her New York twang so effortlessly convincing El could picture the Staten Island walk-up she was raised in, "I'm Special Agent Meena Gupta with the IRS. The *Criminal Investigations Division* of the IRS."

She flashed a gold ID badge in his direction, a four-digit number and a Department of the Treasury stamp emblazoned across it.

"What's this about?" said Wainwright, suddenly panicked - probably, El thought, recalling some of the recent interactions he'd had with law enforcement officials in his own country, and how well they'd ended for him. "Criminal Investigations? Do I need to ring my lawyer?"

"That's really up to you, Mr Wainwright," Sita replied. "There are no formal charges against you right now, although I'm obligated to tell you that situation could change as our investigation moves forward. Right now, we just want to talk. There are a few questions about your last audit that we were hoping you might be able to clear up for us."

"Sounds like my cue to leave," said El, closing the laptop, shoving it back into its case and hastily zipping it closed.

"Can I ask who *you* are, ma'am?" Sita asked her, suspicious.

"Just on my way to an appointment," El said, throwing the case over one shoulder and making for the doorway. "I'll send you that email this evening," she added to Wainwright, almost tripping over her feet in her haste to leave.

"Don't forget, will you?" she heard him shout, as she hit the corridor - and then Sita was closing the door after her, trapping him and the unfortunate office temp inside.

Leaving the Fine Cloth Company in her wake, she headed for the Mission, with a view to grabbing lunch before returning to Presidio Heights. On Folsom Street, where a cluster of motorbike showrooms and auto repair shops segued seamlessly into shuttered bars and steam-filled taquerias, she paused, certain she was being followed, the hairs on the back of her neck prickling - but then, turning, saw nothing but the usual crop of teenagers on skateboards, restaurant workers on cigarette breaks and loud-shirted tourists photographing murals and graffiti.

Wondering whether this new paranoia was the cross *she* had to bear after the Marchant job, or whether it was nothing but a side-effect of geographic dislocation, of being out of the UK and on unfamiliar turf, she lit a cigarette of her own, and carried on walking.

～

It was almost four o'clock when she got back to the house. Only Sophie was there, still in the sunroom but now transplanted to the carpet, where she lay on her back, her thumbs hovering above the buttons of a Sega Game Gear.

"I'm back," El told her - intending to escape to her bedroom, in the privacy of which she could finally shed the second Angela Di Salvo's uncomfortable piercings and excessively baggy slacker-wear before hopping into the shower.

("You have the name already," Sita had insisted of the Angela Di Salvo persona, despite El's objections. "Why not get a little more use from it, before it retires?")

Sophie, though, had questions.

"What's going on with you and my Mum?" she asked, making no effort to get up from the floor but putting down the Game Gear and looking El straight in the eye.

El stopped dead in the sunroom doorway.

"That's a strange thing to ask," she said - uncertain of the kid's exact meaning, much less her motivations, but willing to believe that only snares and pitfalls lay ahead. "Why do you ask?"

"You're being evasive," Sophie said knowingly. "Answering a question with a question. It's what people do when they're nervous or about to lie to you about something."

"Did Ruby tell you that?"

"Sita."

"Well, she isn't always right. Language is complicated.

People are complicated. There's no blanket rule you can apply to every situation."

"Do you like her?"

"Sita?"

"My Mum."

El fidgeted uncomfortably where she stood, horribly aware that the kid would read the motion as a tell. Especially if Sita had been sharing some of her life-lessons.

"Sure," she said, as neutrally as she was able. "She's great."

"But you didn't like it when that woman took her out to the auction. Kate."

Don't panic, El told herself. Everything's fine. She's a kid, not CID. You're not *actually* being interrogated.

"I didn't like it or dislike it," she said, trying for nonchalance and, if the crack in her voice was any indication, failing miserably. "It was part of the job. Had to be done."

Sophie gave her what El's own mother would have called *a very old look* - the deep, cynical stare of an ancient oracle in a cave on the slope of a mountain.

"You didn't *look* like you liked it, when she was here," she said.

"I was just tired," El lied. "I don't know if you've noticed, but there's a lot going on."

"Ruby said she thought you were jealous."

El was, again, outraged.

"*Ruby* said that?" she asked.

"Sort of. She said you had *a touch of the green-eyed monster*, or something like that. But I knew what she meant."

"That's absurd."

"Whatever."

Sophie, no longer entertained enough by El's reactions

to bother carrying on the conversation, turned back to her game.

"I like your Mum," El said, feeling the need to clarify her position. "But not like *that*. Not romantically."

Sophie seemed not to hear her, her attention now entirely focused on the console in her hands.

El suppressed a sigh, wondering again why she'd let herself be persuaded that bringing a teenager along on a job was anything but a terrible idea.

She stepped backwards and out of the sunroom, reaching involuntarily for the cigarette packet in her pocket.

"She'll be disappointed," Sophie called, when she was halfway to the front door, cigarette in her mouth and plastic lighter in her palm. "She likes you, I think. You know... *romantically*."

CHAPTER 17
THE TENDERLOIN, SAN FRANCISCO
SEPTEMBER 1997

El had to take Ruby's word for it that events thereafter played out the way she described them.

But even allowing for the creative licence the old woman had almost certainly taken with the looping thread of her narrative, it seemed to El likely that what had happened was this:

On the morning of the 19th of September - not quite 72 hours after El had left the US headquarters of Fine Cloth, the sensation of being watched pulsing under her skin like a low-level electrical charge - Ted Wainwright took a taxi from his Classical Revival mansion off Pacific Avenue to a small, one-room office above a Vietnamese restaurant on O'Farrell Street, in the altogether less salubrious Tenderloin district.

The woman who buzzed him up and greeted him on the second floor, her handshake firm enough to crack walnuts, could have been the twin separated from Ruby at birth. The eyes were the same, piercing blue and crafty as a raven's, and the same knowing wickedness rippled the corners of her mouth when she smiled, but the rest was different, in both subtle and more obviously quantifiable ways. Her hair was a faded ginger, salt and paprika, tied back in a practical ponytail that had no aspirations to style; her teeth were yellow and tobacco-stained and, though she was white, what even a cursory glance could identify as a lifetime spent outdoors in the Southwest sun had darkened the skin on her face to the leathery brown of a baseball glove and freckled the backs of her hands with liver spots.

She wore stonewash jeans held up by a Longhorn belt buckle, a tan waistcoat over a loose denim shirt and a pair of well-worn cowboy boots, each boot decorated with a tangle of yellow roses.

"Glad to meet you, sir," she told Wainwright, with all the politeness of a native-born East Texan raised on good manners and Southern hospitality. "Why don't you come on inside, and you and me can talk?"

∽

Three days earlier, just as El was taking her slow walk along the mural-lined streets of the Mission, Special Agent Meena Gupta and her associate, the quietly menacing Special Agent Karen Torres (née Baxter) had been laying breadcrumbs.

Flustered by SA Gupta's unexpected, and surely inauspicious, appearance in his conference room, Wainwright had sought to buy himself time - to think, to compose himself, to try to puzzle out what the hell a tax inspector could want with him when he'd barely been a year in this bloody country - by proposing that they retire to his private office on the fifth floor.

SA Gupta had graced the suggestion with a single, thin smile.

"My partner is up there already," she told him, tapping

just once, very lightly, on one of the earrings that Wainwright would have been astonished to discover was connected to the small, circular piece of conductive plastic *right then* resting in SA Torres' left ear canal. "We thought one of us ought to wait there, just in case."

"In case *what*?" Wainwright had asked, flabbergasted.

The thin smile had evaporated.

"You may be surprised to learn, Mr Wainwright," SA Gupta said, "that not everyone is happy to see the IRS when we pay them a visit. Some even try to duck out on us, when they discover we're looking for them. So we find it expedient to consider where they might want to duck out *to*, and make our way there too. Ahead of time."

"So you can ambush them?"

"We're the IRS, Mr Wainwright. We don't ambush. We don't have to. We're very, very good at waiting."

On the fifth floor, alone in a gleaming office suite with a larger footprint than her first flat in Tulse Hill, SA Torres slipped into the In tray on Wainwright's desk two items: a deep purple flyer crammed with bold, black, uppercase text ("LOST SOMEONE CLOSE TO YOU? WE FIND YOUR MISSING LOVED ONES - OR YOUR MONEY BACK. CALL 800-555-LOST") and a business card in the same vivid colour. The card bore similar text to the flyer, with some additional information: a woman's name ("Laurel Hopkins, Private Investigator") and the address of a building not far from Union Square, on the corner of Polk and O'Farrell.

Outside, if the local boys she'd hired three days after she'd arrived in the city had done their jobs, the same advertisement would be leaping out at drivers and pedestrians from five fourteen-foot billboards strategically positioned along key points of what she'd judged to be Wainwright's daily commute from home to Fine Cloth and back again. A sixth billboard, she was pleased to see, had been placed directly opposite his office, and was now not just visible but impossible to avoid from the large back window she imagined Wainwright spinning 'round to stare through every time he took a call or gave dictation.

After a moment's thought, SA Torres removed the business card from the In tray and laid it flat on the desk, beside a pile of papers.

A minute or so later, when SA Gupta and her profusely sweating quarry entered the suite, Torres was standing to attention on the opposite side of the desk - hands on her hips, weapon holstered and badge dangling from a chain around her neck.

"Edward Wainwright?" she asked him, in the generic Midwestern accent that was, she'd previously argued, the best she could muster at short notice.

Wainwright nodded, meek as a terrified kitten.

"I've told Mr Wainwright he's not under arrest at this time," said SA Gupta, "and he's agreed to answer a few questions without his lawyer present."

"Glad to hear it," said Torres. "Why don't you take a seat, Mr Wainwright?" she added, in a tone that suggested refusing to do so really wasn't an option.

Wainwright moved gingerly in the direction of what could only be *his* chair - then, seeing Torres look pointedly down at the seat opposite, the *visitor's* chair, immediately changed paths.

Gupta, when he was seated, began to walk the perimeter of the desk, taking inventory of every fax and scribbled Post-It she found there. Halfway around, she stopped - her bureaucrat's eyes seeming to zoom in on the purple business card.

"A private investigator, Mr Wainwright?" she asked,

neutral curiosity barely covering her suspicion. "What is it you could want with a private investigator?"

"What?" he asked, confused by the question. "What investigator?"

Gupta picked up the card by its edges, as if handling evidence to be bagged and tagged, and turned it to face outwards, until it was only inches from Wainwright's nose.

"'Laurel Hopkins,'" Torres read, giving every impression of seeing the card for the first time. "She work for you, Mr Wainwright?"

∼

"I appreciate you coming out here to see me," the woman in the waistcoat said, hooking a desiccated thumb into the space between her belt and buckle.

"It's no bother," said Wainwright, from the lumpy couch she'd urged him into before pressing an ice-cold bottle of water into his hand. "I've not been here long enough yet to mind poking 'round different bits of the city. It's all interesting to me, still."

"Interesting's right," the woman snorted. "Lot more hookers here than in Nacogdoches, I'll tell you that. That's Texas," she added, for his benefit. "Moved out here in '86 and never looked back since. But forget about me - you sure as shooting didn't come to read my diary. Tell me about you. Tell me what it is I can do for you."

He took a sip from his water bottle; sat up straighter on the couch.

"I've met a lot of private detectives, Miss Hopkins," he said. "Not so many out here, but I should think I've burned through most of the ones in the phone book back at home over the years. Good ones, too. Ex-coppers, ex-

Special Forces - the sort of men who know what they're on about."

"Laurel's just fine," the woman said. "I'm getting a little long in the tooth for Miss these days. But let me stop you right there. These other investigators, back in England - you say they were good. Did none of them get you what it was you were looking for? From the way you're talking, and the fact you're sitting right here with me today and not with them, I'm thinking maybe they didn't."

"And you'd be right. Not one of 'em got so much as a sniff of a lead. Useless, the lot of them."

"The... issue you commissioned them to look into. Would it have anything to do with what landed you in jail?"

This seem to rattle him. His eyes narrowed.

"My work takes me all over, Mr Wainwright," she added mildly, by way of explanation. "I have friends in England, friends at Scotland Yard. And I find it's generally good practice to pick up the phone and make a couple calls before a client comes to see me. So please, don't take offence. I do it with everyone."

He swallowed back more water.

"No," he said, mollified. "Not that. Nowt to do with that."

"What, then, if I can ask?"

"It's my daughter. She was taken."

"Taken?"

"From me and my wife. My... first wife. A long time ago."

"How long?"

Laurel reached for the notepad and fountain pen resting on the side-table by her elbow, flipped it open and began to write.

"Forty two years," he said.

The pen stopped, and Laurel let out a low whistle through her teeth.

"That's a *long* time," she said.

"Yes, it is."

"And this was in England?"

"Harrogate. Yorkshire."

She snapped the cap back on the pen and laid it and the notebook back down on the side table.

"Mr Wainwright," she said, not unsympathetically, "please don't think me insensitive, but you understand that I have to ask: what are you doing coming to me with this, right now? Like I said, I work all over, and like it says on my card, I'm pretty damn good at tracking folks down when they go missing, even if I tell you that myself. But this is the first time anyone's ever come hollering for me to get on a case that happened better than four decades ago and five thousand miles away."

He pressed the water bottle to his brow and held it there.

"Do you need me to put on the fan?" she asked him. "I should have said: I keep it off, even in summer. People say we're in a heatwave right now, but it feels cold as Christmas here to me, always has."

"No," he answered quickly. "No need, not on my account. And as to the other thing... I can see as how it might sound funny, when you put it like that. And if we'd been here talking even a fortnight ago, I'd probably have agreed with you. But this week... I suppose you could say I got given something. New information - the sort of thing you can't very well argue with. And I thought, since *you're* here and *I'm* here and finding people seems to be your bread and butter, it might be that you can help me out."

She took a moment to consider this. Then, appearing to make up her mind about whatever she'd been debating, picked the pen and notebook back up again.

"This new information," she said. "Let's start with that. What is it you were given?"

He reached for the briefcase at his feet, pulled it onto his lap and opened the locks, then put a hand inside and pulled out a crumpled, much-folded piece of paper. He unfolded it and passed it across to her. It was a colour printout of a photograph, she saw - one showing a pale, red-haired woman in her late thirties or early forties, her teeth bared in a tight smile.

"What am I looking at here?" she asked.

"My daughter," he said quietly. "I've not seen so much as a hair on her head since 1955, but I'm telling you, sure as we sit here: it's her. What you're seeing is what she looks like now."

∽

"I don't want you to pretend to *look* for the child," Soames had said, two months and a thousand small deceptions earlier. "Wainwright's been burned so many times, you'd squeeze scarcely a penny from him, if you tried that one."

"What, then?" El had asked.

Soames had run one claw-like hand along his jawline, savouring the moment of revelation.

"What you must do," he said, "is *find* the child. *Be* the child. I know the man well enough to be certain of this: if you present to him a woman, a grown woman, he believes to be his child, he'll give her - or rather, give *us* - anything we want, for as long as she asks him to. He'll empty his pockets and his bank accounts, and he'll do it with a smile on his face and a song in his heart."

∽

Laurel Hopkins studied the printout. Turned it to the side; held it up to her nose, and then far away, assessing it from every angle, every distance.

"This woman is your daughter?" she asked, when she was finished.

"I've good reason to think so," Wainwright replied.

"And forgive me if I'm jumping the gun or presuming too much, but you're fixin' to have me find her for you?"

"If you think you can. It won't be easy," he added. "All you'd have to go off is this picture. I couldn't tell you what name she goes by now, or how she dresses, or where she is - she could be in Timbuktu or Outer Mongolia, for all I know. You ask *some* people, and they'd tell you that you *couldn't* find her no matter how hard you tried, because she's dead already - that she's been dead since the night them bastards took her. They'd be wrong, but that's what they'd tell you."

Laurel held up a finger, cutting him off.

"Wait," she said, leaping up from her seat with surprising agility. "Wait just one second."

She raced across the room, coming to a stop at a cheap, overstuffed wooden magazine rack propped up by her desk. She rifled through its contents and then, with a small hiss of triumph, extracted from it a bundle of paper that was evidently the prize she'd been looking for.

"Here," she said, racing back to him and almost throwing the paper into his lap.

He looked down. It was a newspaper, he saw - that day's edition, dated September 19th, the banner encased in a wide, garish rainbow and the headline image showing two short-haired, long-limbed women in white vest tops draped languidly around one another.

"'The Oakland Girlfriend'," Wainwright read, examining the paper's title. "What's this when it's at home?"

"You got a problem with my lifestyle, sir?" Laurel asked, some of the warmth draining from her voice.

"What?" he answered, flustered. "No! I take people as I find 'em, me. Couldn't care less what they get up to in the bedroom, so long as they shut the curtains. But what am I looking at it for?"

"Inside," she said. "Page two or three, I think."

Wainwright flashed her a look that suggested he was regretting the decisions that had led him to this sofa, this office and this apparently very peculiar woman, but did as he was asked.

And there it was, a small colour photograph on the inside page, part of a wider two-page spread covering a charity function at one of the fancy art museums people kept telling him he needed to visit - above it a headline, reading YES I AM, SAYS ENGLISH ARISTO.

And below it, in a photograph snapped at the auction by a press pass-wielding Karen (and slipped subsequently into the waiting hands of the Oakland Girlfriend's chief editor, one of Sita's many very dear friends, with a promise of immediate publication) stood Rose - head tipped back in delighted laughter, arms wrapped intimately around the waist of the beaming, sharp-suited woman who was evidently her date for the evening.

"Seems to me," said Laurel, as Wainwright took in what he was seeing, "that if you want to find this daughter of yours, you ain't got far to go."

CHAPTER 18

WEST HAMPSTEAD, LONDON

JULY 1997

"I can't," Sita had said, back in London, "from all that El has told us, conceive of a single way forward beyond our doing exactly what he asks of us."

Karen was the first to break the deep, painful silence that followed this pronouncement.

"Maybe I'm missing something," she said, "but what's to stop us just bunging Soames a load of money and *saying* it came from Wainwright? He's not gonna know the difference, not if he's so sick he can't even leave the house."

"He'd know," El replied.

("You'll be tempted, I'm sure," Soames had warned her and Rose, before they'd left him, "to find a way around doing what I've... well, let's say *asked* you, shall we? But I'd have to advise very firmly against it. Wainwright and I aren't as close as we were in our confinement, but we *do* speak. I have his number in San Francisco on speed-dial, and you can tell Mrs Redfearn and the rest of your cabal that I'll be checking in on him more regularly over the next few months. Making sure that our plans are progressing as they should be.")

"You can't just click your fingers and expect us to hop to it," El had argued. "A job like that takes time. It's not a question of jumping on a plane tomorrow and sweet-talking him into writing a cheque. You have to lay the groundwork."

"You have two months," Soames had replied, quickly enough that El thought he'd probably had a timeframe in mind for the con from the beginning. "From now until the end of September. Ample time to get the ball rolling, I'd say. And since you bring it up, I ought to add: it won't only be in *America* that I'll be checking up on you. I have friends here too, as you've seen. They'll be keeping an eye on all of you on *this* side of the pond. Keeping me abreast of how this groundwork is unfolding").

"He's watching us, then?" Ruby asked.

El nodded.

"'Course he is," Ruby said quietly. "*Course* he is. He'll have been doing it a while, an' all - keeping track of where we go, who we see, what sort of calendars we keep to. It's what *I'd* do, if I were him."

The room fell silent again, all of them grappling with the implications of this - not so much the being watched as the certainty that Soames would know, and know immediately, if any one of them put so much as a foot out of line.

"Rose," Ruby said, emerging from her reverie with a jerk of the head that El recognised as a tell - a sign that something had occurred to her, a new idea or a sudden flash of inspiration, and that she wanted to explore it, to follow the thought to its logical conclusion. "Question for you."

"Okay," Rose answered, guardedly - unsure of what was coming.

"That sister of yours, Harriet. You see much of her these days?"

It was a miracle, in El's opinion, that Rose and Harriet Marchant had managed to cultivate any sort of relationship at all.

The youngest of their father's *legitimate* children, the ones born in wedlock to James Marchant's widow Elizabeth (who, to the best of El's knowledge, remained unaware that she *was* a widow), Harriet was by her own admission an odd duck: solitary, introverted to the point of rudeness and borderline obsessive about her work and the handful of hobbies that orbited it. A social psychologist who lived alone and liked it, she'd learned of Rose's existence only a few months before, and had introduced herself to her half-sister in the first instance - at El's kitchen table, early on New Year's Day - by revealing that she not only *knew* that Rose and El and the others had killed her father, but *approved* of what they'd done.

The bond she and Rose had begun to form thereafter was fragile, but significant to both of them. Harriet, El knew, was one of the very few people who'd been allowed to visit Rose - and eventually, to meet Sophie - in their new penthouse fortress; Rose, in return, had earned a standing invitation to the musty flat on Holloway Road that Harriet shared with her cat, a two-room labyrinth of books, academic journal articles and rock music memorabilia that gave no indication at all that its occupant had a personal net worth rising into the tens of millions.

What *Ruby's* interest in Harriet might be, though, was anyone's guess.

"How *much* do I see her?" Rose replied. "Reasonably often, I suppose. When I can."

Ruby scratched thoughtfully at her chin.

"What would you say," she asked, "about giving her a quick call? Sort of nowish?"

CHAPTER 19
PRESIDIO HEIGHTS, SAN FRANCISCO
SEPTEMBER 1997

The morning after Wainwright paid a visit to Laurel Hopkins' office in the Tenderloin, coming up to 6am Pacific Time, the phone in the hallway of the Presidio Heights house began to ring.

It was a novelty handset, a hamburger phone with plastic cheese and sesame seed embossing bought by the owners of the property in a moment of whimsy, but the tone was high and clear, carrying upstairs and along the first floor landing at a volume loud enough to rouse El from shallow, still jet-lagged sleep and propel her down the stairs to pick up the receiver.

Ruby, however, got there first. And seemed, if her daytime clothes and combed, no-longer-ginger hair were any indication, to have been awake for a while.

"You got it?" she was saying down the line, just as El made it to the gossip bench on which the ill-judged hamburger rested. "Yeah? Alright. You done good, girl. Better than good. Now go and get your feet up and a cup of tea inside you. I'll give you a bell once I've told the rest of 'em."

"Tell us what?" El asked, when she'd hung up the call. "What's going on?"

"Do us a favour," Ruby replied, "and go and wake Rose? Sita an' all, if you can tear her from her slumber."

"Why?"

"'Cause it's time, is why. So get a wiggle on and wake 'em. If we're lucky, we can catch Wainwright before he leaves for work."

∼

From a rented Ford Taurus parked across the street from the house, in the shade of a Monterey pine, he watched them – infrared binoculars pressed so hard to his eyes they'd leave bruises around the sockets.

He'd been there all night: tracking them through windows and the gaps in the half-closed blinds as they came and went, moving from living room to kitchen to bathroom and, eventually, to bed.

She hadn't slept, though; had stayed curled up on a sofa, reading and making notes on an A4 pad that never left her lap, stopping only to shower and throw back coffee from a cappuccino cup the size of his head as the others fell away, one by one. As if she were waiting for something – for the phone call that, when it came, had her rushing into the hall to answer it.

In spite of the coffee, he imagined she was exhausted. *He* was exhausted, for all the thin, bitter American chocolate he'd eaten and the flask of cold, sweet tea he'd worked through to keep himself awake, and he was young and fit by comparison, not some wizened old bag who probably needed a rub-down with a tube of Deep Heat before she could drop off.

The other old one didn't sleep much either, he'd noticed in the days and nights he'd been watching – the foreign one with a thing for antiques, so unexpectedly quick and deceptively strong that his balls had ached for a week after she'd kicked him. She'd go upstairs, like the rest of them; make a show of saying goodnight, changing into silk pyjamas or a night gown, dabbing at her face with cold cream and a cotton wool pad. But then, once she was in her bedroom with the door shut, she'd spend hours on the phone, just talking, her mobile pressed to her ear as she gabbed away – though to who, and about what, he had no idea. It made him wonder whether he ought to have tried harder to bug the house; to have sought out some way of listening in, as well as watching.

Too late for that now, he supposed.

He almost felt sorry for the younger ones: the skinny one who'd dyed her hair pink, the one he'd followed to the car show out in Gloucester nearly three months back; the posh bird with the kid and the scar down her arm; the black girl who always seemed to be carrying a screwdriver in her pocket. They weren't to blame, not really; all they'd done was fall in with *her* and her mate. But lie down with dogs and you wake up with fleas – wasn't that what they said?

And here they were.

It seemed to be moving forward, that was the main thing – whatever it was they were doing to that bloke with the big moustache, whatever scam it was they were pulling on him. And the further forward it moved, the closer they were to wrapping it up and heading back to London.

Which was good news for him.

He'd never been to America before – had never had a passport or been out of the *country* before – but he'd had hopes, when he got on the plane, of seeing at least a few of the sights he'd heard San Francisco was famous for, in between keeping an eye on *her* and her crew: Alcatraz, the Golden Gate Bridge, the tower from Vertigo. Instead, he'd spent most of the trip with a camera or a telescopic lens glued to his face, stuck in a rental car with no air conditioning that smelled like hot dogs and wet fur, or following the pink-haired woman from one identikit grey building to another in the baking sun until his legs cramped and the soles of his feet blistered.

He was ready to go home.

When they were all home, of course – him, and them – there'd be more to deal with. Once they'd cleaned the old walrus out of whatever they could get, they'd need to be dealt with. He doubted he'd get a say in *how*, but if he *did*, he'd do them all in one go, take them out in one clean sweep: a fire, maybe, or a traffic accident, if he could make it so all five of them – and *her* sons too, the mixed-race lad in the smart suit and the other one, the one he'd slashed – were in the same place at the same time.

He had no taste for pain or violence, he'd realised since this business had started. He knew why it was needed here, and he understood why he – out of everyone – was the best placed to mete it out. But stabbing the son on his mother's doorstep, feeling the knife go in and hearing the skin pop as it broke the surface... it made him queasy. He'd been sick straight after, pulling his van into a side-street near the Brent Cross roundabout and vomiting into the gutter until the nausea passed – a detail he'd omitted, when he'd recounted later how his mission had gone.

And as for the old girl...

Bad enough, he'd thought, that he had to slash her – even if it *was* just a warning shot, not the whole shebang. Maybe she *was* a con – but she was an OAP, too, old enough to be his nan, and tricking her outside then going at her in the dark with a blade ... it had felt wrong. Shameful. And that was *before* he'd let her take the knife off him; *before* she'd given him a kicking and sent him racing off through Kensington with his tail between his legs.

It was no fun, hurting people. No fun at all.

But sometimes it had to be done, didn't it? Sometimes the world didn't leave you much choice.

PART III
JULY/AUGUST

CHAPTER 20
MATLOCK, DERBYSHIRE
JULY 1997

There were storm clouds over the Peak District when Kat Morgan left Bakewell for Matlock Bath: dark, pillowy malignancies hanging claustrophobically low in the sky, threatening thunder and lightning as well as rain. It had stormed, on and off, since she'd started the trip, an impromptu tour of the northern counties that had taken in what felt like every market town and mining community between Chesterfield and Cleveland; the Mini, which had been sparkling when she'd left London, was now, not even a week later, streaked and smeared, splattered with mud and whatever unholy stew of gravel and dirt and dead animals she'd been driving through.

This village, she'd heard, was a tourist trap, the bustling hub at the centre of a network of theme parks, museums and aquariums penned in by a crop of vertiginous moors and valleys so steep they might as well have been mountains - but she saw no evidence of this today. What she took to be the main shopping drag, a curving stretch of sweet shops and souvenir stands, was all but deserted, the road beside it clear of traffic. Probably the weather, she thought. Clouds like that'd be enough to put anyone off their toffee apples.

The house she was looking for turned out to be not a house at all, but a bed and breakfast - a converted cottage with space, she guessed, for no more than four visitors at a time. It was neat, well-kept and unfussily pretty, the kind that would photograph well for a holiday brochure; a welcome change, at least, from the terraces and bungalows and council flats she'd been shown into, sometimes warmly and at other times grudgingly, since she'd begun her odyssey.

She parked the Mini as near as she could manage to the B&B without ramming the front gate, reached for her sticks and began the process of untangling herself from the driving seat. It took so long now, this untangling; so fucking *long*. A minor inconvenience by the standards of everything else that had come her way since the year before, since the bitch she'd considered an ally, if not exactly a friend, had taken her head apart with a twelve-inch metal bar and nearly killed her in the process: the pounding migraines, the constant ache in her hips, the legs that *wouldn't do what she fucking told them* no matter how much she tried to will them into submission. But an inconvenience just the same, and one that reminded her, every time, of all the other things that were more difficult now than they used to be - and of the *other* other things, though there were fewer of them, that were probably impossible.

Gritting her teeth, she pressed down on the sticks and levered herself to a standing position on the pavement. The ground was flat, and the walk to the doorbell short; all being well, she could make it without losing her balance or falling flat on her arse.

The woman who answered the door when she rang it seemed friendly, though Kat supposed friendliness was a hygiene factor if you wanted to sell yourself as a landlady - and the sticks themselves had a tendency to elicit an initial burst of sympathy in an audience. The wheelchair - which she'd brought with her but which had stayed thus far, fingers crossed, in the boot - even more so.

She was younger than Kat had been expecting - not even sixty, ash-blonde and as modestly immaculate as the guest house she kept.

"Can I help you, duck?" she asked.

"I hope so," Kat answered, falling back into the light-touch Scouse accent and hesitant disposition she'd adopted for the week. "I'm Faye Tuttle, Mrs Otley - with the Wirral Advocate. I was hoping I might be able to talk to you about Ingrid Wainwright."

∼

"I ain't just asking this for me," Ruby had said, when she'd first called Kat to recruit her for the job. "It's me Soames is after, but what he's got - it's on all of us. You included."

Kat hadn't bitten. Not then.

"In case you hadn't noticed," she'd replied, angry as hell at the old battle-axe for reasons that even *she* didn't really understand, "I'm not really up to working just at the moment, what with the crippling headaches and it taking me half an hour to get my knickers on in the morning. Perhaps come back to me when I'm not having to use a Stannah lift to make it up the stairs."

"He'll have us," Ruby had said, not rising to the bait. "I *know* him. He'll have us, and he'll *keep* having us - he's that sort. Doing one job for him once, it won't be enough. He'll want us on the hook for the long haul, dancing to his tune. Unless we do something about it."

"Are you not hearing what I'm saying to you? *I can't*."

"You can't do the *job* - that's what you've been saying. Which I'm not so sure is true, but that's neither here nor there. What I'm asking you to do ain't work - not the way you mean it. It's more like... research."

"Research? What does *that* mean?"

"It *means* you don't need to be conning nobody. Just pokin' around a few places and askin' a few questions."

"And how's *that* supposed to help us dig our way out of this pile of shit you've landed us in, if I may ask?"

"I ain't exactly sure yet. But I'll tell you one thing: I might not've been there with Rose and young El when they went down to see the bastard, but you don't get to my age without a decent nose on you, and this whole thing... it smells wrong. There's more to it somehow - more going on behind the scenes than what he's told 'em. And if we're wading feet-first into the game he's got set up for us, then I don't know about you, but I want to know what that *something* is."

∿

"Ingrid Wainwright?" said Mrs Otley, neither budging from the doorstep nor making any move to let Kat inside. She was suspicious now, bordering on frosty - but at least a little bit curious too, if Kat was reading her right.

"That's right," Kat said. "You might have known her as Little Ingrid? It was a long time ago now, but I understand you were doing some work at the Wainwright house when she was kidnapped? With the horses?"

"Who told you that?" Mrs Otley asked sharply.

You know what? Kat replied to herself, in her own voice. *I don't even remember. I've spent the whole fucking week running up and down motorways chasing interchangeable old biddies who might have been in Harrogate forty years ago and might have known these Wainwrights, whoever they were, and you expect me to remember which one it was?*

If that's what coppers do 24/7, I'm bloody glad I'm on the other side of the fence.

"I'd rather not say, if you don't mind, Mrs Otley," she replied out loud. "She asked me to keep the conversations we had private. But she said she was sure she remembered seeing you there, around that time."

You want to talk to the stable girl, love, that particular biddy had told her - one of the *really* old ones she'd talked to in Knaresborough, or so she thought, though her memory was like a block of bloody Emmental these days, and she doubted there was a physiotherapist alive who could help her out with *that*, no matter how much money she threw at them.

Ada Lee, her name was then. 'Course, that was before she married that Otley boy from Ripon and they moved down south. John? Jack? It'll come to me. Any road, have a word with her and see what shakes out. I weren't up at that house much, just two mornings a week to see to the carpets and give it a once-over with the duster, but I always used to catch sight of her hanging about the place, watching and listening. We all used to think she had a bit of a thing for Ted - Mr Wainwright, I should say. Though if she did, she'd have been flat out of luck. He'd never have strayed, that one. Only ever had eyes for his wife.

"Whatever you're sniffing 'round for, I can't help you," Mrs Otley said. "I've nothing to say to you that I've not already said to the police back when it happened."

You're not closing the door, though, are you? Kat

thought. At least some of you *wants* to talk to me. It's a bit of excitement, isn't it? Probably the biggest thrill you'll get between changing the bedsheets and doling out the scrambled eggs at breakfast.

"It's nothing salacious, I promise, Mrs Otley," she said. "We're running a series on unsolved crimes, and the Little Ingrid case came up as one worth looking into. I'm just after some background - you know, on the house, the family, that sort of thing. Something a bit more human than what we've got already in the archives. I'd keep your name out of it," she added.

And that, she judged - *that'd* be the clincher. *I'd keep your name out of it. You can have your moment in the spotlight - a willing audience, sat there on tenterhooks listening to everything you say. And the neighbours'll never know you told.*

"Alright," said Mrs Otley, opening the door a crack and taking two steps back into the hallway. "Five minutes. That's all I can spare."

"Brilliant," Kat replied, crossing the threshold. "Should be all I need."

∼

Five minutes turned into twenty, then forty five. When the storm clouds finally cleared and the rain began to dry up outside the window of the little front parlour that served as her private living room, Mrs Otley had been speaking, virtually uninterrupted, for almost two hours.

Getting them to open up - that had always been Kat's gift.

She'd known, from her first year at drama school, that she'd never be an actress, not a proper one. There was too much competition: too many genuinely talented - far *more* talented - Lears and Blanche DuBoises and Desdemonas on her course alone, never mind in the years above or already out there with an Equity card. The same way she'd known, since she'd woken up in hospital after that *bitch* Hannah had come at her with the wheel lock, that the cons she used to run out of the casinos around Mayfair and Park Lane and Piccadilly were off the menu - the ones that relied on her showing off her legs in a little black dress and being quick enough to make a sharp exit once her marks were passed out cold on their beds and she'd had a rifle through their wallets. Now, and forever, most likely.

But knowing how to get people to talk to her, to say the things they didn't know they wanted to say - *that* had stayed with her.

"She killed herself, you know," Mrs Otley told her - speaking, Kat noticed, directly into the recording device set up on the coffee table between them. "Mrs Wainwright - the wife. A year or two after the little girl was took. Drowned herself in the river like that writer, that Virginia Woolf."

"Did she?" said Kat, who'd heard some variation on the same story at least four times that week.

"Oh, yes. But I mean, you can see why she would, can't you? Losing her little one like that. Especially when..."

She stopped abruptly, mid-revelation.

"Especially when...?" Kat prompted.

"Oh, I shouldn't say. It was nothing, really. Just gossip."

"Gossip?"

"Folk whispering. You know the sort of thing. Saying this and that."

"About?"

Mrs Otley paused again; looked from the recorder to Kat, and back again.

"And this is definitely off the record, is it?" she asked. "You won't be quoting me, or owt like that?"

"Not unless you want me to."

"Alright. Thing is, see, it's not something I told the police, back then, when they came 'round asking questions. I didn't *lie*, as such. I just... didn't mention it, and they had so many people they were talking to I were *sure* someone else would've brought it up."

"Brought *what* up, Mrs Otley?"

"The gardener, duck. Bob Kingsley. That was the gossip - about what was meant to have been going on with him and Mrs Wainwright, 'round about the time the kiddie went missing."

∼

Ada Lee, as she was then, had started with the Wainwrights only a few months after Little Ingrid was born.

She stuck to the stables, mainly - mucking out the horses, grooming and feeding them, taking them out across the fields that bordered the Wainwrights' big country house. But Mr Wainwright was so handsome, and always so nice to her when he saddled up to go riding, that she'd developed a bit of a crush on him - and so, whenever the opportunity arose to go into the house to request more feed or get herself a drink of water from the kitchen tap, she took it, hoping she might catch a glimpse of him.

It was in the kitchen that she first heard the rumours about Bob and Mrs Wainwright.

"Shocking, that's what I call it," the cook was saying to the housekeeper. Ada stilled by the sink, glass in hand, pretending not to listen.

"Shocking's right," said the housekeeper. "The pair of

them swanning about 'round the garden together, thinking nobody'll have a mind to put two and two together. And her still with a babe in arms, too!"

"If *I* were young Mr Wainwright," said the cook authoritatively, "I'd be going back over my diary to about the time she first announced she were expecting. Checking a few dates, if you know what I mean."

"No!" said the housekeeper, scandalised. "You don't think...?"

"Doesn't matter what *I* think, does it? It's what *he* thinks that's important. And she's got him convinced the sun shines out of her proverbial. But if you're telling me it's a new development, this *thing* with our friend Bob and that little madam..."

Both cook and housekeeper seemed to notice, all at once, that Ada was still in the kitchen.

"What you doing skulking 'round in here, cloth ears?" the housekeeper said, shooing her outside as if she were a stray cat in the larder. "Get back to them horses, 'fore I clout you one!"

∽

"The baby wasn't Wainwright's?" Kat asked, taken aback by this twist in the tale despite herself.

"Those were the rumours," Mrs Otley shrugged. "Bob Kingsley handed in his notice a month or so before young Ingrid were snatched - got a better job at some stately home in London, or so he said. There's no sense rehashing it all now, so long after the fact, but if she *was* his... well, it wouldn't surprise me if it were the guilt over that on top of what happened to the little one that drove Mrs Wainwright into that river. And poor Ted. You just have to hope he never found out, don't you? I know he married again, after - but can you imagine going through all that, losing your only daughter and waiting 'round to pay a ransom that never comes, and then finding out she was another's man's child all along?"

CHAPTER 21

CALEDONIAN ROAD, LONDON

JULY 1997

Briscoe was late. Harriet, who was never late - who left the flat for seminars and lectures and appointments thirty minutes earlier than she needed to, every time, to make absolutely certain of it - was thrown; irritated by his carelessness, but anxious too that his absence from the table would call attention to her *presence*, would announce to the handful of other daytime drinkers at the bar that she was both *there*, and there *alone*. That she'd been stood up, or dumped - or worse, that she was *on the lookout,* casting her net into the sparsely-populated waters of The Golden Lion at four o'clock on a Tuesday in hope of luring in a balding City trader or an alcoholic solicitor with a redundancy cheque burning a hole in his pocket. *What else*, as her father would doubtless have told her, *would a woman your age be doing on her own in a place like that?*

At ten past the hour, when she was on the verge of gathering her things to leave, Briscoe arrived, smelling of cigarette smoke and murmuring half-hearted apologies, his bomber jacket zipped up to the neck – she assumed to hide the uniform underneath.

"My shift ran over," he said, pulling up a stool so unnecessarily close to hers that she was forced to physically veer away, inclining her upper body in the opposite direction at an uncomfortable forty five-degree angle. "Couldn't get away."

"No problem," she said, though it was.

She didn't offer to buy him a drink, and he made no move to order one, which she took as a sign of his desire to get the initial, transactional part of their meeting out of the way before he settled himself in for the long haul. She'd been ready for this; under the table, the envelope was already in her hand, so full she'd had to seal it with sticky tape to keep it closed.

"Here," she told him, pushing it towards him - not to where he *was*, where the bulk of him was encroaching onto her, but where he *ought* to be, across from her and at least a foot away.

He took it; tore open the brown paper with greedy fingers and peered inside, his eyes widening as he took in the contents, then narrowing as it struck him - so obviously she could have laughed - that it would serve him better to play it cool, to try to squeeze her for as much as she'd give.

"Fifteen hundred?" he asked her, though she thought he'd probably done the sums already in his head, multiplied the number of notes by their denominations and arrived at a conclusion.

"The rest to follow," she said.

"When?"

"When we've talked."

"Doesn't seem a lot, for the risk I'm taking."

She held back a sigh; tamped down her frustration at his transparency, at knowing she'd have to suffer the rigmarole of *bartering* before he'd give her what she needed because he wasn't bright enough to have realised earlier that he could take her for a higher figure.

"You're asking for more?" she said, and something in her tone must have startled him - possibly some of the business-like coldness she'd been told sometimes carried in her voice, regardless of how she felt in the moment of speaking - because he drew back hurriedly, recoiling from her as if a tiger snake had risen up from her lap to hiss at him, fangs bared.

"No," he said quickly. "No, it's fine. Just wanted you to know that, you know... I'm sticking my neck on the block a bit here."

And getting two months' salary for the inconvenience, she thought.

"I understand," she told him. It wouldn't pay to antagonise him; not while he could still get up and walk away and take his information with him. "Thank you."

He unzipped the jacket just enough to slide a hand inside and pluck out his cigarettes, treating her to a brief glimpse of a white shirt, black tie and epaulettes that disappeared as soon as he'd lit up.

"Go on, then," he said. "Ask."

"Ask?"

"Whatever it is you want to know."

She thought back to the list of questions she'd made the night before, the neatly ordered bullet points and decision-tree branches she planned to use to guide the conversation, and wished she'd brought it with her, if for nothing else than her own reference.

"You've worked at Hendon since 1987, is that right?" she said.

"I have, yeah. D Wing and Enhanced, mostly."

"And you were Charles Soames' Personal Officer?"

"From '90 to '95, yeah."

"Let's start there, then. Tell me about him – about what he was like when you knew him. Anything you can remember."

∼

"I hate that I'm asking you this," Rose had said, and Harriet had believed her - had believed, moreover, that Rose *wouldn't* have asked her, unless circumstances had absolutely necessitated it. Circumstances, and the probable actions of their *other* sister, the one they tried very hard not to talk about.

"Here's the thing," the other woman had chipped in - the little fat Cockney one with the strange, sharp eyes, the one all the others seemed to defer to. The one Rose said had once saved her life in a fire - a fire their father had set, no less. "We need your help, I ain't denying it. A job like yours... it can open a few doors the rest of us might have to pry open with a crowbar, if you know what I mean."

"My job?" Harriet had asked - entirely disingenuously, since Rose had filled her in already, and in some detail.

"Not the teaching - the research. Rose says you've done a bit of work for the prison service?"

"*In*, not *for*. I did some interviews with prisoners for a project I was running, the year before last. At Wandsworth and Long Lartin."

"And Hendon."

"Yes, as it happens."

"So you know people there. People on staff."

"Some. But I was there to speak to the men inside, not form lifelong friendships with the POs or the Wing Governors. It's not as if we've stayed in contact."

"Still... good enough."

"For what?"

This, too, Rose had explained already: they wanted her to reach out to a PO, a *particular* PO, and mine him for information. But first they needed her to find out *which* PO that was.

She wasn't about to let the little fat one *know* that she knew, though. If she wanted Harriet to do her bidding, she was going to have to explain herself; not just behave, as Harriet had seen her do around the other women, as if Rose's new-found sister toeing the line was some sort of sealed deal.

"For checking into him - Soames," the little fat one had said, impatiently. "Seeing who he might have brought on board to help him stick a knife in one of my boys. And smoking out your Hannah while you're at it – that'd be a nice bonus an' all, wouldn't it?"

∼

"He was never trouble, Soames," Briscoe said. "Even before he had that stroke and his breathing took a turn for the worse. Never unpredictable, either. Some of them, even the old boys - they look for ways to needle you any way they can. We're not just talking verbal here - some of them will go for you, *really* go for you. Or they'll throw things - food and bits of paper, foam they've torn off their own mattress. And that's the *good* end. I've had more shit thrown at me than a zookeeper, doing this job."

"But Soames wasn't like that?" Harriet asked, remembering how the inside of the prisons she'd visited had seemed to her during her interviews: the stench of sweat and disinfectant - and yes, shit - that had permeated everything; the casual bovine cruelty of so many of the officers, even the ones who'd been pleasant enough to *her*; how horribly unlikely she'd found it that so many men with so many complex needs could possibly have lived, and worked, and slept in so small and confined a space.

"Never. He was polite as you like from the get-go. Always said hello, always asked how I was. Always very respectful."

"You liked him?"

"I didn't say that, did I?"

"So you *didn't* like him?"

She suspected he'd think that *she* was needling him too, playing deliberately dumb to goad him, and found she didn't care in the slightest.

"You don't *like* any of them," he said tetchily. "It's basic self-preservation. When you start warming to them, telling yourself they're just another bloke like you and *there but for the grace of God go I...* that's when they get you. Doesn't matter how *nice* you think they are - they've all got one eye out for the moment you start to let your guard down. But I will say this: he was never a pain in the arse. And that made *my* life a damn sight easier."

"How would you characterise him?" she asked, recognising a dead end when she heard one and changing tack accordingly. "Beyond that he was easy to deal with?"

He scratched the back of his head with one hairy hand, pursed his lips and blew a stream of smoke up to the ceiling.

"Slippery," he said, when he'd finished exhaling - delivering the verdict with the learned conviction of an art historian appraising a Rembrandt. "Nice manners on him, but a bit of an opportunist is what I'd say. Not one you'd want to turn your back on."

"You found him untrustworthy?"

He laughed aloud at this - a laugh which descended rapidly into smoke-filled coughing, then choking.

"Untrustworthy?" he gasped, ruddy face reddening further by the second. "They're *all* untrustworthy. They're *cons.*"

"More so than any of the others, then."

He caught his breath; picked up her lukewarm orange juice and, without asking permission, took a deep swig of it.

"No," he said, swallowing. "No more than the others. But he was definitely a funny one. You wouldn't have had him down for armed robbery, that's for sure."

"What do you mean?"

"He was too... neat. Meticulous. And clever, too. You couldn't imagine him just sticking a gun in your face and screaming, not like some of the villains in there. Too thoughtful. Put a suit and tie on him and he could have been the manager of that bank he did over."

"What about friends?" she asked - conscious of needing to bring the conversation back around to Hannah, to know how on earth she could have established contact with Soames while he was locked up. "Did he have any? Or did the other men agree with your assessment of him?"

Briscoe took a second, oblivious swig of her orange juice.

"There *was* one bloke, a few years back," he said. "Another old guy. The Guv stuck him in with Soames on Enhanced. You'd know who he was if you saw him - he used to be on the telly. Sued the papers when they said he'd been cheating on his wife, then got sent down for lying to the judge at the trial. Talk about shooting yourself in the foot."

"Anyone else?"

"Not that I can think of. He wasn't much for company. Liked to read, liked a smoke, but never really got stuck in with any of the usual bollocks you see going on - all the fights and beefs and grudges over who owes who a phone card and whose turn it is to change the channel on the box. You sort of got the impression he thought he was a bit above it all, though that could have been his age. It's normally the younger ones you see looking for an excuse to kick off at dinner time."

"And what about *outside*? Did he have many visitors?"

"When I was there? Not a lot. Had his brief in now and then to work on his case, but they can't have been making much progress - he'd been pleading not guilty since the day he rolled in, and he never once got permission to appeal. Didn't even get paroled, in the end – they let him out on compassionate grounds after he had his stroke. There *might* have been an old dear, once or twice - an auntie or a mother, something like that. And that's it, I think. Unless you count his missus."

"He had a wife?" she asked, surprised. Neither Rose nor the little fat one had mentioned Soames having a partner, in the strange briefing they'd given her before she signed up for their mission.

"I don't know if they were married or not," Briscoe said. "But they were definitely together. Long-term together, too - not one of those prison bride pen-pal arrangements. She'd been coming in to see him from the off - once a week, every week for twenty-odd years. Her and the boy."

"The boy? What boy?"

"Their son – hers and Soames'. Don't look so shocked," he added. "He didn't knock her up while he was inside. The way I heard it, she was already pregnant when he got sent down."

CHAPTER 22
FOLLIFOOT, HARROGATE
JULY 1997

Detective work, Kat was beginning to realise, was nothing at all like the con.

There were points of overlap, certainly. The need to make a study of the other person and their responses; to cold-read cadence and gesture, expression and reaction, and then adapt in the moment to what you'd decrypted. The teasing out of information, slowly and seductively, so soft-footed if you'd done it right that they'd never even know they were being worked over. The obligation to empathise - not just to talk and listen but to forge an emotional bond, a human to human connection that would make them feel better about spilling their guts to a stranger.

But the con was a dance, even if only one of you knew that you were dancing: a lithe, sinuating two-step that lasted only as long as you stayed on the floor but left you flushed with pleasure in the aftermath.

Investigation, by contrast, was a winter marathon: an endless, exhausting plod around the same grey circuit. It was possible, she thought, that there'd be some payoff as she sprinted to the finish line, when she'd uncovered the

Rosetta Stone that would make sense of everything else she'd seen and heard on her travels; some runner's high that would leave her smiling with the satisfaction of knowing that she'd *done* it, that it was *over*. But she was yet to experience it. The ribbon was a long way off, and she was very much still *in* the race, penned in on all sides - figuratively speaking - by panting first-timers and fundraising firemen in chicken-suits.

Ada Otley's bit of gossip had been interesting; useful, even. But all but one of the half-dozen names the woman had passed along to Kat - once Faye Tuttle-of-the-Wirral Advocate had passed *her* a hundred quid in twenties for the tip - had turned up nothing she hadn't gleaned already from her time in the Otley guesthouse. Namely: Ted Wainwright's wife had been having it away with Bob Kingsley, the gardener; the abducted baby might not, strictly biologically, have been *Wainwright's* abducted baby; and, most importantly to Kat's mind, nobody had any bloody clue at all what the hell had happened to the kid, after she was taken. And Kat's patience for the beige rugs and ornamental teacups of the old-lady living rooms of West Riding was growing thinner by the hour.

The last name on the list Mrs Otley had given her - a scattergun Greatest Hits of everyone she could remember who might have known, slept with or been distantly related to Kingsley - was one of his cousins, Lucille Salter: a now-eightysomething spinster still living in a village on the outskirts of Harrogate.

"I couldn't tell you if they were close," Mrs Otley had said. "But there's not many of them left now, the Kingsleys *or* the Salters, so it might be worth a knock at her door. I shouldn't go getting my hopes up, though, if I were you. She could be senile now, if she ever had anything to tell you to begin with."

Lucille Salter's cottage sat at the top end of a cul-de-sac of nearly identical structures, all built from the sort of dark stone that gave the road the appearance, even in sunlight, of a particularly forbidding Central European castle. There was a garage but no obvious car, and a wheelchair ramp and grab handles - of the kind Kat had resisted installing at her own place – that suggested the old lady inside was, at the very least, infirm. Playing the odds, Kat swung the Mini into the driveway and parked up.

The delay between Kat ringing the doorbell and Lucille Salter actually opening the door - once she'd shuffled, centimetre by centimetre, up the hallway - felt to Kat interminable, and not only because of the havoc wreaked on her aching head and stiffening hips by the perpetual northern rain. When, finally, she *did* open it, she kept the chain on - treating Kat to little but a sliver of the corkwood floor and stippled walls inside, and, in the gap between chain and door, a single suspicious grey eye set into a face the colour and texture of a dried apricot.

"Miss Salter?" Kat said, slipping back into the spiel she could have recited by now in her sleep. "I'm Faye Tuttle with the Wirral Advocate. I was wondering if you might have five minutes to spare for a chat? I'm doing a piece on the Ingrid Wainwright abduction, and I was told you might be able to offer a bit of background on the case. We'd pay you for your time, of course," she added - mentally calculating how much an elderly, single woman on a fixed pension would consider appropriate recompense for a bit of forty year old scuttlebutt.

The grey eye narrowed.

"A journalist, did you say, love?" she answered, voice scratching and crackling like tissue paper on gravel.

"That's right, Miss Salter. With the Wirral Advocate."

The apricot-face vanished, momentarily, from view, affording Kat a fuller picture of the cottage interior: a Scandinavian-style kitchen with a surprisingly expensive-looking Aga, and two sets of bookshelves stacked with serious-looking hardbacks.

"Miss Salter?" she said, with genuine hesitation.

The face reappeared, now sporting a pair of thick-lensed, ludicrously overlarge plastic reading glasses.

"Got your press pass on you, have you, love?" she asked amiably.

Press pass? Kat thought. What sort of pensioner knows what a *press pass* is, let alone asks to see it?

She made a show of searching her pockets; opening her handbag and rifling through it.

"I'm so sorry, Miss Salter," she said, when she came up empty, "I must have left it in the car. Do you mind if I don't go and get it? My legs are playing up a bit this morning," she gestured down her body, to the hated walking sticks, "and I'm trying to avoid walking where I can."

It wasn't a gambit she'd had cause to use much, since she'd taken her blow to the head - but it couldn't fail to work, could it? Especially not on a woman who clearly had her own issues with mobility.

Lucille Salter - a home owner, in Kat's estimation, for whom every census-taker and gas meter-reader would need to have their lanyard at the ready if they wanted access to her property - seemed to think hard about this before replying.

"Go on, then," she said, without enthusiasm. "Come in,

if you have to. But you'd best give me a minute to tidy 'round."

Abruptly, the door closed, leaving Kat to twiddle her fingers on the doorstep. When it opened again, what *had* to have been five minutes later, the chain was unfastened, and Lucille Salter appeared to be *holding* the door open for her - crouching half-hidden in the shadows behind it, humped and bowed as a five foot-high vampire bat.

Kat stepped inside, leaning exaggeratedly on her sticks, the old woman still lurking behind her.

She heard the door click closed again, which was when she felt it: something hard and metallic, pressing up between her shoulder blades.

She turned around slowly, letting the sticks bear the brunt of the movement - and there, behind her, so unlikely a sight that she might have laughed out loud in other circumstances, was Lucille Salter, her own stooped shoulder taking the weight of an ancient, long-barrelled and partially rusted hunting gun that was more blunderbuss than rifle. A gun pointed, very firmly, at Kat's face.

"Right, then, cock," she said, her finger resting on the trigger with a practised ease that Kat found alarming. "You're not press, and I don't reckon you're police. So how about you tell me who you *are*, and what it is you're really after?"

∼

"There's no stress," Ruby had said. "You ain't gonna be on the front line with this one. More like... out in the back office. Doing the filing."

So this is the back office, is it? Kat thought now. Explains why you didn't want to do your *own* bloody filing.

"Miss Salter," she began to the lunatic with the musket, "I can assure you..."

"You can drop all that *Miss Salter* rubbish," the lunatic told her, keeping her ridiculous weapon trained on the space between Kat's eyebrows. "*And* that accent, while you're at it. I don't know what you're up to, but I know a Scouser when I hear one, and you're about as Scouse as I am Puerto Rican."

"Miss Salter...," she started, then paused.

Bad idea, she thought. When you're in a hole, *stop fucking digging*.

"Alright," she said, letting Faye Tuttle fall away and hoping the lunatic would prove more amenable to a real Welsh lilt than the high, flat notes of her faux-Scouse. "Got me there, haven't you? I never was that good at dialects."

Neither the lunatic nor the gun moved a millimetre.

"Let's have it, then," the lunatic said. "Who are you?"

Thinking on her feet: that was another skill Kat hadn't lost yet.

A bit of unsolved mystery, she thought. That's what we need here. An unanswered question - something to get her wondering, get her to drop her guard while she asks herself whether or not what I'm telling her might be true.

"I'm an investigator," she said, looking the lunatic straight in her mad, wide eyes. "A *private* investigator, you know?"

"Investigating what?" the lunatic asked. She didn't believe what she was hearing, not quite - but there was a note of doubt in there, something that suggested to Kat that she might be open to persuasion, if the story she was told held up.

"The Wainwright baby. The kidnapping. I can't tell you who hired me, I'd lose my licence. But my client... they think there's more to it than the official story let on. More than what they were told at the time. They think..."

She hesitated - another, altogether more audacious idea coming to her as she spun the tale.

"They *think*," she said, "that she's still alive - the baby. That whoever took her never killed her. Just hid her away somewhere."

She'd expected – had *hoped* - that this new nugget of information would give the lunatic pause; cause her, if nothing else, to lower the barrel of the gun just enough for Kat to duck out of the way and, if her mutinous legs would carry her fast enough, barrel out the door and slam it shut behind her.

Instead, the old psycho *smiled*: a broad, gummy grin that stretched the loose skin of her lower jaw all the way back to her earlobes.

"I *knew* it!" she cackled, triumphantly. "I said, didn't I? I *said* she weren't dead. Not one of them bastards believed me, but I *said*! He never would've killed her, I told 'em so. Not his own flesh and blood. Took her off and away, that's what he'd have done. And he did, didn't he? He *did*!"

Now she lowered the gun; took her yellow-nailed knot of a finger off the trigger.

"Sorry I startled you, cock," she said, friendly again, the feral grin now directed Kat's way. "But you can't be too careful, when you get people coming to the door."

"Not to worry," Kat murmured, entirely mystified by the turn the situation seemed to be taking but still acutely aware that the gun, while no longer in her line of sight, remained very much *in the frame*. "I'd have done the same, I'm sure."

"This investigation you're doing - is that what you wanted to talk to me for?"

Kat nodded in the affirmative - afraid that anything she

said might lead the conversation back down another dark path, one possibly terminating in the unloading of an antique firearm into her forehead.

"I'll tell you this, then," the lunatic said. "You've come to the right place. Forty two years I've been waiting for someone to turn up here asking about that kiddie. So in you come, and I'll get us a brew on. There's a *lot* I've got to say."

∽

"I was older than Bobby," she told Kat, when the tea had been made and the blunderbuss, now divested of ammunition, had been tucked away in its resting place beside the Aga. "A fair bit older. Could've been his mam, if I'd had him early. His *actual* Mam were my Dad's little sister, and there were fifteen years between the two of them. You got big families, in them days."

"He was never much for school, Bobby, but he *loved* plants - growing 'em, tending to 'em, all of it. Proper greenfingered, he was. Not *light*-fingered - not like his Dad."

"Bit of a criminal, the dad, was he?" Kat asked, sensing that some response was expected of her. "Bit dodgy?"

Lucille Salter snorted.

"They *all* were," she said. "Every one of them Kingsleys. Thieves and drunks, the lot of them. Not Bobby, though - he was different. More like his Mam. And when he got that job in the garden up at the Wainwrights... well, it was just *right*, if you know what I mean. You'd never seen him so happy."

∽

Bob Kingsley's first gardening job, taken up a day shy of his nineteenth birthday, was with the *old* Mr Wainwright - Ted

Wainwright's father, over in Wetherby. He'd done well there: kept the rose bushes blooming, the weeds in check, the little hedge maze symmetrical, and - most importantly, at least in the eyes of Wainwright Senior, who secretly feared them - the wider grounds clear of marauding muntjac deer. He was well-liked, and his work roundly respected, and it came as no surprise to anyone that, when the younger Mr Wainwright announced his engagement to a girl he'd met on business in Cheshire, Bob was offered a pay rise and his own small cottage on site in exchange for following young Ted and his bride-to-be to their new house on the outskirts of Burn Bridge.

"Bobby hadn't met the girl when he agreed to it," Lucille Salter said. "I think if he had, if he'd known... he wouldn't have took the job."

It was when he *did* meet her, finally - when Ted Wainwright returned to Harrogate with Gillian, his new wife - that Bob's trouble began.

"He was taken with her from the start," said Lucille. "Smitten, he was. Mooning around like a love-sick puppy. None of us knew what was wrong with him, first off - I thought he might be taking ill, he was that bad. But then he had a few too many down the pub one night with our Kenneth - my brother that was, may he rest in peace - and it all came tumbling out of him. How he'd known from the moment he clamped eyes on her that she was *it*, this Gillian; she was *the one*. How he couldn't stop thinking about her, no matter what hour of the day or night. And how it was *him* she was supposed to be with, not Ted Wainwright."

"It was all one-sided, or so our Kenneth thought - a bit of an infatuation, no real harm in it. But then old Noreen Wicklow, her that used to do the cooking up at the Wainwright house... she said she'd seen the two of them together,

Bobby and young Mrs Wainwright. *Together*, together. Up in the master bedroom one lunchtime, when Ted was out doing one of his factory visits."

Neither Bob nor Gillian - Mrs Wainwright - had known they'd been seen. But Noreen Wicklow wasn't known for her discretion, and it wasn't long before the local tongues were wagging.

"I don't know *how* it didn't get back to young Ted," Lucille said. "Or maybe it did, and he ignored it. Some men are like that, aren't they, duck? Hear what they want to hear, and filter out the rest. Any road, he never *said* anything, if he *did* hear it, and he was always nice as pie to Bobby when he saw him."

"And then she went and fell pregnant, didn't she?"

It was Bob Kingsley's baby. That was the opinion of the village - if not of Ted Wainwright, who waited hand and foot on his wife for the duration of the pregnancy, bringing her cups of tea in bed and calling the housekeeper to check up on her whenever he was out travelling.

"None of us asked our Bobby outright," Lucille said. "But it was obvious he *thought* it was his, the baby, from the way he was flouncing around - beaming his head off, pleased as punch. You'd tell him he looked happy, just to test the waters and see if he'd let you in on it himself, but he'd just give you this *smile*, all enigmatic - like he had a secret, but he weren't about to share it with you. Bit worrying, it was, to tell you the truth. It was all well and good him getting excited about having a little one on the way - but what was he supposed to do after it was *born*, eh? I mean, even if it *was* his, technically - that baby was going to grow up a Wainwright, wasn't it? And there'd be nothing he could do about it."

But Bob Kingsley's smile didn't slip, not even when the

baby was born and christened Ingrid, after Ted Wainwright's grandmother. He continued to strut about the village like the cock of the walk, giving no outward indication of displeasure that his putative daughter was fed and changed and swaddled every night by another man while his lover, the mother of that putative child, slept and woke in that same man's arms.

Until the day he announced that he was leaving Yorkshire for a job in London - not at the end of the month, once he'd picked up his final pay packet from the Wainwrights, but that very weekend, taking the Pullman to King's Cross out of Harrogate station on the Saturday morning with nothing but a suitcase and the clothes on his back.

"Just like that," Lucille said. "He'd never told *us* he'd applied for any job down south, neither. If you ask me, there *wasn't* one. He just wanted folk to *think* there was, and that he was out of the picture, so's nobody'd point the finger at him for what came after."

"What?" asked Kat. "The kidnapping?"

"I shouldn't call it that, duck. It's not kidnapping when it's your own baba, is it?"

"But you think it was him that took her?"

Lucille Salter chewed this over.

"I can't prove anything," she said. "Close as we were - or close as him and *Kenneth* were, anyway - I didn't see hide nor hair of Bobby again after he left on that train. Didn't hear from him, neither - hear *from* him or hear *of* him, not until the day he died and one of the Kingsley nephews down in London rang to ask us to the funeral. 1967, that was, and him just thirty five. Lymphoma. It's a bloody crab, cancer, right enough. Gets its claws in you and never lets go."

"What can't you prove?" Kat pressed.

"There never was a ransom note, you know," Lucille continued, apparently oblivious to the question. "Folk 'round here had it in their heads there was going to be one, that whoever it was that took her did it for a chunk of Ted Wainwright's inheritance. And it was a puzzle, right enough. But not for what they reckoned. 'Cause do you know what *I* think happened, duck? I think they planned it - our Bobby and that Gillian. Staged the whole thing to make it *look* like a kidnapping, so he could take the little one off somewhere. Set it up so's the three of them could get away together, out of Harrogate, and start afresh with poor Ted's money as a cushion."

Kat thought this through. The tale made sense, in its way: Bob Kingsley was never going to make a packet as a gardener, and Mrs Wainwright must have been used to a certain standard of living that her lover could never have afforded to maintain without another income stream, not with a young child to feed, and especially not down in London. There was a simplicity to it; a sort of coherence that she could easily find compelling.

But it didn't fit the *facts*, was the problem, at least not as she'd understood them.

"What cushion?" she said. "What money are we talking about, if there wasn't a ransom?"

Lucille grimaced.

"Like I said, I can't *prove* it," she replied. "And maybe you're sat here thinking I'm nowt but a lonely old woman cooking up some cockeyed story to keep her mind from wandering. But I think they *meant* to send a ransom note, at first. If you ask me, that was the plan from the off: that Bobby and his mates would break in and take that little girl, rough Ted up a bit to make it look proper, then tell him he could have her back if he paid up. And then, when all the fuss died down and Bobby'd got his sackful of money, him and that Gillian and the baby would've been all set to run off together into the sunset and leave Ted Wainwright crying into his porridge."

"But they *didn't*, is my point," Kat insisted. "There never *was* a ransom. Nobody paid up, the kid stayed missing, and Gillian Wainwright topped herself, didn't she? Took a swan-dive into the river."

"Show a bit of respect, won't you, duck? I might not have cared for her or what she did to my Bobby, but the girl's dead, right enough. Whatever wrong she did, she's paid for it now."

"What do you mean?" Kat said. It was becoming her mantra, she realised; her constant refrain, in this increasingly strange exchange that wasn't quite a conversation. "What do you think she did?"

"Isn't it obvious?" the old woman replied. "She got cold feet. Planned the whole thing with Bobby, told him just what to do and why. Then at the very last, just when he'd got the baba stashed away somewhere and he was all set to tell Ted Wainwright where to drop off the money… *she changed her mind.*"

CHAPTER 23
BROMLEY, LONDON
AUGUST 1997

Harriet knew about coercive control - about gaslighting, and lovebombing, and battered woman syndrome, and the hundred adjacent behaviours and responses that fell broadly under the unhappy umbrella of domestic abuse.

Her father had been - though she'd been mid-way through her first degree before she'd put a name to it - an archetypal abuser, maintaining his psychological hold over her mother, and by extension her mother's money, through an unpredictable combination of praise and punishment, silence and carefully modulated rage that left no-one listening in any doubt that she'd let him down, let the children down, let *herself* down.

Elizabeth Marchant was a lonely woman, brittle and easily flustered and not - in Harriet's opinion - particularly easy to like. But she was coming on, in the tiniest of increments, since her husband's vanishing: joining a book club, learning to swim with a group of other older women in the pools at Hampstead Heath, collecting and displaying the absurd Tarot decks she loved but had always felt compelled to stow away in drawers and hidden cupboards around the house while Harriet's father was on the scene.

The woman facing Harriet across the doorway of *this* house, by contrast - if the information she'd learned since her meeting with Briscoe was accurate, and if Harriet's own judgement could be trusted – remained very firmly in the grip of her absent captor. She was small, the woman, and skinny verging on skeletal, but gave the impression of willing herself to become smaller still, to minimise the space she took up in the world. Her skin was tanned an artificial shade of orange, her hair white-blonde and thinning slightly at the crown and temples - from malnutrition, was Harriet's guess. In the glaring midday sun, the bones in her chest and shoulders leapt out from the neckline of her denim dress in such stark, painful detail that it took great effort not to look away.

Chronologically, Harriet knew, she was in her mid to late forties, if Winston Redfearn's estimation of her age when he'd met her in the early '70s had been accurate; on appearances alone she could have been sixty.

"Lois Soames?" she asked - sounding, she was acutely aware, very much like the visiting social workers, neighbourhood police and parole officers that were almost certainly a fixture of the woman's everyday life.

"Is this about the Fiesta?" the woman replied, her accent as thick as Ruby Redfearn's but her voice more timid by far. "Because they told me I had 'til Monday, and my Income Support don't come in until the end of the week."

Diplomacy had never been Harriet's forte; even in interviews and focus groups, her preferred style was bluntness rather than prevarication. There was no benefit, she'd learned in almost a decade of working with charismatic sociopaths and men with aggressive Antisocial Personality

Disorders so extreme they'd pull your eyeballs from their sockets with their fingernails if they suspected you'd wronged them, in telling lies or making false promises, if there was any chance at all they'd be exposed.

For this task, though, Rose had been clear that tact, and politeness, and sensitivity - even outright lies, should they be required - were an absolute necessity. And since Harriet had no interest in doing anything that might harm Rose or Sophie or their interests, even where those interests extended to little Ruby Redfearn and her Merry Women, it was in the spirit of politeness and sensitivity that she responded.

"No, Mrs Soames," she said. "It's nothing to do with cars. I'm here about Charles. Your husband."

The woman's face fell; became a mask of terror.

"Charlie?" she said, the words tumbling incoherently out of her as panic took hold. "What's happened? Has something happened to him? Oh, God - it has, hasn't it? I knew it, I *knew* it would if I weren't there to look after him…"

Harriet felt herself stiffen; felt disgust take hold of her, revulsion at the woman's weakness.

He hits you and bites you and does Christ knows what else to you, and this *is how you react when you think he might be dead?* she thought, in what she'd come to recognise as her father's voice - the cold, pitiless judgement of a man with no patience at all for frailty. *It's pathetic, just absolutely pathetic. Pull yourself together, for God's sake, before you embarrass yourself any more than you have already.*

They were meaningless - the thoughts, the voice. She'd learned that too, through her research as much as through the endless rounds of mandatory therapy she'd had to work through before they'd given her her PhD. They were *just* thoughts; *just* memories. They weren't *her*.

But hearing them, acknowledging them, needing to *tell* herself they were meaningless whenever they struck - it was exhausting, an incessant cycle of *listen* and *recognise* and *accept* and *move on*. She'd like, just occasionally, to be able to *stop*; for her own mind to let her be.

"He's fine, Mrs Soames," she said, straining to infuse her words with kindness, with an un-Marchant-like note of sympathy. "Nothing's wrong. I wanted a quick word with you, that's all. I'm working with the probation service, and they like to drop in every now and then on clients and their families for the first year or two after release. Just to make sure everything's going alright."

It wasn't a lie; not completely. She *had* been working with the probation service that year - albeit on another project, in an entirely different area. And it was entirely possible that the service *did* do spot checks on its clients - especially ones, like Soames, who'd served life sentences.

If Lois Soames knew better, of course, then things were apt to become very difficult, very quickly.

"Oh!" the woman said, holding a palm to her emaciated chest. "*Oh!* You scared me then!"

The panic cleared. She eyed Harriet up and down, with the sort of wary scrutiny Harriet imagined she reserved for public sector employees taking an interest in her husband.

"He doesn't live with us," she said, leaning against the door with both hands - desperate, Harriet thought, to push it closed and scurry back inside, but aware that wasn't an option. "He needs a lot of care, and space for his oxygen and his other things, so it isn't big enough for him here, and even if it was, I wouldn't be any good at looking after all the equipment and keeping it clean enough..."

She gestured inside, to the hallway and living room of a perfectly normal-sized council house that was, it seemed to

Harriet, more than adequate to accommodate a man with Soames' disabilities.

"He's got a place in Kent," she finished. "Out by the sea. It's good for him, the air there. Clean. Better than all the smog you get here."

"And are you there often?" Harriet asked.

"He doesn't like us seeing him, the way he is now," she replied – a touch defensively, Harriet thought.

"Well, it's really *you* I was hoping to speak to anyway," Harriet said, veering away from what was evidently a sore point. "You and your son."

"He's not here. He's gone out."

"Is there a better time for me to call in? Perhaps later this afternoon, when he's back?"

"He's out all day. You won't catch him."

She was creeping back, now - retreating behind the door, pushing it towards Harriet's body. Harriet fought an urge to shove her foot against the frame; to step inside uninvited, impose herself by force on the starving church mouse of a woman, and her objections be damned.

Not that she'd voice them, anyway, she heard her father say. *A doormat like that would let you get away with* anything. *I doubt she's ever said no to anyone in her life.*

"Where is he, can I ask?" she said - still measured, still sing-song gentle. Still intent on proving to herself, whatever the voice might tell her, that someone else's weakness wasn't an invitation to use and exploit.

"He's at college," Lois Soames answered - anxious again now, her utter desperation to *get away* from Harriet, to bolt the door and lock herself in with the curtains drawn so obvious Harriet was almost certain she was screaming inside. "He's got lectures in the day, and he goes out with his mates after. I don't know where. What did you want to ask him that you can't ask me?"

~

"If that screw's right, and Soames has got a son," Ruby Redfearn had told her after her meeting with Briscoe, in an unlit corner of the dingy, smoke-clogged Greek restaurant in Golders Green where she'd insisted they meet in place of Rose's apartment, "then that boy'd be twenty-odd now. More than old enough to set to stabbin' someone if his old man said the word."

"Are you quite sure about that?" Harriet had asked. "Charles Soames would have spent most of his son's life in Hendon. And stabbing someone, a perfect stranger no less... that's no small request, even from your own father. It's rather hard to imagine they'd have a relationship strong enough to elicit that level of blind filial obedience."

"You don't know Charlie Soames," Redfearn had replied ominously. "He's like one of them psychopaths you study. He knows how to pull your levers; how to get under your skin and make you do what he wants. And if his boy's been raised by the same girl my Winston seen to when she come 'round our flat all them years ago, then he'd have grown up not knowing no different than doing what his Dad told him. That Lois... she was *his*, you know what I mean? Soames'. Might as well have had his name stamped on her arm with a cattle iron."

"Is that even possible?" the woman Redfearn had brought with her had asked – El, the maybe-Spanish, maybe-Indian girl with the big dark eyes and the haunted face who'd inadvertently brought Harriet into their strange orbit the previous year, and who'd been throwing lovelorn glances at Rose across the table whenever she had an idea the others weren't looking.

If these are the best liars and dissemblers London has to offer, Harriet had thought, then the fat cats of the City can rest easy.

"Is what possible?" Redfearn had said.

"Keeping that much of a hold on someone for that long, when you're inside. I mean, I believe you when you say he had her under his spell - and we've seen what Soames is like, so no argument there. But could you really control someone - a partner - when you're not with them? Not *physically* with them?"

Redfearn had shrugged.

"I'm gonna pass that one over to the doc here," she'd said, gesturing to Harriet. "What do you reckon, Dr Marchant? Think it's possible?"

"Theoretically?" Harriet had answered. "Maybe. If the initial hold he had over her was entrenched enough before he was convicted. I couldn't say with any more certainty without having met them. But it's not impossible."

"The difficulty, of course, would be maintaining that level of psychological dominance over her without being able to guarantee that she'd *stay* socially isolated - that she wouldn't engage for any length of time with the sort of people who might weaken his hold on her."

"The kind of coercive control that you're suggesting... it would rely to some extent on his keeping her apart from friends, family... really from anyone who might encourage her to think more critically about his behaviour or the power dynamics underpinning their relationship. If absolute authority over her was what he wanted, he'd need to be sure that she wouldn't come into contact with anyone in her everyday life who'd ask uncomfortable questions - or worse still, try to intervene in some way. Try to rescue her, even - or *deprogramme* her, if you'd prefer. The cult analogy certainly isn't *so* wide of the mark, since we're effectively talking about brainwashing."

"What I suppose I'm saying," she'd concluded, "is that for him to *know*, to be absolutely *certain* that he could trust her to stay under his thumb, under his control, even while he was serving a life sentence in a closed prison... he'd have to have had his hooks embedded in her very deeply indeed."

"Stockholm syndrome?" Rose had asked. "Is that what you mean?"

El had nodded vigorous agreement at this. Rose, in turn, had smiled shyly back at her, apparently pleased to have won her approval.

Perhaps it isn't *just* some unrequited crush after all, Harriet had thought - and then wondered, distantly, whether she and Rose were sufficiently close yet that she could ask her about it and find out for sure.

"I wouldn't use that term," she'd answered. "It's not a very helpful descriptor. Stockholm syndrome is really more of a media phenomenon than a clinical diagnosis - it's not in the DSM, for one thing. But I suppose there are some similarities with what we're describing: a woman so completely in thrall to her captor that she'd stay loyal to him through years, even decades of being physically separated *from* him. And then do everything she could to inculcate that same loyalty in their child."

"Raising him to be Daddy's Little Soldier," Redfearn had said.

"I suppose so, yes. His soldier, and his slave."

∽

"There's nothing I need to ask him specifically," Harriet said. "But it would save me having to come back another time, if I could speak to the two of you together."

Lois Soames slunk further still behind the door, leaving only her head and wasted neck visible from the outside.

"You won't be able to catch him," she repeated.

"Perhaps I could come in anyway?" Harriet asked. Ruby Redfearn wouldn't like it, she knew - the woman had near-on insisted that Harriet meet the Soameses *together*, that she assess them as a unit. But if this little doorstep interaction had confirmed anything, it was that Lois Soames was, if not her son's keeper, then his *gate*keeper - and that she'd stand between him and anyone she deemed a possible threat to his safety and security. Except, perhaps, her husband.

Getting to the son, as Harriet saw it, meant getting past the mother first.

Lois Soames hesitated; caught, Harriet surmised, between the compliance she knew she ought to be showing and the urge to protect her husband and her son, to shield them from the scrutiny of the justice system and the further batch of trouble that scrutiny might bring.

Eventually, deference won out, and she tugged the door fully open.

"Come in," she sighed, sounding utterly defeated. "I don't have hot drinks or biscuits," she added, apologetically. "We don't keep them in the house."

"Water's fine," Harriet told her.

It was apparent, almost from the moment she crossed the threshold, *why* there were neither hot drinks nor biscuits on offer. Inside, the house was the closest she'd seen in the flesh to a clean room: every surface polished, every millimetre of floor spotless. The cutlery and crockery stacked in neat symmetrical piles on the gleaming stainless steel sink were, she saw as they passed the kitchen, not only *made of* disposable plastic but *wrapped* in plastic, too - despite the apparent absence elsewhere in the room of any food or drink that might be consumed *on*, or *with*, or *in* them.

(Which could, she reasoned, explain Lois Soames' emaciated appearance - at least, if what she'd read initially as anorexia was actually obsessive-compulsive mysophobia, a germ-aversion so acute that it prevented her from eating or drinking anything she might perceive as contaminated).

What little furniture there *was* in the plain, beige-hued lounge was similarly wrapped - most notably the sofa that served as the room's centrepiece, a brown velour model enveloped in broad strips of transparent cellophane that crinkled as, following her host's lead, she lowered herself onto it. There was no table, nowhere to *put* a hot drink or a biscuit, had Harriet had one; just a small walnut writing bureau pushed against the wall, not swaddled but laid open to reveal box upon box of latex gloves, surgical masks and plastic aprons.

"I like to keep clean," Lois Soames said, seeing Harriet struggle to adopt a comfortable position on the slippery, squeaking cushions.

"Absolutely," Harriet replied in the most empathetic tone she could muster - hoping to communicate that, yes, cleanliness *was* important, and there was nothing unusual or dysfunctional *at all* in striving to maintain a living environment as aseptic as an operating theatre.

"Charlie always liked things kept clean. Clean and neat. Have you got a list?" she added, apropos of nothing, as far as Harriet could tell.

"I'm sorry?"

"Of questions. About us and Charlie. There's normally a list, when you people come 'round."

Harriet kicked herself for not bringing a bag, or a notebook, or anything at all that might speak to an official, legally sanctioned reason for her presence in the Soames house.

"I'm a bit more informal than some of my colleagues," she said, freewheeling madly, and was this how Redfearn and the others played it *all the time*? If it was, she could see herself developing a new admiration for their dexterity, their stamina. Five minutes into the lie, and she was already exhausted.

"What sort of thing is it you want to know? You're really best off speaking to Charlie direct, if it's to do with him."

Ask about the son, Redfearn had said. *Go around the houses a bit so she doesn't twig it's him you're after. But we need to find out. 'Specially if he's still running 'round the place with his dad's grudge and a knife in his pocket.*

"How long have you and Charlie been married?" she asked, glossing over the last entreaty.

"Don't you know all that already?"

"I do. But I'd like to hear it in your words. To get a fuller picture."

Lois Soames's mouth twitched - not in irritation or impatience, as Harriet would have expected of another woman asked to answer the same question she'd doubtless been confronted with a hundred times before, but in fear. Fear of saying the wrong thing; of incriminating her husband - and possibly her son, too - through some unplanned, inadvertent admission.

"Twenty two years," she said. "We done it while he was inside. After we'd had Jay."

She never had him registered, the son, Redfearn had told

her. *There's no birth certificate for him, no child benefit claims, no vaccination records, no national insurance number. My Dexter's checked everywhere, but there weren't nothing to find. Not so much as a passport photo. I doubt she even sent him school, so Christ knows how she managed to get a visiting order for him to go and see his old man inside. Only good news is that anything you dig up, anything at all, is gonna give us more than we've got on him already. As things stand, we don't know nothing. Not what he's called. Not even what he looks like.*

There were no pictures in the lounge, that Harriet could see - no graduation shots or baby photos, no carefully posed portraits of Lois Soames and her son. Just blank, sponged-down walls.

"And does Jay see his father often?" she asked - making a note of the name and storing it away for further use.

"When he can," Lois Soames answered, more elliptically than Harriet would have liked. "He loves his dad."

Something caught Harriet's attention, a flash of light on metal in the corner of her eye: a silver picture frame, balanced on the window ledge to her left.

She squinted; focused, until the picture inside came into view.

It was an old photo - late '60s or early '70s, she guessed, from the fading and desaturated colour as much as from the clothes and hairstyles of its subjects. There were two of them in shot, their faces turned to the camera like the dour farmers of Grant Wood's American Gothic: a man in his twenties or thereabouts, one she recognised from the clippings Redfearn had shown her as Charles Soames, his suit ironed and immaculate and a bow-tie fixed below his collar. And beside him, pressed into his side, a girl, blonde and sallow and no older, it seemed to Harriet, than eleven or twelve years old.

It was difficult to know for sure, even from a distance of only a few feet - the picture frame was small, and her eyesight was less than 20/20 even when she remembered to wear her glasses, which she hadn't today.

But she thought the girl was Lois Soames.

PART IV
SEPTEMBER/OCTOBER

CHAPTER 24

FLIGHT EXK 255 (SFO TO LHR)
SEPTEMBER 1997

"You're a fool to yourself, you are."

El debated the merits of responding. She wasn't asleep - had woken up somewhere over Saskatchewan - but had planned to feign unconsciousness at least until they hit the Atlantic.

Ruby, evidently, had other ideas.

"I'm sleeping," El said, her eyes still closed.

"No, you ain't. You don't snore so bad as Karen, but I can always tell when you're having a kip - your breath goes in and out like one of them iron lungs. You can hear it from all the way back there."

She opened one eyelid, tentatively, and saw Ruby gesturing behind her to her own, now unoccupied seat three rows along the cabin.

"Go on, then," she said wearily, still reclining against her headrest. "You might as well get it off your chest. Why am I a fool?"

"You *know* why. All that business with Rose. I don't know what you think you're playing at, but if you don't start pulling that head of yours out of your arse, you're gonna miss the boat altogether. She's a nice girl, a patient one an' all, but she won't keep waiting 'round for you to work out if you want her or not. And when she *does* lose interest, there won't be nothing me or Sita can do to sort it out for you."

She bolted upright at this; scanned the mostly empty cabin, panicked at the prospect of Karen or Sophie - or worse yet, Rose herself - hearing anything that Ruby had to say about her love life.

The others, thank God, were asleep, or otherwise occupied: Karen, her legs propped up on her footrest, stretched out under a blanket and, yes, snoring; Sita, sipping champagne and resplendent in the jewelled vermillion sari she reserved for airline travel ("it's pure Bollywood, darling - guarantees celebrity treatment"), making animated conversation with a high-cheekboned, impeccably-suited businesswoman across the aisle; Sophie, separated from the world by the enormous black headphones covering her ears, and Rose, resting lightly against her daughter's shoulder, her face shielded against the overhead cabin lights by an emerald sleep mask.

"You know your trouble?" Ruby said - then, not waiting for El to reply, continued: "You think too much. Tie yourself in so many knots trying to work out what you *should* do or you *shouldn't* do, you never get round to actually *doing* what you thought you might want to do in the first place. Me and her over there," she gestured this time to Sita, now laughing heartily - and, in El's estimation, not un-flirtatiously - at something the businesswoman had said, "you think we got where we are by worrying if we were doing it right?"

"Doing *what* right?" El asked.

"Anything. *Everything*. I like to plan, don't get me wrong - more than *she* does, that's for bleedin' sure. I need to have my ducks in a row when I'm on the con. But it ain't cerebral, grifting, or it shouldn't be, not when you get right down to it. It's instinct. And you... you're good at it, at trusting your instinct on the job. Always have been, ever since you were a kid. So why you don't do the same and just trust yourself when you're *off* the clock, I'll never know."

A flight attendant, her trolley loaded with wine and spirits, wheeled her way towards them.

"A drink for you, Lady Westholme?" she asked Ruby, with the confidence of a woman who'd memorised the First Class passenger manifest and wasn't about to be thrown by something as minor as a change in the seating plan. "And you, Ms. Di Salvo?"

El shook her head. Ruby, though, was more ebullient.

"Do you know, my dear," she trilled, in the plummy if slightly inebriated tones of the elderly society widow whose name she'd been travelling under since they began their American adventure, "I believe I will. A little of the Bordeaux, if you wouldn't mind."

"What I'm trying to tell you," she said, when the attendant had moved on, "is that you ain't got time to sit around wringing your hands and *umming* and *ahing*. If you're interested, then you best tell her so, and pronto. Besides which: it were bloody agony last night, watching you mope around the house like a kicked puppy, and I ain't keen on seeing that again for a good long while if I can possibly help it."

∽

El saw her point.

The previous day, their last in the city before flying back to London, had begun well enough - all six of them convening for an outdoor lunch on the long bench under the eucalyptus trees in the backyard, a lunch only slightly marred by the low thrum of tension that had kept all of them faintly jittery since their final meeting with Wainwright.

Sita had left first, wrapping a shawl around her tunic and disappearing into the back of a yellow cab bound for parts unknown, or at least unknown to El.

"She's gone to sell the Taj Mahal," Ruby had said, when Karen asked. "Met some oilman from Alaska coming out of Trader Joe's the other day, and now she's got him on the hook she reckons she can seal the deal before he sods off back to Anchorage. You know what she's like, always trying her luck. Don't tell me none of you have noticed all the sneaking about she's been doing?"

El *had* noticed - but, knowing Sita's propensity for cultivating her own side projects even in the middle of a job, had considered it barely worthy of attention.

"Tell you what, though," Ruby had added, "she'll be a bleedin' *nightmare* if it works. Be the second time she's managed to offload that charnel house - we'll have her crowing about it for *years*."

The first sale, to El's recollection, had been to a Russian oligarch named Yahontov, a rapacious and unscrupulous man with a taste for plundering Islamic antiquities. First Sita, presenting herself as the undersecretary to the Chief Minister of Uttar Pradesh, had invited him - after much groundwork had been laid - to proffer a bid for the mausoleum when it came to auction, as it soon would. The auction, she'd explained, would be kept secret, the Minister having no desire to incur the wrath of UNESCO or the newspapers or the Wakf Council or the nationalists; all bids would be sealed, and all participants required to sign a non-disclosure agreement so complex and so binding it would reduce even the most affluent of them to ruin were they to violate its terms.

Later, and so tacitly Yahontov was unsure at first of what she was actually suggesting, she'd made a second offer: in exchange for a small percentage of the bid - something as negligible as, say, £500,000, sterling - she could ensure that *his* bid not only made it to the top of the pile, but was higher (if only by an equally small percentage) than its nearest rival, thus securing for him ownership of the jewel of India.

He'd leapt at the former offer readily; then - after scarcely a day's deliberation - accepted the latter one, too.

Sita hadn't elaborated further on how things had unfolded thereafter. But El had been left with the distinct impression that Yahontov still considered himself, despite all evidence to the contrary, the rightful landlord of the Crown of Palaces.

"Who is she for this one?" El had asked Ruby, reaching for the last of the bread.

"Some UN delegate, she said," Ruby had replied. "Wish I could tell you what sort, but I don't know no more than that myself. She's been cagey about this one - properly cagey. Christ knows why - it ain't as if I'm looking to get in on the action, is it? I got my own fish to fry."

Karen had gone next, excusing herself to go and call Fergus ("before he falls asleep playing Transport Tycoon again"); then Sophie, who had her Game Gear out of her pocket and her thumbs on the controls before she'd even left the table. And finally, Ruby.

"I'll just take this lot inside, then, shall I?" she'd said, picking up a salad bowl in the crook of one arm and a bottle of olive oil in the other and levering herself up from the bench. "Leave you two to it."

She hadn't tipped them a wink as she left, not quite, but

El found herself embarrassed anyway; looking anywhere but at Rose, her eyes fixed on the red and white cotton of the tablecloth and her hands wrapped tightly around the neck of her beer bottle.

"How are you feeling?" Rose had asked.

"What?" El had replied, startled - terrified that Rose had not only picked up on her embarrassment but elected to tackle it head-on.

"About the job," Rose had clarified. "Soames and Wainwright."

"Oh, right. That. Okay, I think. For now. It's the next bit I'm worried about."

"You're not alone. I feel as if I've spent the last fortnight doing nothing but bite my fingernails."

"And bidding on yachts at fundraisers. And opening up your closet to the San Francisco art community."

"I daresay I had the readers of the Oakland Girlfriend clutching their pearls at that one."

"Still, though. Big step."

"Hardly. I can't say I care *who* knows, now that Sophie and I have talked it through. The secrecy, before - it was never about my private life. It was about *him*. Keeping him in the dark and away from us."

Him, El had known, meant Marchant: the father Rose had hidden from for almost all her adult life.

"Any plans tonight?" El had asked, more to change the subject than because she thought Rose might have made any. They were all exhausted, close to spent; there was nothing left to do before they flew out but rest and recharge, and get themselves as ready as they could for the next stage of the game.

"Actually... yes," Rose had answered - awkwardly, fingers tracing the scar along her wrist and forearm the way El had noticed they tended to when she was nervous, or anxious, or upset. "I'm having dinner with Kate. There's a Cindy Sherman exhibition that I mentioned wanting to see before we left," she'd added, what might have been apologetically, "and she called last night to say she'd got us tickets, so I thought..."

Something like a boulder had fallen, hot and heavy, in El's stomach.

"Sounds great," she'd said, and finished the beer.

~

It was morning again when they touched down at Heathrow, as light as it had been when they'd left California.

She stood; stretched; pulled her backpack from the overhead locker and made for the aisle.

She found herself waiting, in the elongated stretch of time between the extinguishing of the seatbelt sign and the suction-*thwock* of the airlock releasing, directly behind Sita and the businesswoman in the suit - an American, she learned from the conversation she couldn't help but overhear, and a lawyer, one of the senior partners at a West Coast firm with an international client base.

"I'm staying at the Kendal, over on Great Portland Street," she was telling Sita, her voice Mid-Atlantic-clipped and cigarette-husky. "We should get dinner, while I'm here."

"I'd love to, darling," Sita said. "I'm afraid I'm promised elsewhere this week, but how's Saturday? There's a little place in Soho that does the most *remarkable* butternut terrine, if you're game."

The lawyer took a pen and a soft, suede business card from her purse, scribbled something on the back and passed it across the aisle to Sita.

"Here's my cell," she said, with a wide, even-toothed smile. "My *personal* cell. Call me when you're free."

"I certainly shall," Sita replied, taking the card and returning the smile.

How does she do it? El wondered, marvelling at Sita's charisma, the ease with which she seemed to navigate the world even when she wasn't in character. How the *hell* does she do it?

When the cabin door finally opened, she surged to the exit, through the bridge, up the escalator and along the walkway to Passport Control, breaking free of the others and putting as much distance as possible between her and them - between her and *Rose*, if she was honest with herself - before the limo Ruby had arranged to drive them home threw all of them back together again in yet another confined space.

She was the first from their flight in the queue, catching the tail-end of a glut of passengers disgorged from what she took to be - from the accents she could hear, the Lakers jerseys and Dodgers jackets she could see, the smattering of Bear Flags decorating sundry pieces of luggage - another West Coast flight.

Tiredness, incipient jet-lag and a gnawing discomfort that she refused to recognise as jealousy meant she didn't register him as familiar, even when she saw him ahead of her in line: a white man, of entirely average height and build, dressed in jeans and an unmemorable t-shirt, his unremarkable features mostly hidden by the Giants cap pulled low over his face.

Then the queue moved forward, catapulting him into the waiting arms of a bored-looking customs officer - and before she could blink, he was gone.

CHAPTER 25
HERNE BAY, KENT
OCTOBER 1997

Satis House hadn't improved in the time they'd been away. If anything, El thought, it had deteriorated: the weeds and rushes grown higher and denser, the windows more thoroughly caked with grease and dust.

"Good God," Sita muttered, as they made their way up the path to the main entrance. "It's the Castle of Otranto."

"Yet somehow exactly right for a man like Soames," Rose replied, taking Sita's arm and helping her across a particularly unyielding patch of nettles. "I wouldn't be at all surprised to find some young girl locked up in a dungeon inside."

Jared the home-help answered the door when they knocked, his eyes widening when he recognised them - then widening further as he took in Sita behind them, dark-suited and radiating authority.

"You're back?" he said - less friendly and more hostile this time around, a sentry rather than an usher. "What's happened now?"

"We need to talk to Soames," El told him, all business herself.

"Do you know what a state he was in after you left before? He could hardly catch his breath. He doesn't need you lot upsetting him again."

"Open the door, please," Sita said, her delivery suggesting the *please* was no more than a nicety, and one that might easily fall away, should Jared fail to comply. "He's aware that we're coming."

Jared gawped at them, aghast at their rudeness - then, apparently realising the futility of remonstrating any further, turned around and stalked away, leaving the front door open.

"He's in the conservatory," he shouted down to them, his back turned as he stomped away up the stairs. "You know where it is."

Soames was waiting for them - still hunched and vulturine, his chair now turned towards the conservatory doorway as if in anticipation of their arrival.

"Mrs Acharya!" he rasped as they approached him, pulling the oxygen mask from his mouth. "Such a lovely surprise. I'd expected it to be just me and the younger ones for this part of the proceedings."

Sita didn't answer him, but seemed instead to see *through* him - her gaze fixed on a single point a metre or so above his head.

He disgusts her, thought El, who'd rarely seen Sita broadcast such outright revulsion, even in the face of marks so objectionable they'd left her own stomach sickened. She can't bring herself to look at him.

"No Mrs Redfearn today, though, I see," he added.

"She's ill," El said. "Has the flu."

"That'll be the flight home taking its toll," he said. "She must have picked something up on the aeroplane. It's rather a hazard of air travel, as one ages. Wouldn't you agree, Mrs Acharya?"

Sita continued to stare through him, her face so impassive it might have been cast in marble.

∼

A hundred miles away, in her duplex flat in West Hampstead, inside the spare bedroom that her sons had carefully remodelled into a temporary sick bay, Ruby slept - covers pulled up to her chin and a box of paracetamol on the nightstand beside her.

From his hiding place behind the wardrobe, Jay watched her toss and turn in her sleep; heard the small, soft noises she made as she - he supposed - dreamed.

The butcher's knife in his hand felt heavy as lead; so heavy he wondered if he'd even be able to lift his wrist, when it came to it.

He'd never had a grandmother, on either side of his family. But if he *had* had one, he could see her looking a bit like *she* did, now: tired and wrinkled, bags on top of bags under her eyes; hair like greased-up candy floss, sticking out in all directions on her pillow; lips dry and cracked, parched tongue darting out to try to lick them moist.

Old, and weak, and vulnerable.

Even she-devils got old, of course. He knew that; he wasn't stupid. And that was what she was, no question - no-one but a she-devil could have done what she did to his Dad. Twenty three years inside, nearly as long as Jay had been alive now, and for what? To make extra sure that Jay's old man would keep his gob shut about the cons she was running, the mob medicine her husband was administering from his kitchen table?

It beggared belief: the lengths she'd gone to, just to shut the old man up. The depths of her cruelty.

She stirred again; called out for someone. A man: someone named Winston. Her dead husband, most likely.

He was grateful, today, that the husband *was* dead. It was an unkind thought, and not one his Mum would approve of, because it wasn't this *Winston's* fault, what his wife had done, and from the way Jay's Dad told it, he - Winston - was all but under *her* thumb anyway. But being dead meant he wasn't *here*, now, in this bedroom; meant he wouldn't interfere, wouldn't get in the way of what Jay knew he was there to do. Wouldn't, thank God, need Jay to take care of *him* as well as *her*.

The sons were gone, both of them: to work, or so Jay had gathered from the snippets of their conversation he'd overheard while he'd been crouching, armpits sweating and knees buckling, in his last but one hiding place, a linen cupboard under the stairs that housed the boiler as well as the towels. They'd be out all day; would be back - or so the nerdier, more serious one had told the other - in time to cook a rosemary chicken for their sick Mum's dinner.

Jay would be gone by then; long gone. At home, in his own bedroom, with a beat 'em up game on the PlayStation - clean and showered, his clothes in the wash on the hottest, longest cycle he could find on the machine. Or better yet, down in Kent with the old man - the two of them talking and sharing a celebratory bottle of single malt in front of the telly, once the home-help had knocked off for the day and Jay could stop pretending he was there to clean the house, or weed the garden, or whatever lie the old man had told about what Jay did around the place so the little queer wouldn't go sticking his nose into their business.

And - touch wood, fingers crossed - his Dad could rest a

little bit easier knowing some sort of justice had been done. Even if it *was* twenty years too late.

∼

"We've got your money," El said, her voice as expressionless as Sita's face.

"How did you find Wainwright?" Soames asked, smiling. "Easy to get along with? I suppose he must have been, or how would you have taken his cheque? And he sounded very excited about meeting *you*, Lady Winchester, when I last gave the old chap a call. I assume the family reunion went well?"

"Karen's transferring it now," El told him, ignoring his questions. "It should be in your account in the next few minutes."

"I'll get Jared to check on it then, in that case. Not that I don't trust you."

The pager in El's back pocket beeped: once, twice, three times.

She held it up to the light; read the message picked out in capitals on the little green screen.

"That's her," she said - to Rose and Sita, as much as to Soames. "It's done."

∼

Jay wrapped his other hand around the knife handle and raised it to his ear - like nunchaku, or a Samurai sword.

He was ready, he told himself. He could do this.

With his shoulder, he nudged the wardrobe door open a crack; not much, but just enough for him to slide out and into the room if he sucked in his stomach and flattened his back.

He'd left his trainers in the linen cupboard, before he crossed the landing. That would help him now; would keep his feet from making a sound as he crept across the carpet. She'd be half deaf, if she was anything like the other old people he'd met, but he didn't want to risk taking chances. Not now; not when he was so close to finishing it.

He snaked one sock-clad, shoeless foot through the crack and let one, tentative toe sink into the carpet.

She stirred again. Only not in her sleep, not this time. Now she was awake - wide awake and sitting up, getting ready to *get* up and out of bed, her arms rising up above her head in a long, yawning stretch that made her bones crack and her jaw click.

He panicked; yanked his foot back into the darkness of the wardrobe and held his breath, praying she wouldn't sense his presence in the room with her as she untangled herself from the covers and slid her own feet into a pair of slippers, her arms into a blue flannel dressing gown.

She stood; shuffled to the door and out into the hallway - over the landing and down the stairs.

He let himself breathe. Listened; waited until her could sense her moving around in the kitchen, could hear the opening of drawers and the clanging of spoons on cups. Then he leaned forward; let the wardrobe swing open and stepped out of the darkness to follow her.

~

"You know," Soames said, "you really *should* have brought Mrs Redfearn with you."

"She's ill," El repeated flatly.

"Still. I can't help but feel it might have been better for her to be here than at home. Safer."

"Safer?" El said. "What do you mean, *safer*?"

∼

Downstairs, barely six feet away from her, he paused. The mirror in the hallway, from where he stood, was positioned in such a way as to give him a clear view into the kitchen: he could see her inside, filling up the kettle at the sink, spooning sugar into a coffee cup.

Her back was turned to him.

If he was quick - if he ran inside and did it now - she might not see him. Might not know he was there at all until the knife went in.

∼

Soames didn't answer immediately, but reached for his mask and inhaled - slowly and deeply, filling his lungs with the oxygen they couldn't take themselves from the air.

"I don't mean to imply that I find you in any way stupid," he said, when he was free again of the mask. "Certainly not *you*, Mrs Acharya - I'm more than aware of *your* accomplishments. But I *do* have to ask myself: did it really seem likely to you all that the money would be enough, after twenty three years? Twenty three years of odour and filth, of a dozen men screaming through the walls at the top of their voices from the moment you wake until the moment you sleep, if ever you *can* sleep?"

"I was a young man when I was sentenced - not even forty. And now look at me. I'm barely alive at all. All because of your Mrs Redfearn."

"So how is that she believes - as all of *you* seem to believe - that I'd be satisfied with what you've just given me? She took my *life*. Did it not *once* occur to you, to *any* of you, that I might want hers in return?"

El considered this. Looked to Rose, who said nothing, and then to Sita, who nodded - a gesture so slight it was almost undetectable.

"As it happens," El told him, her own smile surfacing, "it did."

∼

She dropped a tea bag into the coffee cup - something herbal that reminded him of flowers, echinacea or hibiscus. Held it up to her nose and inhaled, then, satisfied with what she smelled, reached for the kettle and filled the cup to the brim with boiling water.

He took a step forward, then another; pulled the knife backwards, behind his body, with all the strength of his triceps, preparing to drive it into her ribs, her neck.

"You don't want to do that, son," she said, not turning around - her voice not the sickly tremor he might have been expecting, if he'd thought he'd hear her speak at all, but tough and determined and clear as a bell. "I promise you, and you best believe me when I tell you that *I know what I'm talking about* when I say this... What you're gearing yourself up to do now - you don't want to do it. So how's about you put that knife of yours down, eh? There's a good boy. Put it down, and me and you can have a talk."

CHAPTER 26

WEST HAMPSTEAD, LONDON
JULY 1997

"I been thinking," Ruby had said to El, before they'd flown out to San Francisco. "About Soames. What I said to young Kat about him wanting to keep us dangling, keep tugging our strings."

"What about it?" El had replied, unclear on where Ruby was heading.

"I ain't so certain I was right, when I said that was what he wanted. Or *all* he wanted. I reckon there's more to it - that it ain't just Wainwright's money or a little bit of power over us lot that he's after. I reckon he wants *me*."

"Wants you how?"

"Dead, girl. Wants me dead. And maybe not *just* me, neither. Could be he thinks the rest of you are guilty by association."

El had given this a moment's thought: weighed up the violence Soames had rained down already on Michael and Sita through whatever proxy he'd been using against the delight she was sure, having met him, that he'd take in watching Ruby – watching *all* of them - suspended on the hook indefinitely.

"What makes you say that?" she'd asked.

"He's petty, Soames is. Controlling, but petty with it. Not the sort of bloke you can imagine letting it go, if he thought someone had done him wrong."

"Didn't we know that already?"

"Alright, smart arse - *yes*, we did. *I* did. But don't it strike you as a poor sort of revenge, having us run round the States doing his donkey work for him? A bit... I don't know, *insufficient*, if it's payback for twenty-odd years inside? Especially when he's already had someone go after Sita and my Michael with that bleedin' penknife of his?"

"Maybe. When you put it like that."

"What I'm thinking is, he's got something else lined up for me when we get done with Wainwright. I don't know what, exactly. But *something*."

"Let's say you're right, then. What are you thinking we ought to do about it?"

"I ain't so certain of that one either - not yet. But leave it with me. I want to see what Kat drags up before I start working things out. Her and that Harriet both."

~

Jay froze, the butcher's knife still clenched between his fingers.

How had she known he was there? How the *fuck* had she known?

And why, when he was standing half a foot behind her and about to stick her with a blade that could've sliced her into pieces before she'd even known what hit her, was she so *calm*?

"I'm gonna turn around now," she told him. "I'll do it slow. And I'll keep my hands out, so you know there's nothing in 'em that can do you no harm. I don't hurt you, and you don't hurt me. We got a deal?"

A *deal*? he thought, completely disoriented by her reaction. She was about a hundred years old, on her own in the flat, with no weapon and her back turned to him. He was young, fit, strong; he was literally holding a knife to her. What sort of *deal* did she think she could make?

And suddenly, while he was still trying to work out what the hell she thought she was playing at, she was spinning around, the unplugged kettle in her hand - and then the knife was on the floor, her slipper-covered foot pressing down on one edge of the blade to keep him from retrieving it, and his arm was a fireball of agony, the bones in his wrist throbbing in time to the pulse of his blood.

"Sorry about that," she said conversationally, returning the kettle to its place by the sink and picking up the knife by its handle. "I ain't normally one for dirty tricks, but it's easier to have a proper chat, I find, when you're sat down with a cup of tea and a biscuit and neither one of you's trying to gut the other with a machete."

"My wrist!" he howled, clutching at himself with his undamaged hand. "You fucking cow, you broke my wrist!"

She took a sip of the herbal concoction in her coffee mug; swallowed.

"Doubt it," she said. "There's hardly any water left in that kettle - it's light as a feather, look. And keep a civil tongue in your head when you're talking to me, if you don't mind. I don't take kindly to being sworn at in my own kitchen."

She took a step towards him; instinctively, he backed away.

"You're alright," she told him - soothing now, as if she really *was* his gran and he'd fractured his scaphoid helping her lift a piece of furniture. "Like I said, I ain't intending to hurt you - no more than I have already, anyway."

"What do you want?" he said, hating the way he sounded, the pathetic mewling tone to his voice - the tone, not of a man in charge of the situation, but of a sad little kitten, begging its owner for a bowl of milk.

"I want you to know you don't have to do it - whatever it is your old man's told you to do. You got choices. And one of them choices is walking away from this, now. Before any more harm's done."

He almost laughed, despite the pain in his arm and wrist.

"*You're* telling *me* that?" he said. "After what you did?"

"I know what you must think of me. Christ knows, I know it. But the stories I'm betting your old man's told you - they ain't true."

"What, so you *didn't* do it, then?" he scoffed - sounding, he was pleased to hear, more confident now, more in control. "*Didn't* set him up for that robbery?"

"Oh, I done *that*. Stitched him up, right and proper. All them years he done inside - they're on me, not that I'd do things different even if I could. But did he ever tell you *why* I done it? *Why* I had him put away?"

She paused; took another swallow of her tea.

"No, 'course he didn't. Telling you that - it wouldn't fit the yarn he's been spinning you. Wouldn't *align with his self-image*, as a friend of mine might put it. Well, I *say* friend... I wouldn't put money on her thinking of me that way, though that's neither here nor there at the moment. What I'm getting at is: your old man, he's been keeping things from you. Big, important things, things that might make you think different about whether or not I'm worth taking a swing at with that bloody great carver of yours. And what he *has* been telling you, the poison he's been dripping in your ear since the day you were born - it's got your head so twisted up I expect you ain't ever learned how to think for yourself."

That stung - that she thought she knew him, knew anything at all about him or his Dad or the way the two of them were together. Against his will, his cheeks reddened as his anger rose.

Stupid cow, he thought. Stupid fucking lying cow.

And somewhere inside him, a half-formed voice spoke up - the same voice that used to whisper to him when they'd go to Hendon for a visit and Jay would spend the hour listening to his Dad tell his Mum she'd put weight on, or accusing her of flirting with the POs on duty even though, he said in the next breath, she was so ugly no-one but him would ever want her.

You sure about that, Jay? it asked. *You sure she's lying?*

What if there is *more to it? What if the old man* did *do something you don't know about, to her or someone else? What if he has been dripping poison in your ear, like she says?*

"These things he ain't told you," the old cow said, "they're things you ought to know. Things you *deserve* to know, really. But I got a feeling they ain't likely to sound that plausible, coming from me. I reckon I got a... what would this friend of mine call it? A *credibility problem*, so far as you're concerned. So it strikes me that it might be better for both of us for you to hear it from someone a bit closer to home. What do you reckon?"

She waited - and, when he didn't answer, ran a hand into the fluffy folds of her dressing gown and pulled out a small, folding mobile phone. She looked quizzically at it for a second, as if she wasn't quite sure how it worked or what she should be doing with it - then opened it up, pushed one of the buttons on the handset and held it up to her face, at least three inches from her right ear.

"He's ready," she said, when whoever she'd rung had answered. "Bring her through, would you? Door's unlocked."

She flipped the handset down again - but before he could ask her what the *fuck* she was doing, who the *fuck* she was talking to, he heard it: a click and a scrape and a sudden rush of noise from the corridor, the up-down rhythm of footsteps coming his way.

"We're in here," the old cow called out to whoever it was.

And there, suddenly, was his Mum, her face red from crying and a terrified look in her eyes, flanked on one side by a younger, grim-faced woman in a Metallica t-shirt.

"I'm sorry, Jay," she told him, reaching out to him and wrapping her thin, white arms around his shoulders. "I'm so, so sorry, baby. I didn't know. I just... I didn't know."

CHAPTER 27
WEST HAMPSTEAD, LONDON
OCTOBER 1997

Harriet was uncomfortable with casual touching: the hugs, cheek-kisses, back-pats and hand-squeezes that the rest of the world deemed so essential to functional social interaction. The few boyfriends she'd had over the years had found her cold and unaffectionate - had told her so, in several cases - while colleagues, acquaintances, even distant family members regularly took umbrage at the urge to flinch and recoil she could never quite hide when they darted towards her, lips and open arms at the ready.

Rose, she'd been pleased to note, was neither a hugger nor a kisser, and Harriet had wondered as early as their first meeting - their first *real* meeting, at a Charlotte Street coffee shop, and not their strange initial encounter at El's kitchen table in the arse-end of the Midlands - whether it was this, more than anything else, that had laid the foundations of the rapidly-accreting affection she felt for the older half-sister (and by extension, the niece) she hadn't known she had until the year before.

If ever she'd considered anyone in *need* of a hug, however - of the reassurance of a friendly hand on the shoulder or the comforting warmth of a light press of one body against another - it was Lois Soames, in this moment.

"It's time," Harriet told her, as kindly as she could, when the call she'd been waiting for had ended. "Are you ready?"

Lois shook her head, but reached for the door handle anyway and - without Harriet even needing to prompt her - stepped forward, into Ruby Redfearn's flat.

~

Harriet hadn't been at all convinced, the second time she'd visited Lois at the house the thin, frightened woman shared with her still absent son, that she was up to the task Redfearn had given her. Not, Harriet was quick to remind herself, because of any lack of confidence in her own professional abilities, but rather because of the Herculean enormity of the task itself. Namely: winning the trust of someone who, as she understood it, had spent not years but *decades* - the majority of her life, effectively since childhood - utterly under her partner's control. And thereafter, as if the first part of this task weren't challenge enough, persuading her to *break free* of this control.

The allusion she'd made in conversation with Rose and Redfearn and El-the-inside-woman with the puppy-dog eyes to *deprogramming* - a concept, with all its faintly fascistic, pseudo-scientific connotations, that Harriet absolutely loathed - hadn't been entirely wide of the mark; nor, though she found the term so broad a description as to be almost meaningless, was the suggestion she'd made of Charles Soames having *brainwashed* his wife and offspring.

The expectation that she'd somehow be equipped to undo so many years of damage in one fell swoop felt...

unreasonable, to say the least. Even with the ammunition she apparently had at her disposal.

Nevertheless, she'd tried. For Rose, and for Sophie.

The initial part of that second visit had been, by any estimation, a failure: the strange, unlikely story Harriet had to tell - about Charlie and their son and the mission he'd given him, about the convoluted corkscrewing of history that had brought Harriet to Lois' doorstep - falling on ears that were not so much deaf as actively resistant.

No, Lois had told Harriet, when she'd finally spoken. *No, that's not true. I don't know what you've got against my Charlie or why you'd want to say those things to me, but you're talking rubbish.*

And I'd like you to leave now, if you don't mind.

Okay, Harriet had replied, staying calm - very calm, her voice as even and emotionless as a speaking clock. *I'll go. But before I do, there's something I'd like you to do - not for me, but for yourself. It won't take a moment, I promise. You do it, and I'll leave, and I won't bother you again.*

What? Lois had said, angry affront bleeding into confusion. *What are you on about? What do you mean by that,* do something?

Come outside, Harriet had told her. *Come outside, and you'll see.*

~

"I didn't know," Lois was telling her son, her face half-buried in his chest in the middle of Redfearn's kitchen. "I didn't know."

"Didn't know what?" the boy said, pulling away from her, horrified. "*What* didn't you know? What are you even doing here, Mum? You shouldn't be here."

"Nor should you, sweetheart," she told him, stretching up to cup his jaw with her hand. "Neither one of us should be."

Harriet stayed silent: watching them from the kitchen doorway, watching *Redfearn* watch them.

"What's going on?" he asked - looking, Harriet thought, terribly young, and terribly bewildered, and terribly frightened by the many things he was beginning to realise he didn't understand. A fairy-tale child, lost in the woods; nothing at all like a man who'd break into an old woman's home with the express purpose of doing her harm.

"You're a good boy," Lois said, still cradling his face. "You are, I *know* you are, and I won't have no-one tell me different. But you're here because of your Dad, because he said to come and do... what it was he *said* to do. And that ain't right. *He* weren't right to ask you. No father ought to do that, send his own son out to put a knife to the throat of an old lady. Even *her*."

She threw a poisonous look at Redfearn, who saw it but - at least as far as Harriet could tell - seemed not to react to it at all.

"He didn't *need* to ask me," the boy argued, defiant now. "I wanted to do it. Not just for him, for *all* of us - you and me. She took him from us, Mum - you know she did. She might as well have killed him, for what she did to him."

"Yeah," said Lois thoughtfully. "Well, maybe she should have done. Maybe she should have done, at that."

∞

It was seeing him that swung it, Harriet thought later.

On the surface, they couldn't have been more different, physically: he large and hairy and ruddy from the sun, she as pale and skeletal as a corpse. But there was *something*: an obvious but somehow indefinable quality both shared - the shape of the mouth, perhaps, or the set and colour of the eyes - that marked them out as alike. As kin.

Lois saw it, Harriet believed; saw it, and knew - however much she hadn't *wanted* to know - that at least a part of the far-fetched tale Harriet had told was true.

He saw it, too: his caterpillar eyebrows knitting and his lower lip beginning to tremble under his thick grey moustache as he looked at her through the doorway, as he took in the worry-lines etched into her cheeks and forehead, the bones threatening to break through the surface of her skin.

"Lois," Harriet had said, when she'd judged it appropriate, "this is Ted. Ted, this is Lois. Your daughter."

~

"What?" Jay spluttered, peeling his mother's palm away from his face with his uninjured hand. "Why would you say that?"

"He's your Dad," Lois said softly. "And he'll always *be* your Dad. But he ain't who you think he is, Jay. He ain't who either of us thought he was. What he's done, what he's kept from us..."

She broke off, apparently struggling to find the words to encapsulate the sentiment, much less the explanation driving it.

Jay's expression flickered from anger to puzzlement and back again - a textbook illustration of *conflicted*.

"Stop saying that!" he shouted, pushing her away so hard she fell back against the doorframe. "Stop fucking saying that! What sort of wife *are* you, saying that about your own husband?"

Now Redfearn spoke; *now* she intervened.

"You're upset," she told him, "and I get that. It ain't easy to hear, what your Mum's trying to tell you. But you're in *my* house, son. *My* house. And I don't hold with people laying hands on each other under my roof. So if you know what's good for you, you'll go on over there and help her up before I remember that I seen you put her down there, and you'll do it now."

"Or what?" he snarled, curling his fist. "You'll hit me with a kettle again?"

"Leave it, Jay!" Lois begged him, pulling herself to her feet. "Please, just leave it!"

"You're defending her now, over me? Her who had my Dad locked up?"

"Calm down, son," said Ruby, evenly. "You just calm down."

"Shut it!" he yelled. "You don't get to speak, after what you did! You don't get to fucking speak!"

"Maybe I *should* defend her, at that!" cried Lois, almost screaming to be heard. "'Cause I'm *glad* he went down! He deserved to go down, after what he did!"

"What does that mean, *what he did*?" Jay screamed back at her, his head swinging left and right like the tail of a caged tiger. "What is it he's meant to have done?"

"He *took* me!" she bawled, her voice so raw Harriet wondered if her vocal cords had torn. "He took me, him and his mate and the man who called himself my Dad. Shut me away, so I wouldn't know no better than what he did or the things he said to me. Wouldn't know right from wrong. You want to talk about people robbing people of their lives, Jay? Then you look at me. You have a *good* look. 'Cause your Dad, he robbed mine."

CHAPTER 28

PACIFIC AVENUE, SAN FRANCISCO

SEPTEMBER 1997

El had never done anything like this before; never even come close.

The very thought of it had made her nervous. *Very* nervous.

"If this goes bad," she'd said, "we're going to end up inside. And not Holloway, either. It'll be some state prison out in the desert with open dormitories and guards with machine guns in the watchtower. You do realise that, don't you?"

"Been watching too many documentaries, you have," Ruby had told her, more amused than El would have expected given their situation. "And it ain't *going* to go bad. When are you lot gonna learn to trust me?"

Even Rose, whose apprehension had rendered her mute for the entirety of their walk to Pacific Heights, had rolled her eyes at that one.

"It'll all come right," Ruby had said, as they'd made their way through the unlocked gates and up to the entrance of the mansion proper. "You wait and see."

"Are you sure you're okay to do this?" El had asked Rose,

placing a reassuring hand - almost before she was aware that she'd done it - in the small of the other woman's back as Ruby grabbed and then released the roaring lion's head ornament that served as a door knocker, sending low vibrations racing through the heavy wood of the door.

"Not remotely," Rose had replied - leaning, or so El had thought, very lightly into the touch.

Wainwright's expression, on encountering the three of them waiting under the Grecian canopy of his porch-way, had run exactly the gamut of emotions that Ruby had anticipated they would: surprise, at seeing the woman he'd met as Laurel Hopkins appear unannounced so early in the day; surprise and confusion, at seeing El with her, and finally, on seeing Rose, a sort of wary, parched-mouthed yearning that had struck El like a punch to the solar plexus.

He hadn't said a word.

Rose would do the talking first; that was the plan. Anything else would seem to Wainwright, then or later, either the revelation of an earlier lie or its continuation into the present. Everything he knew as far as they were concerned, Ruby had reminded them - though El, at least, had needed no reminding - had been part of the con: how they looked, the way they spoke, what they wanted with him.

And from here on out, as they'd agreed way back in London, there wouldn't *be* a con.

Hereafter, what they'd tell him would be nothing but the truth.

"Good morning, Mr Wainwright," Rose had begun, haltingly. "I know this must seem very strange, but do you think we might come in?"

∼

He'd let them in, of course. And let them speak.

For a time, when Ruby was speaking - in her own voice, the voice that had shocked him so completely when she'd first unleashed it in the high-ceilinged sitting room he'd shown them into - El had thought he might do more than that: that he'd shout, or throw a plate, or come at them with a handgun or one of the decorative swords hanging from the walls of the entrance hall.

But instead, he'd sat quietly and listened, until Ruby was done.

"And what makes you think," he'd said, when she was finished, "that I won't get straight on the phone to the police and have the three of you took away in handcuffs, now you've told me all that?"

That's the question, isn't it? El had thought. Why *wouldn't* you?

"Because we *know*, do you see?" Ruby had told him. "We know where she is, your Ingrid. And we can take you to her."

~

Going back to London after all that time up north, Kat had told El, had been a relief she hadn't felt since the day she'd traded sex work in South Wales for drama school and a waitressing job in Bloomsbury.

The London branch of the Kingsley clan, Dexter had told her - once she'd fed back Lucille Salter's bit of intel, and left him to work whatever magic it was that he worked on his local authority contacts - was scattered mostly across the north west of the city, in and around the unlovely suburbs of Dollis Hill and Neasden, Wembley Park and Kenton. They were, he warned her, fewer than they had been, their numbers diminished by the deaths, chronic illnesses and unexpected emigrations that had beset them since the '60s. Of the remaining London Kingsleys, only two were old enough to remember *Bob* Kingsley - an aunt, now into her nineties and in the early stages of dementia, and another cousin, two and a half decades younger and, Kat hoped, with somewhat better recall.

The cousin, Harry, was a retired bricklayer, twice divorced and living, for the time being, in a rental flat in Kingsbury after declaring bankruptcy the year before. It was his financial situation more than anything else that persuaded Kat to readopt her journalist persona when she approached him, this time minus the Scouse accent Lucille Salter had found so unconvincing; if he really *was* as skint as he sounded, she reasoned, then a few hundred quid from a woman he'd never have to see again in exchange for a bit of dirt on a long-buried relative he probably hadn't even been that close to in the first place would probably strike him as a pretty sweet deal.

What she hadn't seen coming was the religion.

The inside of his flat - the flat he'd invited her into so readily that she worried at first he might be a serial killer on the lookout for his next victim - was a cramped mess of pan-denominational Christian paraphernalia: prayer beads and crucifixes, King James Bibles and Books of Common Prayer, embroidered aphorisms in cheap plastic frames and poster-sized reproductions of the face of Jesus. Most disturbingly, and doing little to dispel her serial killer anxieties, there was a font of water - *holy* water, she assumed - by the front door: a white resin basin in the shape of a cherub into which he dipped his fingers as he re-entered the hallway, spritzing himself with the liquid as he showed her to the living room.

"Are you a follower of Christ?" he said, offering her the

remaining water on his fingertips as easily as another host might ask if he could tempt her to a chocolate digestive.

Best fudge it a bit, she'd thought. Get him on side.

"Methodist," she told him, hoping like hell he wouldn't start quizzing her on John Wesley or the nuances of low church liturgy.

He nodded.

"Bet you were brought up in the Church, weren't you?" he asked.

"I was, yeah," she replied. *If that's what you call two funerals and getting dragged to the Midnight Mass at Christmas*, she added silently.

"Not me," he said sadly. "We didn't have none of that at home when I was growing up. Weren't 'til late last year that I came to God."

Ah, she thought, light dawning. A *convert*. A *late-life* convert, no less. No wonder he's getting so extreme with it.

"I was wondering," she began, hoping to steer him away from God, "if I could ask you a few questions about Bob - your cousin? I'm putting together a story on the abduction of a little girl in Harrogate in 1955, and Bob's name came up in conversation with a couple of the people I've been speaking to..."

It was intended as an opener - nothing more. She hadn't *meant* it to sound accusatory, or even mysteriously ambiguous. But she might as well, from the reaction it elicited, have accused him of taking the child himself.

"Oh, God," he said, taking his crumpling face in his hands. "You *know*, don't you? You *know*."

∾

"You've seen her?" Wainwright had asked - the tiniest green shoots of the hope El had just seen crushed under the wheels of a steamroller springing to life again. "You've seen my Ingrid?"

"Not personally," Ruby had conceded. "It was my husband that met her, a long time ago. But we got someone with her now - a friend. Someone who wants to help her. Her and your grandson both."

Wainwright had gasped, losing his breath at the word *grandson*.

He'd remarried after his first wife died, El had recalled. But he'd never had kids; probably never let himself consider the possibility he might ever be someone's grandfather.

"How do I know that's so?" he'd said, reigning himself in - remembering who he was speaking to. "How am I supposed to know that *any* of it is? You've told me nothing but a pack of lies up 'til now."

"If it's concrete proof you're after," Ruby had told him, "then you ain't gonna get it, not while you're all the way out here. I daresay you can get a load of blood tests ordered once you're back home, for her *and* you, and they'll tell you everything you want to know. But in the meantime, I reckon you'll have to take us at our word."

"You'll have to pardon me for saying so - Ruby, was it? - but I trust your word about as far as I could throw it."

That's it, then, El had told herself. It's over. Alcatraz, here we come.

Ruby had paused; scratched at her chin, apparently deep in thought.

"It's funny," she'd said. "Something occurred to me, when we was on the way over here. I didn't mention it to the girls, 'cause, you know... when you get to our age, not every thought you have is worth sharing, is it? But it *had* occurred to me, before, that you might need a bit more convincing than what we can give you. And that got me thinking that there *could* be something I could show you, at that. Well... perhaps not *show* you. More like: help you recollect what you knew already, but you might not've *known* you knew. If you see what I mean."

I don't, El had thought. So how the hell is *he* supposed to?

"I don't follow," Wainwright had said.

"No, I expect you don't. So instead of me *telling* you, how about I *ask* you something instead. You remember it well, do you, the night your little one got took?"

"I don't believe I'll bother answering that," he'd replied, anger flushing his red cheeks redder still.

"Right enough. I'm not sure I would, either, in your place. But I'd ask you this: do you happen to remember what they *sounded* like, them men that took her? When they were tying you up and hitting you, you and your wife?"

Wainwright didn't answer immediately.

He's playing it back, El had thought, watching his expression as he sifted through whatever impressions he'd been left with of that night, after he took a blow to the head. He's trying to remember - not just go back over what he told the police when it happened, or what he's been telling *himself* happened ever since, but really *remember*.

He's trying to relive it.

"It was only two of 'em that spoke," Wainwright had said distantly. "I didn't think much on it at the time, but I expect you want to tell me it was 'cause of who the other one was. That it were Bob Kingsley under that ski-mask, and he didn't want me recognising his voice."

Ruby had nodded.

"I'd say it probably was, an' all," she'd told him. "But it

was the other two I was thinking of. One of 'em sounded different from the other, did he? Bit younger, maybe?"

Wainwright closed his eyes, apparently pushing himself to remember.

"Yeah," he'd said. "He did, now you say it. Never struck me before, but... yeah. Younger. Like his voice had barely broke."

"It weren't just that, though, was it?" Ruby had pressed. "There was something else, weren't there? Something else about his voice, the young one."

There'd been another pause; another sharp intake of breath.

"Yeah," Wainwright had said, barely whispering. "There was, at that."

"Could have been it sounded different then than it does now. More pronounced. I expect that's why you didn't see it sooner - didn't put two and two together, even while you were inside. But he had a lisp, didn't he, the younger one? Just like Charlie Soames."

∼

It was guilt, Kat thought: a reservoir of it, bubbling just below the surface of the man's mind like pus gathering at the head of a boil. Whether it was *new* guilt, brought on by his religious conversion, or *old* guilt, festering for decades, maybe even the reason *for* his conversion - that, she couldn't say. But however long it had lain there, dormant, it was spilling over now, at only the slightest provocation - the confession dislodging itself from his imperilled soul with the propulsive force of a volcano.

"I didn't go with 'em," he said, still holding his head in his hands. "Bob asked me, he did, but by Almighty God I swear, I told him no. He had the idea in his head that it'd go easier with four of us. But I told him no. I'll be the first to say I wasn't a good man then, before I was received into His grace. I lied, and I stole, and I cheated. I didn't know any better, although that's no excuse, I know. But as much of a sinner as I was, even I had standards. And snatching a little baby from the arms of its mother... it was too much. Too much to ask."

The story as Harry Kingsley told it was fractured, nonlinear - the guilt and his apparently boundless capacity for proselytising sending him off down any number of rabbit-holes and digressions. But Kat's eventual understanding of what had happened before, during and then after the incident at the Wainwright house in 1955 was this:

Bob Kingsley had been having an affair with the wife of his wealthy employer up in Harrogate - a young girl, Gillian. And not *just* a fling, Harry had been keen to emphasise - no, Bob was in love with her. Wanted her to leave the husband and move down to London with him so the pair of them could shack up together somewhere nobody would notice or care that they were living in sin - but with his Dad's side of the family on hand, if they needed them.

When the wife fell pregnant, unexpectedly - with a baby she assured Bob *had* to be his, during the pregnancy and then after, once the girl was born - Bob sprang into action: putting into motion the beginnings of a plan that would end, as he saw it, with the two of them and their child safely ensconced in Northwick Park or Stanmore, away from the extensive reach of the cuckolded husband.

"Poor sod," Harry said - then slapped a hand over his mouth in shame, mortified by his momentary lapse into un-Christian language.

"Why?" Kat asked.

Harry muttered something that Kat took to be a prayer and crossed himself before continuing.

"I assumed he knew - that Bob did. *We* knew, 'round here - his Dad'd told my Mum, I expect in confidence, but she wasn't exactly one to keep a bit of gossip to herself when she heard it, so it did the rounds of all of us lot before we even knew what to make of what she was telling us. But *his* Mum must not have told *him*. Must've thought it was, you know... not something you said to your son, if you wanted him to grow up feeling like a man."

"Told him *what*?"

Harry shuffled awkwardly in his chair.

"He'd had an infection, when he was little. Too little to remember. In his, you know... Down *there*."

He gestured, mortified again, to his own crotch.

"He was infertile?" Kat asked.

"That was how we heard it. *You be careful what you do with that thing of yours, or you'll end up like your cousin Bobby* - that was what my Mum used to tell us."

"But he didn't know?"

"Couldn't have, could he? Or he wouldn't have done what he done."

The problem with the plan Bob had devised, Gillian had pointed out to him, was that it left them effectively penniless. She'd never worked, and didn't come from money, and as talented a gardener as Bob was, he was never going to bring in the kind of salary that would keep not just both of them but their baby comfortably afloat.

Fortunately, she'd been thinking, and had come up with a plan of her own.

"A kidnapping," Harry said. "Bob'd get a gang together to break in and take the little girl so he could hold her to ransom - get the husband to pay up however much they thought they could get him to shell out to have her back. He'd get one of his lads to do the handover, swap the baby for the pay-out - then, once all the fuss had died down, the wife'd pack a suitcase, wrap the kiddie up in a blanket and jump on the train to London to meet Bob. Who by then would've used his share of the ransom money to get things set up for the three of them at this end."

"Except there *was* no ransom money," Kat said - edging, she thought, close enough to the truth of what had happened now to see its outline, the basic shape of the thing, but not quite close enough that she could name it, not yet. "Or any ransom at all, the way I heard it."

"No," Harry agreed. "They were all set to wait to send it out - forty eight hours was what Bob told me, when he was trying to rope me into it. Forty eight hours to make sure the husband was desperate, then hit him with the ransom note when he was in such a state he'd say yes to anything if it brought the little girl back. But somewhere between them taking her and when they were meant to send out the note, the wife... she changed her mind. Decided she was going to stay with the husband after all."

"And Bob... he didn't like that. Nor did the rest of them, for that matter."

An idea - not quite a suspicion, but almost - took hold of Kat.

"These others, the ones who did the break-in with him," she asked, with a casualness she hoped would go some way towards disguising how *much* she wanted to know. "Mates of his, were they? Of Bob's?"

Harry raised his eyes to the heavens and crossed himself a second time, his lips moving as he whispered another prayer she couldn't hear.

"Not mates," he answered. "Relatives."

He hesitated.

"'First remove the beam from your own eye,'" he said, "'and then you will see clearly to remove the speck from your brother's eye.' It's a good lesson."

"Sorry?" said Kat, momentarily regretting her younger incarnation's decision to abandon Bible school and textual analysis of the Scriptures in favour of Sunday morning TV and a lie-in.

"It means you shouldn't judge others. Shouldn't call out their sins before you've looked deep at your own." He paused again. "But their sin... it's *my* sin too, do you see? And I can't tell you mine, tell you what poison I've known and kept hidden all these years, without telling you theirs too."

"But Bob's dead, isn't he?" she said - not sure anymore if he even remembered she was supposed to be a journalist sniffing out a story, or if the fact of her presence in his flat had transformed her, in his mind, into some sort of mother-confessor. "If it's *his* secrets you've been protecting... well, there's no sense in doing it now, is there?"

His lips moved soundlessly a third time, and she wondered - with a pang of guilt of her own - if he wasn't just volatile but actually ill; if this compulsive purging of sins was symptomatic of a deeper hyperreligiosity that might itself index some sort of psychotic disorder, and that she'd just happened to appear in the right place at the right time to capitalise on its expression.

"Not just Bob," he said eventually. "Stuart, too. He's... he *was* my brother. Half-brother, on our Dad's side. I said no, when Bob asked if I'd help him, but Stu... Stu said yes."

"And he's... not with us?" Kat asked carefully - paranoid now that anything she said might set him off down a potentially frightening path.

"Congestive heart failure," he answered, to her relief comparatively calmly. "He went home to the Lord five years ago now."

"And the other man - did he... pass away, too?"

This elicited not the further wince of inner conflict she'd expected, but a peal of laughter, cruel and bitter.

"Oh, he's been judged," he said. "But not by the Lord - that judgement's still to come for him. He's doing time, or he was, last I heard. A long stretch, too."

The not-quite-suspicion she'd been nurturing exploded into certainty.

"Is he?" she asked, with such deliberate disinterest that it occurred to her that he might not even register the question.

"Yeah. Got life for an armed robbery he done back in the '70s. If you'd asked me before... asked the man I *used* to be, I'd have said he didn't have it in him. But I suppose I never really knew him that well. His Mum and mine were sisters, but she died having him, and it was his Dad who brought him up, out in the East End somewhere. And he was always a peculiar one, Charlie. I never did much care for him."

∽

"Soames?" Wainwright had said - torn, El thought, between his own recollections and an unwillingness to believe the worst of a man he'd considered a friend. "Charlie Soames took my Ingrid?"

"It's looking that way," Ruby had replied.

"And you didn't think to let me in on this from the beginning, instead of stringing me along like some bloody idiot?"

"We haven't known for very long ourselves," Rose had interjected. "Not for sure. We've been waiting for... confirmation, from London."

"Besides which," Ruby had added, "it wouldn't have been safe to tell you straight off."

"What the bloody hell are you talking about, *safe*?" Wainwright had said, almost shouting in her face as his temper rose again.

"Safe for *us*, I should've said. He's had eyes on us since we've been here, Soames has. Young El here's felt it, when she's been out and about, and I've felt something similar myself more than once. We don't know who he's sent to do the watching, not for sure, but I know *him*, and his kind don't like to leave much to chance. He'll have rung you an' all this last fortnight, I expect? Asked how you're doing, what you've been up to?"

Wainwright's face had frozen.

"Twice," he'd said quietly, after a moment. "Once last week, and once the night before last. Said he'd been worried about me, on my own all the way out here."

"And he asked you about El and her magic computer program, I should think?"

"I brought it up - told him all about it, at that. He was very kind about it - not a bit doubtful like some would've been. Said it sounded like the miracle I'd been waiting for."

"I'm sure he did. Them calls... they weren't him seeing about *you*. They were him checking up on *us* - making sure we were on the con the way we said we'd be, not straying too far from what we'd told him we'd be doing. And if he'd got so much as an inkling we were going off-piste... Put it this way: the *best* case scenario would've been him sending Interpol after us with a search warrant."

∼

Bob Kingsley had kept the child; had raised her as his own.

"I don't think he did it to spite Gillian," Harry said. "That might have been a bit of it, but he really did love that little girl, blood or not. And once he had her, once he'd held her in his arms and convinced himself he'd never have to give her back..."

"I understand," said Kat, who didn't entirely, but suspected it was in her interests to play along with whatever sentiment he expressed.

"Do you know what she did, afterwards - Gillian?"

"I do, yeah."

"And you know it's a sin, suicide? A mortal sin?"

"I've heard people say as much," Kat replied - the half-dormant memory of her father hanging by a rope from an oak tree in the woods behind their house carving rough grooves at the edges of her voice.

"A woman who'd do that, who'd spit in the face of God like that... She deserved to be punished. And she's *being* punished, now and forever, as Matthew tells us. But what about the ones who drove her to it, and the ones who held their tongues when they should have cried out for justice? What punishment is there for them? For *us*?"

Kat didn't trust herself to speak; to keep her *own* tongue in check.

"Stu and Charlie weren't happy, when they found out Bob wouldn't be getting them the money he'd promised," Harry continued, careering away from the possibility of his own eternal damnation and back to concrete historical reality. "Charlie especially. I reckon that's why Bob tried so hard to get him involved in the little girl's life - so Charlie'd see what a lovely kid she was, and maybe come to realise for himself that having her around the place was worth more than a fifty grand pay-out."

They settled in Harlesden, Bob and the child. With the

help of the Kingsleys' less law-abiding connections, he changed her name, procuring her the necessary paperwork for barely more than a month's salary - a deal he considered a bargain, for the doors it would open as she aged.

And they lived together happily enough, as Harry saw it. Until the day Bob went to the doctor with a stomach ache he couldn't shift and found out shortly after that his little Ingrid - little Lois, as he'd rechristened her, after his own grandmother - would be left without any parent at all before too long.

"Nobody could work it out, why he asked *Charlie* of all people to step in and take care of her after he was gone," Harry said. "But *we* knew, me and Stu. Because who else could he have trusted to keep her hidden from her *real* dad, if he ever came looking for her?"

∽

"He must not have known *what* to think, the first time they stuck you in that cell with him in Hendon," Ruby had told Wainwright. "I mean, what are the odds of it? Of the bloke whose kid he snatched all them years ago, whose kid he'd been grooming to be his child-bride or what have you almost all her life, just rocking up in the bunk above his? About a million to one, I reckon."

Wainwright's anger had begun to dissipate by then, his indignation replaced by the queasy dawning realisation that what he was hearing was, very likely, something like the truth.

"I expect he was lying there one night listening to you talk away above him, and he had the idea of how he could use what he knew to fleece you - perhaps when you told him how much you'd spent on private detectives, and he got a sense that you'd shell out a hundred times that making up for lost time with your Ingrid, if you could just see her again. And he'd have been sure there was no danger of the *real* Ingrid showing up and spoiling things, wouldn't he? 'Cause he knew exactly where *she* was. And better than that: he had her so far under his thumb, she'd hardly dare go to the bathroom without his say-so."

"We know he'd been turning over what I done to him, and how he was gonna get back at me if he ever got out. I doubt it took much to get him thinking on how he'd put both of them things together - how he'd use *me* to get to *you*. Use *us*."

They hadn't told him *what* dirt Soames had on them, and how he'd happened to come upon it; what leverage, exactly. And Wainwright hadn't asked.

But it was, El had considered later, the one loose end they hadn't managed to tie up; the one question to which no obvious answer had presented itself. Because despite everything else they knew, despite everything Ruby and Dexter and Kat and Harriet had been able to uncover - they still had no idea at all *how* Soames had known what he'd known about the death of James Marchant. Or who, more specifically, had been the one to tell him.

CHAPTER 29
HERNE BAY, KENT
OCTOBER 1997

"Do you have any idea how hard it is," El told Soames, still smiling, "getting a woman like Ruby to stay in bed? She can't stand being sick, even when she *is* sick, so persuading her to lie there like the English Patient until your son caught sight of her through his binoculars and decided she was weak enough for him to make his move..."

"Was rather an ordeal," Sita concluded, smiling back at her.

∼

"And you're sure he's watching, are you?" Ruby had asked Sita earlier that morning.

"Absolutely certain," Sita had replied, tucking her into the duvet and plumping the pile of pillows behind her. "You'd see for yourself, if you looked. He's directly across the road, on the roof of that monstrous building site your council seems to have abandoned to the elements."

"It's not like we ain't complained," Ruby responded, halfheartedly. "Michael rang up someone at Environmental Health the other week, but they kept fobbing him off."

"Are *you* sure about this, Mum?" Dexter had said, apprehensively. "What if this Jay changes his mind, or decides he'd rather throw a petrol bomb through the window? What if Soames has someone else on hand for the break-in, and the son's just there to stand guard?"

Ruby had beckoned him closer, patting the unoccupied side of the bed until he sat down beside her.

"I know you're worried," she'd told him, taking his hand. "But you got to trust me, alright? It'll be him that does it, this Jay – Soames has had him doing his running 'round for him from the get-go. And much as the boy might *want* to chuck a Molotov cocktail through the letterbox, he ain't *going* to. Soames'll want it done up close and personal. He'll want me to *know* about it, when it's happening."

"As to the timing, darling," Sita had said, "I'll concede that there's a degree of guesswork involved on our part. But it's educated guesswork, not a blind shot in the dark. Soames is a sadist; we've all seen as much. He likes to dominate. It won't be enough for him to simply have your mother removed from the equation. He'll want the rest of us to know about it when he does. He'll want to see our reactions, when he tells us what he's done. And since he's insisted that we visit him *today, this morning* no less, I find it difficult to imagine that he won't be taking the opportunity to tell us all *about* what he's done - or what he believes he's done. If only to see the looks on our faces, as he's bragging about it."

"You listen to your Auntie Sita," Ruby had said, not loosening her grip on Dexter's hand. "I might do her head in sometimes, but she ain't about to offer me up for sacrifice."

"Not today, at any rate," Sita had added. "And I can

assure you, there'll be something far better than *this* in it for me, if I ever do."

～

"What the *hell* are you talking about?" Soames demanded - tendrils of unease wrapping around the words as he spoke them.

"Ruby - she's not dead," El told him. "Not even close. Your son's with her now, in fact - having a cup of tea with her in her kitchen, was the last I heard. Your wife's there, too."

"She took none too kindly to the revelation of her parentage," Sita said. "Nor to the realisation that her husband and the man she'd long assumed to be her father had conspired all her life to keep her from discovering that parentage. *Nor*, I would add, to learning that that same husband had recruited their only son to commit murder on his behalf. Though I can't *think* why."

El had been prepared for him to shout, to scream bloody murder at them. But he didn't.

Instead, he began to laugh - a dry, corrosive rattle that rose up from his chest like the grind of rusted gears and left him gasping for breath.

"Will you be letting us in on the joke?" Rose asked him, the high-handed timbre of her voice at odds with her body language - the clench of her teeth and the anxious, erratic scratching at her wrist.

"I'm sorry," he wheezed, pulling on his oxygen and wiping at his spittle-flecked mouth. "I'm just finding it rather funny that you seem to think you've *pulled one over on me*, somehow."

Rose shot her a look of frightened incomprehension. Sita seemed barely to react at all.

In another time and place, El might have been impressed by her stoicism.

"There'll be some small degree of inconvenience," he said, "if you really *have* succeeded in turning Lois against me - although I shouldn't take even that for granted, if I were you. We've been together a *very* long time, as you know yourselves. And my idiot son may have shown himself to have less courage and fewer of the little grey cells than that bum-boy Jared out there – though I can't say even *that* surprises me immensely, he never *was* Brain of Britain. But inconvenience will be the worst of it, you see. There'll be no other adverse consequences - at least, not for me. Good as it may have made you feel to solve the mystery of the Wainwright baby and snatch your Mrs Redfearn from the jaws of death, it hasn't served your cause well in the slightest. I still know what you did to James Marchant, the six of you - or had you forgotten? All *this* conversation has done is suggest that it might be preferable for me to see you in prison for it, rather than out in the world plotting my downfall."

Sita's lips twitched.

"You intend to call the police?" she asked.

El thought she caught something, beyond the conservatory: the sound of a heavy door, opening and closing; the whisper of voices echoing faintly along the hallway.

"I do," Soames replied, seeming not to hear them.

Another door opened, this one closer by, and then Karen was standing in the conservatory doorway – hemmed in on one side by a cowed-looking Jared, and on the other by an older white man with a bald, egg-like head whom Dexter, had he seen him, would have been surprised to recognise as Gerry The Eagle, Gary Hartwood's long-suffering business manager.

"And the cavalry arrives," Sita said.

The bald man stepped forward, not stopping until he loomed directly over Soames in his chair.

"Charles Soames?" he asked.

Soames stared up at him mutely, not comprehending.

"Mr Soames," the man continued, reaching into his back pocket for his handcuffs, "you're under arrest on suspicion of kidnapping and false imprisonment. You do not have to say anything, but it may hurt your defence if you do not mention when questioned something which you later rely on in court."

CHAPTER 30
EMBARCADERO, SAN FRANCISCO
SEPTEMBER 1997

To properly appreciate the dynamic that had underpinned Ruby and Sita's professional relationship for so many years, El had learned, you had to understand this: Ruby sometimes overreached.

Not often - certainly not often enough for it to be a problem. She was a planner, a strategist; she thought things through. But occasionally, however intricate her planning, she'd miscalculate: underestimate a mark, or overestimate the capabilities of a colleague, or fail to notice a crack in the foundations of a con that might bring the whole house tumbling down.

And Sita - Sita liked to spread her bets.

She wasn't as meticulous as Ruby; was more inclined to impromptu decision-making and seizing opportunities as and when they presented themselves. But she believed very firmly in contingency measures; in, as she'd reminded El as recently as the Marchant job, not putting all her eggs in one basket.

Which meant that, when Ruby *did* occasionally overreach, Sita would almost always have an extra card up her sleeve to help them capture the pot.

The card, in this case, had very literally fallen into her lap.

They'd been in San Francisco for less than a day when she first saw him, snapping pictures of her and El and Rose as the three of them stretched their legs along the waterfront, an absurd orange baseball cap covering the shining - and, she imagined, easily sunburned - surface of his head and an equally ludicrous Hawaiian shirt swaddling his upper body like a mu-mu. It was very nearly endearing, she'd thought, how sure he'd seemed that he'd go undetected; that if any of them *did* register his presence, he'd appear to them as innocuous as any other starry-eyed, pink-skinned tourist gobbling chilli dogs and fighting off marauding seagulls on Fisherman's Wharf.

She hadn't confronted him then, nor mentioned to either girl that he was there and what his presence might signify. Rather, she'd made a mental note to keep an eye on him - to track his movements and divine from them some indication of what he was up to before challenging him outright.

The confrontation, such as it was, had happened less than two days later, scarcely a block from the home they'd rented by the national park.

He'd been following *her* that afternoon; perhaps, she'd thought, because the others had sensibly elected to shelter indoors from the unexpected heat that seemed to have engulfed the city since their arrival. She'd led him to a - thankfully well air-conditioned - Japanese supermarket wedged between a synagogue and a hardware store on Lake Street; lingered a few minutes by the edamame and then, when he lowered his head to check his camera, had dashed outside through the fire door, leaving him *inside* to scratch his newly-shaven chin in confusion.

When he made his own exit, she was waiting for him outside, half-hidden by a pillar. She'd... perhaps not quite *leapt* out at him, but the effect had been much the same as if she had: he'd jumped several inches in the air, ending up virtually on top of her and almost knocking her to the ground.

"Gerald, darling," she asked, when he'd adjusted his clothes and modulated his terror, "is it too much to enquire what *exactly* it is you're doing here?"

~

She'd met Gerry Adler in much the same manner she'd come to know so many of her police contacts: through work.

It was the early '80s, and she'd been in the latter stages of a not especially lucrative but enormously satisfying talent agent scam on an aspiring film actor down in Wimbledon - an arrogant, supercilious boy whose narcissism far outstripped his only moderate good looks, and whose father, unbeknown to her at the time, served as the go-to solicitor and *consigliere* of an organised crime boss masterminding a heroin-smuggling enterprise from his Limehouse base.

In the course of a Met investigation that saw the younger, trimmer Gerry go undercover as a demanding new client of the *consigliere*, their paths had crossed - specifically at a garden party celebrating the son's 'discovery' by a major Hollywood producer. She'd spotted him immediately for what he was, his sharp suit and coconut-oiled side-parting not disguising the innately *rumpled* look that characterised every policeman she'd ever known, though it had taken him somewhat longer to identify *her* as something other than that which she purported to be - and, when he had, to assure her that, providing she abandoned the con immediately and did nothing to interfere with his own operation, he had nothing to gain by unmasking her.

When their paths crossed for a second time the following year, while she and Ruby were mid-way through offloading Waterhouse's Lady of Shalott onto a Filipino dignitary Gerry had been assigned to for the duration of his stay in London, she wondered whether fate might have had a hand in it - she was, after all, between husbands at the time, with no steady partners to speak of, and the younger Gerry wasn't so terribly unappealing.

When it happened for a third time, though, at an Easter festival hosted by the Ghanaian High Commission in Belgravia, she suspected that not fate but Gerry himself was responsible; when he began to throw decidedly doe-eyed looks her way over a platter of artisanal pastries, her suspicions were confirmed.

Although perhaps, she'd thought then, fate *was* trying to tell her something. Were there not certain advantages for a woman such as herself, after all, in capturing the affections of an officer of the law, particularly one whose star appeared to be rising within the Met?

The friendship that developed between them thereafter, somewhat one-sided though it was, had distinct benefits for both parties - Gerry enjoying the pleasure of Sita's company from time to time, as she saw fit to bestow it upon him, and Sita establishing a channel of communication with the British police that would long outlast any physical relationship between them.

Pursuing her across continents for no other reason than

to *watch* her, however, seemed to her a bridge too far, even for a man as devoted as Gerry.

∾

"Bloody hell, woman," he panted, clutching at his chest through the polyester shirt, "are you trying to give me a heart attack?"

"I'm not at all sorry. And I ask again: *what* are you doing here, and *why* are you following me?"

He was reluctant to tell her, at first; perhaps in the spirit of protecting his dented pride, and perhaps because he was still inclined, despite all evidence to the contrary, to believe himself the kind of man who *wouldn't* just release confidential operational details to decidedly un-law-abiding members of the public at the drop of a hat.

But he *did* tell her, of course. And *what* he told her was… eye-opening.

∾

He'd been back undercover for the better part of the year, assigned to a washed-up pop singer out in Essex who'd taken to topping up the royalties from his music by buying and selling high-end motors that passed through his hands by less than savoury (and more importantly for Gerry's purposes, less than legal) means.

The singer, a Gary Hartwood, had begun more recently to dabble in extortion - snapping up vehicles from unwitting sellers for the lowest price they'd accept, claiming a week or so after the sale that the odometer of *this* Bentley or *that* Aston had been manually altered and then threatening with violence any vendor resistant to the prospect of returning the money Hartwood had paid them. Most were too frightened of the promised retribution to refuse, and many chose to cut their losses altogether once they'd made the transfer - leaving Hartwood with the cars they'd 'sold' him, as well as the cash he'd ostensibly paid them to begin with.

It had been working very well for him, Gerry had observed, until Dexter Redfearn had turned up with his Jag.

He hadn't known for sure who the bloke was, when he'd first come out to Hartwood's gaff in Saffron Walden. There'd been something familiar about him, for sure, something about the wide, knowing grin and the glint in his eye that reminded Gerry of someone, though he hadn't put his finger on who that *someone* was until a bit of backroom nosing around had thrown up the name of the lad's mum: Sita's mate Ruby. Her *best* mate.

From there on in, his interest in Redfearn Jr. and his Jag - previously strictly professional - had turned that bit more personal.

He'd tracked the bloke down to a posh-looking flat in West Hampstead he apparently shared with his mum and brother, and to a more run-down office up near Temple Bar. He'd kept eyes on both for a while, juggling the Hartwood operation with surveillance of the flat and office where he could - waiting for Hartwood to pull his signature move on Redfearn, and curious as hell about how the *older* Redfearn and Sita herself would react when he did.

Except that he'd noticed, while he was watching them, that someone else had eyes on them too: a young lad, tall and skinny and so fair he looked like he'd hardly even need to use a razor, peering out at the Redfearn flat through a pair of binoculars from the driving seat of a Transit van.

He'd considered telling Sita there and then that there was someone on the Redfearns' case - then decided against it, reasoning that it might be more sensible to wait a bit, to draw the lad out and see what exactly it was that he wanted.

He hadn't been there the day Michael Redfearn had been stabbed - had been up in Baldock with Hartwood, negotiating the purchase of an Alpine GTA - but had gathered from the subsequent comings and goings at the flat that *something* had gone on in his absence.

He *had* been there, though, the night the young lad went after Sita - had followed him from West Hampstead to her apartment in South Ken, and had been all set to burst out of his Audi and take the little shit down with his baton when Sita had stuck a wrist lock on him and then launched a pointed toe, with a precision of movement that elicited in Gerry a peculiar combination of fear and arousal, straight into the bastard's bollocks.

He'd kept an even closer eye on Redfearn Jr. and the women, after that - spending nigh-on every night parked up in South Ken or West Hampstead, ready to slap a hand on their stalker's shoulder the second he took another step out of line, but secure in the knowledge that if anyone could take care of herself, it was Sita.

When he saw her and Ruby Redfearn and the younger ones in their gang nip into a luxury travel agency on Cromwell Road, his curiosity was piqued; when he saw the knife-happy blond bastard walk into same travel agency not long after, red flags started waving and didn't stop. A flash of his warrant card and a few questions to the booking agent later, and he had a flight destination for them both. The *same* destination, no less: San Francisco.

The Hartwood job was *his* operation, and he'd had the foresight to line up another UC to step in for him, if he ever needed to back away. He'd pled a family emergency to the Guv, one that *had* to be dealt with there and then; the old man hadn't been happy, hadn't been happy at all, but Gerry had got his way.

And with barely time to pack his suntan lotion and his passport, he was off to the airport, bound for Los Angeles and, one short layover later, for San Francisco International.

∽

"To recap, then," Sita said, steering Gerry through the doors of the tea-room opposite the hardware store with a prod to the back. "You've been watching us for months, without declaring yourself. You've witnessed the young man you described not only *stalking* us, as you put it, but physically attacking me, with a weapon no less - again, without making your presence known. You've *tailed* us across the ocean, once again without informing me - or indeed any one of us - that you planned to do so. And now, having been rumbled in the midst of this entirely unethical - not to say positively *sinister* - surveillance mission, you mean to tell me that we may, in fact, *remain* in danger from my attacker? Gingseng Green, please," she added, addressing the startled-looking girl who'd appeared at their table with an order pad. "And my friend will have a pot of the genmaicha, if he ever closes his mouth sufficiently to allow it passage through his gullet."

"You're missing the point," he said, when the girl had gone, no less startled for having taken their order. "I've seen enough to know you're up to something, you and your girls. But that boy, the one who's been keeping tabs on you - my gut says *he's* up to something, too. Something that might end badly for the lot of you."

"I can assure you," she told him, affronted, "that things are very much under control. While I will confess to not knowing exactly *who's* been following us, I was certainly aware that we were *being* followed. And *why*, moreover, this was so."

"And if he comes after you again, the boy? Kick him where it hurts again, will you?"

"He won't. My understanding is that he's here in a purely observational capacity. To make sure none of us deviate from the... well, let's say *instructions* we've been issued."

The girl returned to the table, placing cups, spoons and a pair of teapots onto the tablecloth before scrambling, very quickly, away.

"*Instructions*? Christ almighty, Sita - what have you got yourself caught up in? Since when do any of your lot take *instructions*?"

"It's under control," she repeated, coldly.

"Bollocks is it. What's happened?"

She sighed, and stirred her tea. Then, wondering how long it would be before she began to regret it, offered as much of an outline of their present situation as felt prudent - omitting certain salient details around past cons, decades-long miscarriages of justice and, particularly, recent unlawful killings in which she may or may not have participated.

"So, he's got you dancing for him, this Soames?" Gerry asked, when she was finished. "He's blackmailing you into going after this Wainwright bloke for him?"

"So it appears."

"And the boy, the one who's after you...?"

"His son, or so we believe. It's rather difficult to know for certain, but the evidence certainly points that way."

"And you're telling me you've got it all under control?"

His scepticism riled her; goaded her into revealing more than she intended.

"We have an endgame in place," she told him. "You need not concern yourself with my welfare."

He took a long, graceless slurp from his own cup.

"This endgame," he said slowly, sounding out each syllable. "It finishes with your man Soames back inside for the kidnapping, does it?"

In fact, it didn't: the con, as they'd envisaged it before leaving London, would conclude with the tables turned, the threat Soames posed neutralised and his hold on them destroyed, but they'd yet to decide on whether an anonymous tip-off thereafter to the Met or the North Yorkshire Police regarding a forty year old cold case would yield much beyond rolled eyes and insincere promises to look into the matter. Sita had privately weighed the benefits of a word in the ear of one of her more senior contacts on the force - but had dismissed the idea almost as quickly as it had struck her. She'd pulled on that particular page of her little black book with more frequency than she'd have liked, in recent months. And dropping hints about a decades-old child-snatching, in another jurisdiction no less, would very likely raise questions she was disinclined to answer, even among the most trusted of her uniformed acquaintances.

"Certainly," she lied.

He actually scoffed, which riled her further.

"That's a no, then, is it?" he said.

She stared at him, eyebrows raised witheringly - a gesture that, were he not so absolutely convinced of the rightness of his position, might have reduced him to flustered apologies.

"Fine," she said irritably, when he failed to react as she'd anticipated. "No, it does not."

"Because you thought it'd be too old for anyone to

bother taking it further, this kidnapping, if you reported him for it?"

She gave a small, tight-lipped nod.

And he'd *beamed* at her - a delighted, self-satisfied Cheshire Cat smirk that was virtually an *invitation* to reach across the table and slap him. Beamed at her, and winked.

"In that case," he said, "I'd say it's a bloody good thing you've got an interested copper in your corner, wouldn't you?"

CHAPTER 31
HERNE BAY, KENT
OCTOBER 1997

"Kidnapping?" Soames said - doing, El thought, a remarkable approximation of outraged bafflement. "What are you talking about, *kidnapping*? And what's *she* doing with you?"

He pointed one bony finger towards Karen, who responded with a *who, me?* shrug of her shoulders.

"I can't say that I know her, sir," Gerry answered. "Nor any of these other ladies here. But as to the charges: I can tell you that they relate to the taking in 1955 of Ingrid Wainwright, also known as Lois Soames."

"Lois Soames is my *wife*," Soames said, oxygen deprivation reducing what would have been a roar to a muted half-shout.

"So I understand, sir. Are you able to stand, or do I need to call in one of my officers to help you to the car?"

"You did this, didn't you?" Soames cried, turning to El and Sita. "You sicced your... *pet* here on me?"

"I'm going to pretend I didn't hear that, sir," Gerry told him - still rigidly polite, but something like a warning now entering his voice. "Stand up, please, if you can."

Soames pulled the mask to his face and sucked. The air

seemed to soothe him; to *change* him. When he next spoke, he was calmer; a different, and far more reasonable man.

"Since you're here, Detective - or is it Sergeant? I'm never sure about police ranks."

"Detective Inspector," Gerry replied impassively.

"Of course. As I say: since you're here, Detective Inspector, I wonder if it might be worth us having a small chat about another case I believe your colleagues are investigating? A more *recent* case. It's possible I have information they may be interested in hearing."

"Information?"

"Yes. About that businessman who vanished last year, James Marchant. It's possible I may know what happened to him."

Gerry's brows furrowed.

"Marchant?" he asked, surprised. And legitimately so, El thought - Sita, as far as she knew, hadn't let him in on that aspect of their problem, despite their many clandestine calls and meetings in the Bay Area, nor on the way that Ruby had planned to deal with it.

"Yes. I'm sorry to say...these ladies, they had something to do with his disappearance. Indeed, I believe they may have been responsible for his death. His *murder*."

The bemusement on Gerry's face intensified.

"I think you may be mistaken, sir," he said.

"I'm certain that I'm not. In fact, if you'd like to take a seat, I can share with you exactly what I know, and exactly how it was I believe they came to murder the man."

Gerry looked from Sita to El to Rose, as if trying to reconcile what he was hearing with what he knew of them.

"No," he told Soames. "No, I don't think so."

"If you imagine they're not capable of such an action," Soames began, "then I can assure you..."

"No, sir," Gerry said, stopping him mid-sentence. "It's not that. It's just... well, perhaps I shouldn't be sharing this, but it'll be common knowledge soon enough once the press get hold of it. James Marchant – he isn't dead. He's very much alive."

∽

"Are you absolutely sure you want to do this?" Rose had asked Harriet the day before.

Rose's worries, El had thought at the time, weren't entirely misplaced. Harriet hadn't *looked* sure; had looked, in El's opinion, somewhat nauseated at the prospect of doing what she'd committed to do.

"Will it help you?" Harriet had replied. "You and Sophie?"

"More than you know."

"Then I'm sure. Absolutely sure."

"Right, then," Ruby had said. "Now we've got that out the way, here's what's gonna happen..."

The call, when it came, would be placed not by Karen, as Ruby had originally suggested, but by Sita's good friend Alanza, based currently in the Leblon neighbourhood of Rio de Janeiro. It would last roughly five minutes: long enough, Karen had assured them, to be certain that anyone attempting to trace the call after the fact could identify Brazil - and, if they were competent, Rio specifically - as its point of origin.

"Alanza's a very nice girl," Sita had added. "The perfect combination of loquacious and discreet. Which is exactly what we're in need of here, I'd say."

"When she's finished gabbing away and you've hung up," Ruby said, "don't pick up the phone again straight off.

Go and make yourself a cup of coffee; watch a bit of telly. Leave it an hour - more, if you can manage it. You want to make it look like you weren't sure what you ought to do about it, when the call came in. Like you were sat there biting your nails trying to work it out."

"That... makes sense, I suppose," Harriet said.

"And then," Sita said, "when you're confident enough time has elapsed..."

"I dial 999," Harriet finished. "Ask for the police, and tell them that I need to speak to the person in charge of the investigation into my father. That he's been in touch."

∽

"No!" Soames said. "No! Marchant's dead. These women here *murdered* him. Stabbed him to death with a kitchen knife."

"I can assure you, sir," Gerry told him, eyeing Soames now with a faintly uneasy look that suggested to El that he was harbouring concerns his suspect might be laying the groundwork for an insanity defence later down the line, "he's alive. We received information yesterday that confirmed as much. Some of my colleagues are liaising with Interpol as we speak to work out how we can expedite the extradition process, just as soon as they track down where he's hiding."

Soames stared at him; at all of them.

"That's impossible," he said. "Impossible."

Gerry stared back at him.

"I don't know where you're getting your information," he replied eventually, with a finality that told El, if not Soames himself, that this particular portion of the conversation had gone far enough already, and would go no further, "but whoever you've been talking to... I'd say they've been winding you up. I just hope for your sake that you haven't been using what you *thought* you knew to make life uncomfortable for these women, or anyone else for that matter. Because I wouldn't take kindly to that, sir. Not kindly at all."

CHAPTER 32
LANCASTER GATE, LONDON
NOVEMBER 1997

It was Sophie, not Rose, who answered the intercom; Sophie who opened the door to the apartment when El knocked. But still, she seemed taken aback to find El standing in front of her.

"You want Mum?" she asked, in lieu of a greeting.

She'd dyed her hair since California, El noticed - the canary-yellow-streaked red now a mousey, characterless brown that struck her as a peculiar choice for a teenager. Her clothes too were oddly characterless: a plain white t-shirt, blue jeans and unbranded black trainers that said nothing, made no statement at all.

"If she's in?" El said.

Sophie gave what could have been a nod, or just a twitch of her head, and melted away into the vastness of the apartment, leaving El to make her own way inside.

It was nothing at all like the cluttered, eclectically organised Notting Hill house that she'd come the previous year to associate with Rose - to see as a reflection of her tastes and interests, the rhythms of her life. It was barren, impersonal; so under-decorated that it seemed barely lived in at all. Not one of Rose's prints or paintings hung on the tastefully off-white walls; none of Sophie's books or magazines or computer games littered the pale-wood floor the way her toys and clothes and school-work had at Ledbury Road.

They're not staying here long, she thought. This isn't a home - it's a way station. A safe house.

Rose found her nosing around what was probably intended to be the study, a pleasantly beige non-room with an electric faux-Victorian fireplace as its centrepiece.

"This is unexpected," she said, coming up behind El as she took in the view of the park from the window. She was smiling, El saw as she spun around; her eyes wrinkling in a way that suggested the surprise visit wasn't entirely unwelcome.

"I was in the area," El replied. It was at best a half-truth: she'd driven in that morning to have lunch with Ruby and Sita in Highgate, forty minutes and a dozen sets of traffic-clogging roadworks away. But seeing Rose while she was down in London had seemed important; not something she ought to put off for much longer.

You're a fool to yourself, you are, Ruby had told her. And perhaps, El considered, she hadn't been entirely wrong in that assessment.

"Sophie looks different," she added.

"You can blame Ruby for that," Rose said, still smiling. "I'm afraid my daughter has decided - against my deeply-held and explicitly communicated wishes to the contrary, I might add - that she wants to be a grifter when she grows up."

El, too, had to smile at this. It occurred to her that, really, it was a development both of them should have seen coming. Sophie was a bright kid, pain in the arse though she could be, and it had been a while since Ruby had taken a protégé under her wing. The two of them together were a perfect match.

"Hence the clothes?" she asked.

"Hence the clothes. Apparently camouflage is key, in your line of work? She's learning how to blend into the background. And if the pound coins that keep disappearing from my wallet are any indication, how to pocket-dip, too."

Surely it's *our* line of work by now? El thought. Then realised, having thought it, the implication *of* the thought. That whatever new life she'd imagined for herself in the wake of the Marchant job, whatever fantasies she'd harboured about retiring from the con and retreating to her cottage to grow herbs or keep bees or write a screenplay, they were just that: fantasies. Grifting wasn't just what she *did*; it was who she *was*. And perhaps that wasn't so terrible, after all.

You know your trouble? she heard Ruby tell her again. *You think too much. Tie yourself in so many knots trying to work out what you should do or you shouldn't do, you never get 'round to actually doing what you thought you might* want *to do in the first place.*

She hadn't been entirely wrong about *that*, either.

~

"It's a worry," Ruby had said, tucking into her Lobster Thermidor with eye-watering gusto.

"What is?" El had asked, poking at her linguine with considerably more restraint.

"Soames. Not knowing how he heard about us, how he got his information."

It *was* a worry; El had no argument there.

Though currently out on bail on medical grounds,

Soames no longer - or so Ruby and Sita believed - represented much of a threat, to them or to anyone. His family were gone, his hold over his son broken, and - in light of James Marchant's recent contact with his daughter - his means of blackmailing *them* into submission had effectively dematerialised. He was powerless, now; just a weak, sick old man waiting to stand trial for crimes of which, Gerry Adler had assured them, he would almost certainly be found guilty. Eyewitness testimony was unreliable, especially so many years after the fact. But the DNA evidence provided by Lois Soames and her father - not Bob Kingsley, as she'd always thought, but Ted Wainwright, the father from whom she'd been stolen - should, Gerry had said, be enough to guarantee a conviction.

The question of who had given Soames the details of the Marchant murder and their involvement in it, however, remained entirely unanswered. And Soames himself, El suspected, would take whatever secrets he knew back to prison with him - and, in the fullness of time, to the grave.

"It *was* her, though, wasn't it?" El had said. "It was Hannah. It had to be."

Ruby had shrugged.

"We're making enquiries," Sita had said, downing two Jersey oysters in quick succession.

"Good at that, she is," Ruby had added sourly. "Sneaking around, interrogating people down dark alleys."

"Must this forever be a bone of contention?" Sita had sighed.

"It ain't right, that's all I'm saying - going behind people's backs like that. Ain't right at all."

El hadn't been sure how much of Ruby's irritation at Sita conspiring with Gerry Adler in San Francisco - the excuses, the late-night phone calls, the fabricated Taj Mahal story -

was real, and how much was feigned. Probably, she thought, the deception *had* stung, at least a little. But that it had proven so pivotal, so necessary to neutralising the danger Soames had posed ... *that*, she suspected, had cut deeper.

Sita had sighed again - a loud, grande dame suspiration that was more performance than catharsis.

"To move away from this, if we may," she'd said, when her breath was spent. "El, darling - how are *you*? Have you been seeing very much of Rose?"

~

"I thought I'd stop by," El said, galled by her own nervousness, the roiling churn of her stomach. "See how you are."

"We're fine," Rose said lightly. "Settling back into the swing of things. Though I will say that I'm in no rush to return to California any time soon, after this year's adventure."

"Not even to see Kate?" she asked before she could stop herself - clamp a muffling hand, perhaps, over the jaw that seemed, suddenly, not entirely under her control.

Rose moved back a step, and fixed her with the same appraising stare that Sita had used on her earlier in the day.

"No," she said, sounding both puzzled and faintly amused. "Not even to see Kate."

"And how's Harriet?" El continued, feeling a pressing need to manoeuvre things in an alternative direction, to reverse them out of the humiliating conversational cul-de-sac into which she'd steered them.

"She's well. Taking everything that's happened in her stride, I'm happy to say."

This tallied with what El had heard already over lunch. Harriet Marchant, Ruby had told her, had seemed surprisingly unfazed both by her involvement in the Soames affair and by the lies she'd recounted subsequently for the police - and presumably for Interpol - around where exactly in the world her father might be found.

("She's a cold fish, that Harriet," Ruby had said, "but she's got a good head on her shoulders. Can't fault it").

"Is she still in touch with Lois Soames?" El asked.

In part because of her job, and in part - or so El thought - because of the sense of responsibility she felt towards both Lois and Jay after having sprung Ted Wainwright on them, Harriet had offered herself to all three of them as an informal counsellor and confidante - until, as she took pains to emphasise, an appropriately-qualified (and wholly impartial) therapist could be located to work through their respective issues, one-on-one and, where relevant, together.

Lois, to everyone's astonishment - including, Harriet said, her own - had dealt the best of the three of them with the revelations that had confronted her the month before: the combined impact of Wainwright's arrival on her doorstep and the realisation of what her husband had done, what he was *still doing* to her and her son apparently enough to pull the scales forcibly from her eyes. She'd be testifying at Soames' trial, she'd told Harriet; was prepared, now she recognised it for the abuse it was, to tell anyone who'd listen what she'd suffered over the decades at his hands.

"She's resilient," Harriet had said. "I don't think she sees it that way, but she is. He had her for nearly thirty years, and she survived. If I were to guess, I'd say she'll survive the rest, too."

Jay Soames's recovery, she'd said, would likely be a longer and more challenging journey - his desire to protect and avenge his mother still warring with the lifetime of conditioning he'd received from his father.

"He knows what the right thing to do is, and what he ought to think," Harriet had added - the small catch in her throat as she spoke suggesting to El that it might not *just* be Jay she was talking about. "But there's still a voice in his head telling him a different story, a more toxic story altogether. A sort of... demon on his shoulder. He'll learn to stop listening, I've no doubt of that. But that voice... I'm not sure it'll ever quite leave him."

Wainwright, she thought, was still shell-shocked - his newly discovered daughter and grandson still seeming to him not quite solid, not quite *real*.

Nevertheless, Harriet said, he had no plans to return to the Bay Area for the foreseeable future, and would be staying instead in England - not in London but in Yorkshire, far enough from Lois and Jay that his presence wouldn't be felt as oppressive, but close enough that he could be on hand as and when they needed him, as they began the slow, painstaking process of getting to know each other.

Just as importantly, as Harriet had observed: his substantial personal fortunes meant that *paying* for the treatment all three of them so desperately needed would present no problem at all.

"She's found her a therapist," Rose replied. "A good one, I think - a friend of hers from university, one who specialises in domestic abuse. And another for Jay. She wouldn't tell me much more that, for obvious reasons, but Harriet knows what she's doing - she'd never recommend someone who wasn't every bit as capable as she is."

She's proud of her, El realised - proud of her accomplishments, her competence.

The idea pleased her. If, she thought, Rose and Harriet could be close enough, after not even a year of knowing each other, for Rose to take a sisterly pride in what Harriet did and was, then perhaps there was hope, after all, for Lois and Jay and Ted Wainwright.

"Did you hear about Karen?" Rose asked, when no further reply from El was forthcoming.

"Got the invitation yesterday," El said.

She hadn't quite believed what she was seeing, when she'd opened the envelope - a thick, gold-trimmed slab of ivory that had weighed more than her last utility bill.

Mrs Eleanor Baxter, the ornate and disorientingly formal script on the folded note inside had read, *requests the pleasure of your company at the marriage of her daughter Karen to Mr Fergus Ian Armstrong, hosted at Allemore Castle, Loch Lomond on Saturday 10th January at 2pm.*

Karen's getting *married*? she'd thought, so shocked she'd nearly said the words aloud. Karen's getting married in a *castle* in the *Highlands*?

"Apparently Fergus missed her while she was away," Rose said, the smile creeping back to her eyes and mouth.

"Isn't she a bit young for it, though?"

"She's older than I was, when Seb and I got married. And she and Fergus are *actually* in love, at least as far as I've been able to tell. Besides - you could hardly accuse her of not knowing her own mind, could you? I'm sure they'll be absolutely fine."

The reference to Rose's husband - the best friend with whom she'd shared a life and a daughter, if not a bed, before his premature death - seemed to nudge some part of El's brain into action; to remind her of why she was there, in the apartment. Of what she'd come to ask.

If you don't start pulling that head of yours out of your arse, Ruby had said, *you're gonna miss the boat altogether.*

She won't keep waiting 'round for you to work out if you want her or not.

"I actually..., " El began - and stopped abruptly. Coughed, ran a hand through her no-longer-neon-pink hair and started again.

"I was wondering," she said, "if you might want to go for dinner sometime this week? Just me and you?"

Rose's smile spread, pulling the skin of her forehead tight and deepening the crow's feet in the corner of her eyes.

"Before I answer that," she said, sounding for a moment almost exactly like her daughter, "I feel I should probably clarify what you're asking. This dinner - is it a catch-up between friends, or are you intending that it should be something more...?"

She trailed off, seeming to lose her nerve.

You ain't got time to sit around wringing your hands, Ruby had said. *If you're interested, then you best tell her so, and pronto.*

"Romantic," El replied - wishing, improbably, that Sophie were there to hear her say it. "Something more romantic."

ALLEMORE CASTLE, LOCH LOMOND
JANUARY 1998

The castle was cold and ugly: a Draculian ruin of a place, only slightly improved by the multi-coloured bunting someone - she assumed the mother of the bride - had strung haphazardly across the dark stone walls.

Her own wedding, she remembered, had been a far more inviting affair - a High Church orgy of light and gold and incense, the priest a veritable peacock of unnecessary colour. Nothing at all like the celebrant running the show today: a tall, shaven-headed boy barely into his twenties, his bare arms invisible under tattoo ink and an unnatural red glow emanating from the implants - *implants*, of all things - embedded in the skin around each of his knuckles.

The groom was unremarkable if comparatively inoffensive in a crushed velvet suit, but the bride, at least, had made an effort: her hair - longer now than it had been - expertly braided, her makeup subtle enough to augment rather than distract from her looks, her ivory gown more traditional than might have been expected of someone so unorthodox, but expensive and well-fitted; a choice she might have made herself.

They were there, of course - the whole lot of them.

Ruby and Sita, seated side by side in one of the middle rows: Ruby dressed for comfort above effect and Sita the diametric opposite, the feathers of her fascinator so tall they threatened to block the view of any guest unlucky enough to have been placed behind her.

Kat, her head wounds healed but the walking sticks that were her constant companion these days resting on the ground beneath her feet.

El, in a dark black suit more appropriate for a funeral than a wedding - and beside her Rose, one hand resting proprietorially on El's leg and the other wrapped around the shoulders of her sullen-looking daughter. She, too, it appeared, had opted for maximalism above discretion, her body sheathed in an unpleasantly shimmering silver number better suited to a cartoon mermaid released onto the mainland than a middle-aged woman.

The car was a nice touch, though - she'd give them that. She was no expert, but she thought it might have been a Bugatti - a vintage, undeniably elegant monochrome panther of a vehicle, low-slung and open-top and as long as a limousine. She had doubts about the level of comfort it afforded its passengers, and how pleasurable Mr and Mrs Armstrong would find it when it conveyed them later from the castle to their honeymoon cabin on the other side of the loch. But it *looked* good, and perhaps that was what mattered.

The celebrant glanced down at the order of service in his glowing hands and, with a nod to the mother of the bride in the front row, declared the happy couple husband and wife, for as long as they both should live.

And Hannah, satisfied with what she'd seen, drew her own dark veil over her face and crept quietly out of the hall.

ABOUT THE AUTHOR

Natalie Edwards is a cultural analyst and researcher with a long-standing interest in cons and con artists. A former lecturer, copywriter and semiotician (among other things), she lives in Leicestershire with her partner and two children.

twitter.com/NEdwards1952

ALSO BY NATALIE EDWARDS

The Debt

Printed in Great Britain
by Amazon